THE POWER AND THE GLORY

The POWER AND THE GLORY

CLINT KELLY

BETHANY HOUSE PUBLISHERS
MINNEAPOLIS, MINNESOTA 55438

The Power and The Glory
Copyright © 1999
Clint Kelly

Cover illustration by Fran Gregory
Cover design by Dan Thornberg,
Bethany House Publishers staff artist.

Portions used from the poem "Constantinople" by Lady Mary Montagu were
obtained from "Representative Poetry On-Line (Toronto)."

Published by Bethany House Publishers
A Ministry of Bethany Fellowship International
11400 Hampshire Avenue South
Minneapolis, Minnesota 55438
www.bethanyhouse.com

Printed in the United States of America by
Bethany Press International, Minneapolis, Minnesota 55438

Library of Congress Cataloging-in-Publication Data

CIP data applied for

ISBN 1–55661–956–1   CIP

To my daughter Stephanie,
with love,
for always championing the underdog.

ABOUT THE AUTHOR

Clint Kelly is the author of *The Landing Place* and *The Aryan*, as well as a publications specialist for Seattle Pacific University. A former forest ranger, Clint's inspiration for his novels comes from his wife and four children and from the landscape of the Pacific Northwest where they make their home.

CHAPTER 1
Autumn 1920

She let the curtain fall back on the inky darkness. For the hundredth time that evening she snapped open the gold enamel casing of the fine pocket watch given her by the brave American.

Ten-fifteen. Her husband was never this late. They had an agreement. The streets of Stambul were not safe under the moon. Something had to be wrong.

Terribly wrong.

The dark memories flooded in. Children reduced to skeletons, barely able to stand or speak; grandfathers butchered for the gold in their teeth; young virgins used for sport and then left for the vultures. Her grandmother, father, friends, all gone. Hundreds of thousands of her people forced to march to exile in the deserts of Syria. A great many perished en route. The official policy of the government of which they were citizens, the grand Ottoman Empire, was to destroy the Armenians. Tens of thousands died in their homes and villages, many executed on the flimsiest of charges without the pretense of any legal cause whatsoever.

The destruction had come with breathtaking vengeance. While a world war raged elsewhere, well more than a million souls had perished at home.

Turkey, the floundering "sick man of Europe," had at last declared war on itself, killing its citizens of Armenian descent.

The watch face began to vibrate in unsteady hands, and Adrine Sarafian snapped the case closed. She gripped the timepiece in the palm of her left hand, tightly cupped in her right.

Slowly squeezing, she stopped the trembling as she always did by rubbing a thumb over the smooth greens and browns of the fantastic enameled hunt scene painted on the outside of the casing.

Surrounded by pearl-set bezels, the painting revealed a golden lion springing toward the cringing form of a European conqueror, his sword lying useless on the ground beside him. Riding to the rescue, an East Indian on horseback held his rifle aimed at the fierce cat's head as a white-turbaned servant boy sat astride the thick neck of an angry-eyed elephant, whacking the pachyderm with a long stick.

Adrine winced, recalling the sting of the Turkish military commander's riding crop that he had used on her and the other female Armenian camp slaves. Then, as if dropped from heaven, a fearless hero had come into town on horseback to save them—Tatul Sarafian, alias the Fox, cunning young Fedayee, rebel warrior of the Armenian resistance.

"I'm a mere cowherd from Erzurum," he had insisted before rescuing her and a hundred other women and their children from certain death. He had had his insecurities and his crises of faith, but she'd gladly married them all. For nearly three years the two of them had lived a wilderness existence, smuggling their people to safety inside Russia from the stronghold of the Fedayeen high in the Caucasus Mountains along the Turkish-Russian border.

The monastic brothers at Mesrop and St. Timothy's had linked arms with the Fedayeen rebels. In league they formed an effective pathway to freedom, what the Americans called an "underground railway." Most Turks avoided the Christian holy men, fearing that "the hooded servants of the bloody Christ" would cast crippling curses upon them, steal their children, perhaps even cannibalize them. It was rumored, though never proved, that rather than evangelize the oppressor, the monks preferred to buy protection for their own by playing on peasant superstition.

Adrine smiled, remembering the brothers' kindness and the rough affections of the Fedayeen warriors. Until Mehmed the VI, last of the Ottoman sultans, sued for peace on October

30, 1918, she and Tatul had lived in caves and run with the wolves. Those people they smuggled over the border to safety were met by veteran Armenian refugees and helped to find places to live and work in Russian villages farther north—some eventually being given safe passage to America.

For the next two years the Sarafians helped organize the movement for justice and the return of the Armenian homeland. They'd formed the Committee for a Restored Homeland (CRH) out of the few hundred Armenian patriots in Stambul who stubbornly clung to their rights as citizens of Turkey and refused to leave. Most of them were uneducated peasant farmers and street vendors who spoke from their passions rather than their intelligence. But they cared and would fight—and die—in the blink of an eye for blessed Armenia. They had even gained a small voice in local politics but feared to meet too openly lest they be accused of sedition. The chief of police was a ruthless pragmatist who believed that Armenians should cower like the conquered minority they were.

The Sarafians fought for stability among the brash and resentful Armenian remnant in Istanbul. The workers at the American consulate were sympathetic and dropped everything to aid those who wanted to emigrate to the United States. But for those wishing to stay and rebuild, little could be done officially. One consulate worker unofficially passed them cash gathered by Armenian sympathizers in the U.S. who wanted to sustain the Committee for a Restored Homeland. A portion of the foreign collection and the modest proceeds from Adrine's produce stall were what the Sarafians lived on. That and their hope for the day to come when the official status of the CRH would allow them to give powerful testimony in a war crimes trial.

At first, it looked as if the tide had turned strongly in favor of their people. Adrine's eyes had flooded with tears at the sight of Allied warships steaming into the harbor at Istanbul and the handsome British, French, and Russian officers striding down the streets in their colorful uniforms, speaking their equally colorful languages. The news that steamed in with them was startling and as hopeful as any the battered Armenians had heard in a thousand days: Russia was to be rewarded possession of Constantinople.

But the Allied warships and the Allied officers with their good Allied intentions eventually left, and in their wake other forces prevailed. A "secure sovereignty" had been promised Turkey and it could not be realized without the strategic location and the security afforded by Constantinople. So it remained in Turk hands. Similarly doomed was the independent Armenia that Woodrow Wilson had called for in the Treaty of Versailles just one year ago!

Adrine squeezed the watch case angrily. Easy, so easy, for men of power to talk of this body of water and that swatch of land as consolation prizes in contests of war. But what of the people who fished those waters and plowed that land, wanting simply to feed their families and make modest plans in peace? Did anyone ever ask them what was in their best interests?

She repeatedly stroked the casing of the beautiful watch, allowing the feel of the exquisite workmanship to spread its healing.

A distant drunken shout made her start. The trembling returned, and she snapped open the watch with the irrational hope that it would somehow read earlier.

Ten-twenty.

An inner cold crept across her shoulders, and icy were the memories. Artillery shells bursting in night air, lighting the rugged Turkey borderland an unearthly gray. Worker priests like giant ravens moving stealthily about in their holy black raiment.

Stepping into the shallow wooden box, stealing a last glimpse of her beloved. Then the horror of the lid descending. Stifling darkness. Hammer blows.

Nailed in.

The creak and sway of the death cart. The thud and bang of adjoining caskets beside and below. Surrounded by the truly dead.

Across the Russian border to "Uncle Christian"—the place of safety. Farewell, my homeland.

Tatul's work was too dangerous. He held too many secrets

and confided in her less and less for fear the knowledge would place her in jeopardy. Like the peril of where he was at the moment, and with whom! She wanted to share his danger and ride by his side, but it was as if he had declared those days finished. He wanted her to enjoy a home again with walls and a roof, to form a community of friends and sisters who worshiped together, laughed and encouraged one another, performed acts of kindness and looked after one another's babies.

Adrine took a deep breath and steadied herself. She placed a palm flat against her belly and gently pressed. After a few moments, the nausea passed. Was it fear inside her ... or something else? *Something else, please God.* Something she had lain awake nights hoping and praying for. They both had. But it was difficult in these times of high anxiety and mistrust. So difficult.

Plenty of others had counted the cost too high and had left their homeland. The Sarafians, too, should go to England, or to America, or back to the mountains where the freedom fighters hatched their plans and launched their raids in the meager hope that the ruthless Turks would rue the day they had voted to kill the People of the Book.

Anything but stay in the whirlpool of civilizations and ideologies named Constantinople by the Romans, Istanbul or Stambul by the Turks, but forever known to the world by its ancient name of Byzantium, the scandalous repository of forbidden delights. For better or worse, it was the capital of Turkey and the cosmopolitan crossroads of the world.

Ex oriente lux, said the Latins. All light comes from the East.

And all debauchery, she thought, lifting the curtain again and seeing no more than she had the last time. *Little of* this *war has disturbed her satin rest.*

She paced the dining room, turned up the lamps, smoothed her brocade dress of black Genoan velvet, and prayed. *Father God, protect my husband. Keep him—keep us—from evil. To you be all power and glory.* One thin but firm hand reached absently to caress the smooth finish of the mahogany dining table, two places set, the dinner of lamb, walnuts, and the sesame seed sweets he so adored, long since cold and congealed.

The glow from two shortened beeswax candles bathed the dining table and chairs in a yellow peace. She thought to snuff them out but instead carried them to the window. She threw back the curtain and set the tiny beacons on the sill.

Adrine Sarafian stood before the windows defiant, arms folded, immovable. The dark would not swallow her. Her people would be redeemed. Her husband was coming home. If Satan wanted any one of them, he would have to get past Father, Son, and Holy Ghost.

The longer she stood in the window, the more her eyes adjusted to the silvery night shimmering off the Bosporus strait. It was a twenty-mile stretch of water connecting the Black Sea and the Sea of Marmara. Its shores rose to two hundred meters in places and were lined with a profusion of palaces, ruins, villages, and gardens. It was exotically intoxicating, and its mysterious appeal was as alive by night as by day.

No, Adrine could not deny the strange allure of the great city and its setting. She and Tatul had come to Constantinople seeking justice, and if it was to be found in all of Turkey, it would be found in Stambul. The Allies had pledged to make the perpetrators of the Armenian slaughter pay for their crimes.

The ink on the armistice agreement had barely dried when the acting Ottoman government under Sultan Mehmed VI called for trials of the accused in Ottoman court. More than one hundred suspects were named. But Armenians lost hope each day as the international trials promised by the Allies failed to materialize. After all, how much justice would Turks exact from other Turks in a civil trial?

Word spread that the Ottoman authorities, while appearing sympathetic to the Armenians, were actually trying to curry favor with the Allies so that things would go easier for them at the peace conference in Paris. And it was no secret that the sultan and his grand vizier, Damad Ferid, were no friends of the former Young Turk government or the strong movement toward Turkish nationalism under Kemal Pasha, later known as Ataturk. As the old Ottoman order had been victimized by the Young Turks, so the sultan and his governors now hoped to extract their own kind of revenge by using the Armenian situation to their advantage.

"No one loves Armenians except Armenians" was Tatul's grim conclusion.

But he had redoubled his efforts to solidify the political base of the Committee for a Restored Homeland. He spoke as passionately at rallies attended by two or three people as at those that drew a hundred. He befriended Turkish politicians, however small their station, and tried to model responsible Armenian nationalism. He fought to remain untainted by the bands of rogue Armenian toughs—many of them members of the Marxist Hunchaks—who fervently believed that the only sincere Turk was a stone-dead one.

Tatul did not revile all Turks, for many were as horrified by the atrocities as were the Armenian victims, although few spoke ill of their leadership, fearing retribution. For the love of Adrine, Tatul even attempted to act charitably toward the enemies who had torn his family—and his people—asunder. And he fought hardest of all to remain true to his faith when sometimes what he really wanted was to strangle the life from the guilty and to blame God for the unexplainable disaster that had befallen Armenia. He went out each day and encouraged the remnant, counseling patience. He met with priests and shopkeepers and government agencies in quest of food and medicine and compassion for his struggling people.

Another shout erupted from the street, followed by a hail of curses. A torch flame flashed in the night somewhere near the corner. Adrine stepped closer to the window, her lips moving silently at first, then the words coming aloud and increasing in volume. "Thanks be to God, who always leads us in triumphal procession in Christ and through us spreads everywhere the fragrance of the knowledge of Him."

Should they go or stay? Constantinople was as abominable as it was fascinating. Desperate Turks. Spiteful Armenians. Postwar opportunists. And everywhere the gendarmes—brutal, arbitrary, triggers ready. The one constant: danger. Adrine couldn't help at once loving and loathing her adopted city.

She automatically snapped open the watch, painfully aware of the time.

Ten-thirty-two.

Slender fingers with clear-lacquered nails shakily picked at the inner lid of the watch. *He said I should open the hidden compartment only when I know without a doubt that he is dead. My head tells me to open it, for he has never been this late; my heart says if I open it, then he will surely die because I lack faith. My Lord, I am sick with doubt. Please help me!*

Adrine snapped the watch closed again and quickly crossed the room. She slid open the top drawer of the table-ware cabinet, placed the watch behind a set of soup ladles, and closed the drawer with finality. "There." It was a word that declared the matter closed, according to Mother Agop at the orphanage.

The boys were just babies. Why did the chief of police harass the orphans and threaten to shut down the only home they knew? Because they were survivors, she concluded. Survivors, young and determined, had established whole nations over the centuries and brought about many earthshaking reforms. Each time an Armenian boy was taught to tie his shoes or lift his eyes to heaven, the spine of his people straightened.

It was a long moment before she could force herself away from the cabinet, heart hammering. Not reading Tatul's hidden message gave her strength to believe that he was alive, that there was a more innocent explanation for his absence. Perhaps he was studying some ancient manuscript in order to amaze her with his arcane knowledge of the ancient city.

A crash, followed by a heavy thud against the house, jerked Adrine from her reverie, and before she could retrieve the loaded pistol Tatul made her keep ready whenever he was out, the front door burst open, admitting a loud confusion of voices, dirty, wild-eyed men, and her battered husband carried between them.

He was covered in blood.

"Christ heal us!" she exclaimed, rushing to them. They brushed her aside in their plunge to the dining room, swept up table settings, centerpiece, and a stack of books she'd been sorting, then stretched Tatul Sarafian full-length on the exposed table.

She forced her way in and bit her lower lip to keep from crying. Dear Tatul was a bruised and torn mess. His nose and lips were split and swollen, his eyes blackened. Blood streamed from matted and blood-soaked hair. His shirt and cloak hung from him in tatters, his chest a mass of cuts and welts. Tears streamed from his eyes, and his ribs rose and fell in the effort to be free of his restraints.

But the roar that came from him was one of frustration, not from pain of injury. "Let me free, you donkey waste! You'll not hold me down like some sick farm animal!"

He moaned and thrashed in their grip, but there were too many of them for him to make good his escape.

"What is this, Andranik?" she demanded of a short, burly member of the CRH. "Where were you when this was going on?"

Andranik's eyes did not meet hers. "We were to gather at Seraglio Point, but he came stumbling out of the dark at us like a creature from the pit. I swear to you, good lady, your impetuous husband received his thrashing well before we saw him. That's what comes of his recklessly keeping appointments with all manner of vermin without anyone by his side."

"I will not live my life in the company of bodyguards!" Tatul bleated through a rapidly swelling mouth but with far less resistance than before.

Her cool fingers tenderly wiped at the blood on his forehead and softly patted his cheek. She bent over him, making soft shushing sounds, and finally he calmed. "Vahram, cloths soaked in cold water," she ordered. "Bring a pail back with you. Ephraim, go raise the iceman and tell him two blocks without delay. If you have them back within the half hour, there is double the fee in it for both of you. Bayard, I need you to remove all my husband's clothes. Andranik, I ask you to forgive my accusatory tone. Would you kindly find the doctor and have him come and suture the deepest of these cuts? The rest of you, please understand. I would ask you to go home."

The water arrived and she took a cloth and gently bathed Tatul's face. "Thank you, Vahram," she said to the water bearer, who anxiously hovered nearby. "A safe night to you. We shall send news in the morning."

"But, good lady," Vahram replied with genuine concern, "such a beautiful dress should not be soiled by blood. I would be honored to clean the Fox for you."

"Thank you, no," she answered firmly. "The dress is of no consequence when my husband—" Her voice caught and she had to stop and swallow hard. Bayard finished undressing Tatul, laid a towel of modesty across his friend's middle, and stood back. "Thank you both," Adrine said. "You are good friends. Leave us alone now. We shall have you over soon for stuffed mackerel and chicken pudding. Greetings to your wives. Good night!"

The men left, though reluctantly, Adrine knew, and fearful for their fallen leader. As soon as the door closed behind them, Adrine rushed to lock it, then removed the candles from the sill and closed the curtains. She turned down the lamps in the sitting room and stood a few seconds, hands tightly folded, praying for courage and strength. She hurried to Tatul's side and resumed bathing his wounds.

"They waited for me in Taksim Square, and when I emerged from the underground railway, they rode me to the ground like some unweaned calf!" Tatul sweated, gritting his teeth in anger. He pounded scarred fists on the table, the frustration pouring from him. "Me, a member of the mountain myths, Fedayeen-trained, adopted son of rebel leader Kevork Chavoush, the Black Wolf! How could I let myself be ambushed that way? I am soft, domesticated, gelded by my own comforts … aaagh!" He groaned again as Adrine roughly lifted his right arm and swiped her cloth at the elbow scraped raw.

"I suppose I am largely responsible for the creature comforts that have brought you low, mighty Fox!" she snapped, letting his arm fall back. "If you prefer a rock for a pillow and cold nights spent caressing a rifle stock, then I urge you by all means …" She felt his fingers press against her lips, and a strong hand take her wrist, guiding the cloth in a much gentler path.

"Mmmmmm," he murmured, eyes closed, "an angel in the infirmary. Tell the doctor when he comes that I am in the best of hands."

She leaned close and kissed him carefully on the forehead. Tears slid down her cheeks, one dropping alongside his nose.

"We'll have to get that leak fixed before winter, my little eggplant," he said, thick lips parting in a weak smile.

Adrine burst into weeping. "Why are we so hated?"

Tatul shushed her and reached up to gently pat her cheek. "Not while I'm in agony," he said, wincing when the cloth touched his ribs. "Sore, but not broken," he reassured her. "They simply wanted to wear me down. And you know what bleeders scalp wounds can be."

He could sense fear in her, mingled with pride and sorrow. He'd sworn to himself as they'd made their escape into Russia that he would be her protector, that by his side she would never have to fear again. He'd tried, but they had returned to Turkey, and in the rolling boil that was Stambul today, he was not always a successful champion. Five hundred years in a shared house and still the Turk and the Armenian remained unreconciled. Thank God the Creator had made his beloved strong and resilient. And his rib cage. But when could they hope for a family of their own in such an uncertain climate?

It would only be when together they had made a child and it stood before them spotless and full of promise that Tatul would truly believe that the restoration had begun, that Armenia would live again.

And until he had settled the case of the Armenian Judas who lived in luxury under the political protection of the Turks just four streets away, the chances of Adrine calming enough to have a baby were thinner than a fly's wings.

He watched her as she worked and wept over him, emptying the bucket of murky red water and bringing fresh. Despite himself and his aching body, he felt desire building beneath her touch but sensed that now was not a good time to seek her embrace.

"You must guess." He whispered the now familiar preamble to the announcement of another amazing fact about Constantinople.

That brought a smile from her despite her anxieties. She sniffed and wiped her eyes dry. "What have you learned today, O grand inquisitor?" she chided.

"The secret to the intense red jam produced right here a hundred years ago and attested to by one Dr. James Dallaway, a semireliable Britisher," he whispered. He pulled himself up by her arm and looked about conspiratorially. "Is it safe?" he inquired.

She giggled. "It is safe, O thou of the bulging brains."

"Rubies!" he rasped, sinking wearily back to the table. "Precious rubies ground to dust and mixed with the fruit. They called it conserve of rubies. As heaven is my witness." He crossed the left half of his chest. "I say we go to that thief of a jeweler across the aisle from you at the bazaar and trade him your sweet fig compote for all the rubies in his collection. Kings and presidents will kneel on your doorstep, my little turnip!"

She laughed musically and he could feel the tension in the room ease. He motioned her close and she bent near. "Good lady," he said, low and confidential, "did you know you have a naked man on your dining table?"

Without hesitation, she whispered back, "That is odd. Last I looked, it was just my husband."

Tatul smiled and lay quiet beneath her careful ministrations. His body felt as if he'd been hurled from the castle wall and left for dead, and yet, by her touch, life aplenty pulsed just below the bruised surface.

He dreaded the moment she would ask for details of the beating. She had been silent for some time and he chanced to look at her. She stared back, fire in the dusty brown eyes he adored.

"We must bring to justice the Turks who did this to you, Tatul. Don't argue with me. To allow them to go unpunished in the name of some greater reconciliation later on is no justice at all. I'm tired of the political game. I want you to bring charges against them. There are newspapers in this city that will print your story. A photographer will take your picture in the morning; then all the good citizens of Constantinople can see how the merciless Turks negotiate."

She was trembling again, but this time it was not out of anxiety. This time it was rage. The Ottomans had once more reached into her home and this time damaged the man she loved, the man she had prayed for, the man God had graciously provided. She believed in finding a way to love her enemies, but would the harassment never end? Could she not have just this little bit of happiness?

"I cannot do that," he said flatly and would not look at her.

"What?!" she cried, face flushed with hurt and dismay. "What do you mean you cannot? Have you so soon forgotten the national bully who tore your people and mine in two? We are beginning to make some small headway, my husband. Give the Turk this victory and we may as well pack our belongings and flee to Outer Mongolia. We will have no place here, and Armenia will fade to a distant memory!"

He turned his face from her. "They were not Turks."

The words came so faint and so coated in remorse that she thought at first she had imagined them.

"Oh, Tatul! If not Turks, then who? Who did this to you?"

He looked at her with a deep sadness, and she knew.

"Armenians," he said. "Brothers of the Cross."

Chapter 2

His wayward heart thudded against its chamber with all the force of a demon hammer. After all the Turks had done to his people, why now should his heart quail in darkness, afraid to take its revenge on so vile a human being?

The Armenian Judas was the bloodiest betrayer in the history of the homeland. And for his treachery he was rewarded by the Turkish officials with a mansion, promises of protection, and a lifetime government pension. The bloated Judas leech grew fatter by the minute off an ocean of Armenian blood spilled by his pen.

Three hundred of Armenia's finest leaders had found their way onto the Judas list, labeled insurrectionists. The cream of Constantinople had been delivered over to the enemy by one of their own, offered up without remorse like so many sweet lambs to feed the ravenous pashas.

O my brothers in Christ's blood, this horror shall not go unpunished! You shall rest in your graves this day, for the honor of Armenia shall be avenged by my hand!

He dared to breathe then, gulping the midmorning air, steadying his resolve.

Assassin.

He recoiled from the word at first. Then with practiced determination, he pictured the fat contours of Harootoun Mugurditchian, whom he had observed from a distance on three occasions. The man was not begotten in the image of God, but rather was a mistake of nature. He had no conscience. No soul. The Judas laughed through a little round hole of a mouth encrusted with the blood of three hundred brother Armenians. A little round blowhole of a mouth that snuffled with glee, ate greasy mutton, and affectionately sought the cheeks of innocent children.

He shuddered and tried to blot out the memory of that leering mouth. What must it be like to be kissed by the devil?

Forgive.

The thought buckled his knees. He stumbled and went down, half bowing on the street before the Armenian Apostolic Church of Constantinople. It was a beautiful Sabbath morning, the services about to begin.

Only the meek would inherit the earth. The biblical maxim had been told him by a dozen different lips—parents, grandparents, aunts, uncles, brother, sister—all saying the same thing, all convinced of the rightness of the Way. Christ's way.

The impossible way.

What kind of way did not allow for justice in the present? There would be no justice for the Judas. Not here in 1920 in the heart of enemy territory. No, the assassin would have to help God and render justice that otherwise would be mute, unless someone broke from the Way long enough to exact retribution.

A dead Judas would immediately come before God and immediately pay the ultimate price for sending three hundred countrymen to their destruction.

A few rows from the altar, he listened to the familiar recitation of the Mass, letting the hallowed reverence steady his nerves. He had never before walked up and shot a man in his home in the midst of his family. The fingers of his right hand searched inside the left breast pocket of his coat and flinched at the coldness of the steel. The length of an open hand, the stocky Mauser 7.65mm automatic pistol weighed just over a pound.

German made. His face twisted in irony. He would bring the Judas down with a weapon manufactured by Turkey's wartime ally.

His head snapped in the direction of the priest giving the sermon.

"Harootoun Mugurditchian supplied Talaat Pasha with the names of our heroes in exchange for material wealth. That mass-murdering Turk next ordered our philosophers, our artists, our scientists herded into groups of fifty and thrown into filthy cells. Packed together like maggots, they were denied water, food, and medical attention and used by their drunken jailers for sport. All but one were murdered. Only good Bishop Krikorees Balakian survived."

The priest, obviously overcome by the thought of so great a loss, paused, head bowed. "Let us pray for these martyrs and for their eternal rest and exalted place in the highest heavens."

It was all he could do to remain still while the priest intoned the names of the dead, one by one. It was the roll call of Armenia's finest minds and stoutest hearts from Ashubashian to Zakarian. Each name was a mule kick to the stomach. Wonderful to think of their contribution to man's understanding, but awful the waste of so many meaningful lives.

" . . . Varoujan." The name of arguably Armenia's greatest poet unleashed the flames of hatred inside the assassin. *God grant me the strength to complete the deed, to punish and forever silence this Judas as surely as you brought down that other Judas who betrayed your Son and sent Him to the cross to die.*

" . . . and finally, we beg God's mercy for Mugurditchian and—yes—even for Talaat the Terrible himself, who ordered the very destruction of Armenia."

He could bear to hear no more. Mercy was for priests and mothers with small children.

He lurched to his feet, afraid that if he stayed twenty seconds more, he would scream at the priest to stop talking, throw off his holy robes, grab a gun, and make a Sabbath visit to the home of every corrupt Turkish minister of government.

A young priest stopped him with a gentle hand on his arm, only inches from the gun. *"Koo guskeeds zanoenk yaid chein gurnahr yaid berell,"* he said in Armenian, a sad but kind smile wreathing his face. "Your grief will not bring them back."

He pulled away from the young priest and hurried to the rear of the church. He fled down the steps, certain every suspicious glance penetrated his coat to the weapon in his pocket. He felt as if the Angel of Death rode on his shoulders.

The news vendor took the coin and handed him a copy of *Jagadamard*, an Armenian paper. While the Turks made a great show of Istanbul as a model city of unrestricted freedom for Armenians, the editor of *Jagadamard* was forced to run certain government press releases. They almost always dealt with postwar Turkey in a favorable light, portraying her as one of the world's great humanitarians, as magnanimous in loss as in victory. And yet the Turkish press ran story after unflattering story about Armenians arrested for denouncing government informers, unemployed Armenians caught stealing food for their malnourished children, and Armenian orphanages—the supposed breeding grounds of pickpockets, disease, and, of course, more insurrectionists. Orphanages that only existed because the Turks had slaughtered all the children's relatives!

He hurled the paper to the ground and set his face toward the mansion of Harootoun Mugurditchian.

God help me.

Ten minutes later, he sat by the corner front window of the Armenian wineshop and sipped the sweet vintage, begging the jitters to be still. He stared across the street at the iron fence encircling Mugurditchian's estate.

In times of peace he would abhor the assassin's bullet as much as the next man. But some kind of violent insanity had been unleashed against Christ's own here in the twentieth century that made even the bloody Romans and their lions' dens of A.D. 70 look like benevolent benefactors.

A Roman holiday, he thought. A time of enjoyment derived from the suffering of others. A savage and spectacular entertainment reminiscent of the staged public battles of Roman gladiators. Well, the Turks had had their Roman holiday. It was time now to balance the scales with one small stone.

The money that purchased the gun and the resolve to use it had crossed two continents and an ocean but had originated with the Armenian Defense League in Los Angeles, California. None of the wealthy benefactors knew what the money was being spent on, but he seriously doubted that they would disapprove. He was a kind of accountant balancing a ledger. His employers would not lose a shred of their respectability, yet would receive an excellent return on their investment. They might even raise a monument to his courage.

A movement in the corner of the gated yard caught his eye. A sturdy boy in curly black hair and costly silk clothes swung the gate open and ran across the street to the wineshop.

His arrival brought all activity in the shop to an icy standstill. No more singing. No clink of glasses. Two old men playing *tavloo*, an Armenian form of backgammon, stopped their good-natured ribbing and raked the boy with looks of utter contempt.

The son of Judas.

He was a strikingly handsome boy, with perfect white teeth flashing a radiant smile and impossibly long lashes framing beautiful raven eyes. If he sensed a chill at his presence, he showed no sign.

"My father hosts a party for Tekir Pasha, the chief of military police," he said importantly in a voice strong and clear. "He would like five bottles of your best Martel wine!"

The shopkeeper hesitated, scanning the faces of his older customers for permission. Though finding none, he thought better of turning down the purchase of five bottles of his best. The boy made a show of paying the shopkeeper and hurried away cumbersomely hunched over, five bottles cradled carefully against his chest as if they were five kittens in danger of being crushed.

The assassin watched the boy stagger home with the wine. He hated to leave fatherless one so fair. But as he watched the boy disappear through the massive ornate doors bought with Armenian blood, he felt like firing from where he sat. Let the devil sort the innocent from the guilty.

"Thank the good Father he bears little resemblance to that bloated pus bag of a father!" snorted one of the backgammon players derisively. The wineshop patrons erupted in laughter, breaking the tension. But the mirth came sour.

"Mugurditchian should have more sense than to entertain

Turkish security so openly!" exclaimed the other player, rubbing one rheumy eye with a yellowed nail. "Doing so could cause acute lead poisoning!" That brought another gale of forced laughter in which the assassin did not participate.

The rest of the patrons waited. The sweating assassin at the corner table knew they wanted him to show himself one of the true remnant. To not laugh at the expense of a traitor yanked one's own reputation into question. Perhaps they assumed he lived in a hole in the ground and was not yet aware a Judas lived among them.

Or perhaps they thought he was a Turk. Or worse, a Turk sympathizer.

The assassin stood, threw money on the table, and faced them. "You sit here, play games, drink wine, suspect everyone, and do nothing. That is why we died. We were docile, easy prey, and for that we are now barely a people. Stay out of my way, or I might be tempted to shoot you myself!"

He stormed from the wineshop, a whirlwind of hope and dread. More death was unlikely to solve much, but he could not stand the thought of spending the remainder of his days playing table games, sipping wine, and making wry political comments to someone who couldn't hear any better than he could.

But why had he threatened his own people? The living were as much victims as the dead.

Maybe he was just sick of being defenseless.

He crossed the street, stepped up to the wrought-iron fence, and looked into the large room clearly visible from the street.

The hugely obese Armenian Judas, Harootoun Mugurditchian, emerged from behind parted drapes, brandy glass in hand, and entered the grand room lit by a hundred fluttering candles. He strode to the banquet table in the center of the room, smiled at his dinner guests, which included Stambul's Military Police Chief Tekir Pasha, raised the deep red liquid high, and rapped importantly on the table with his spoon. The fat man's thick lips moved in a toast, and the revelers thrust their glasses toward the crystal chandelier in boisterous unison.

Was it the easy demise of three hundred gifted Armenian citizens of Turkey they celebrated?

In that moment, the lone figure beyond the iron fence surrounding Mugurditchian's mansion raised the German Mauser automatic and took aim through the dining room window. Although there were eight cartridges in the magazine, one would be enough. One pull of the trigger would settle the case. Maybe this is what the Turks had wanted all along—Armenians to murder Armenians.

But he was not a murderer. He was an assassin.

Whatever he was, he quieted his heart and squeezed the trigger.

CHAPTER 3

Adrine Sarafian awoke with a start. Something was amiss. Tatul was not beside her, nor was his side of the bed even faintly warm.

It had been a long night, although only a few hours of dark remained once they had finally settled down to rest. Tatul could not get comfortable and had spent the night groaning in a futile attempt to find relief from the cuts and bruises he'd sustained in the beating.

Adrine had slept little, perched at the far edge of the bed for fear of touching him and adding to his misery. She winced now at the sight of dried blood on his side of the bedclothes. Where had he gone?

She must have sensed the space caused by his leaving and subconsciously settled into it from sheer exhaustion. How could she have been so callous to sleep through like that?

Adrine reached for the pocket watch she'd placed on the nightstand the night before and saw that it was almost noon. She had not gone to church that morning, emotionally and physically drained as she was from the previous night's ordeal. And worse, she was still in shock that the damage to her husband had been caused by their own.

He was not anywhere in the house. She looked and called for him until the night fears gave way to a daylight dread. Given his condition, this disappearance was even more puzzling than his actions twelve hours before.

Maybe they had come for him. The Covenant of Noah—the most likely group to have attacked Tatul—was a small

31

band of independent Armenian roughnecks who believed Armenia's only hope of recovery was to take advantage of postwar turmoil in Istanbul. Their strategy was to go for Turkey's jugular by eradicating old leadership and hunting down the Young Turks in exile in Germany, by disrupting commerce and communications, by subverting the military—in short, by keeping the chaos alive. Then while the Turks were otherwise occupied, they would take back the homeland and raise the flag over an independent republic of Armenia. That there was no Armenian government, no Armenian military, and barely any Armenian population with which to accomplish the task seemed not to deter the young idealists in the least.

And woe to anyone who consorted with the enemy on any other terms. Almost any kind of negotiations—peace resolutions or written treaties notwithstanding—were tantamount to treason. Add to Tatul's sins that of having a wife who traded with the enemy—nay, profited by it—and Tatul Sarafian was viewed by Covenant hotheads as more a suspect than an advocate.

What the Covenant failed to realize was that Armenia had no clout on the world stage. The fight for Turkish nationalism was centered in the interior of Anatolia, where Kemal Pasha was showing occupying Greek forces the bottom of his boot. No one had time or energy to listen to the weakened Armenians and their talk of an independent state. It could come in time, but not yet. Citizen rights first. Basic human dignity and respect for the oppressed.

Patience was called for. But patience was something the Covenant knew little about.

Adrine's feet were cold, and she folded slender legs inside her plain cotton nightdress and tightly hugged her shins. She had recovered quickly once they had escaped to Russia. It had been a rapid return to the smooth, caramel complexion of youth, the lissome figure of one well kept, and the lustrous smoky black hair she liked to wear pulled back and tied with lavender ribbons. It was still a wonder to stroke that hair with a tortoiseshell brush and to marvel at how long it had grown. Her fondest memory was of the tender way in which Tatul the

Rescuer had held her in the River Euphrates, the way he had scrubbed clean the matted tangle of her hair, and how he had given her, an Armenian camp slave, new life.

Her next favorite memory of those days was that of the faces of her Armenian sisters of slavery when at last they crossed the border into the arms of "Uncle Christian." Meeting their adopted Russian families for the first time, they had fallen to the ground, weeping at such kindness. And when they saw the little carved wooden crosses on the walls and necks of the Russian "angels," they bathed the rude symbols of redemption and freedom with their kisses. Each time a door opened to a tattered refugee and closed to a friend safely settled, the Fox and his lady rode from them like the wind, high into the hills, and reported to the Black Wolf that another sister, or three or five, had found the Fedayeen promise of freedom to be as true as the rising and setting of the sun. And liberty delivered, Tatul and Adrine took their rest beneath bear hides in trees or caves, where they slept the deep night of the righteous.

" 'For we are to God the aroma of Christ among those who are being saved and those who are perishing. To the one we are the smell of death; to the other, the fragrance of life.' " She liked the sound of that and said it again. The apostle Paul's letter to the church at Corinth could as well have been to the Armenian church. When Tatul had wanted to execute the Turkish officials responsible for mistreating the Armenian women at Hekim Khan, Adrine had urged restraint. She believed then, as she did now, that the way in which the surviving church behaved toward its persecutors could mean a significant difference in how many actually tasted eternal life.

Maybe Tatul's idea to farm a little patch of fertile land in the shadow of Ararat was the wisest course of action. Then they could have their babies, let them run with the wind, and be content with the simple life of field and forest. Her children could play with foxes and study the ways of the eagle. She and her husband could lie down beneath trees heavy with golden fruit and let free their love without fear, instead of living tight with the knowledge that friend and foe presented two faces of the same danger. Anxiously, Adrine bit a knee through the cloth of her nightgown. Three years they had been married, and children had not come. But the nausea of the last few days ... perhaps it was too early to be sure. ...

Should she tell Tatul?

She turned onto her belly, as if to protect it from unseen forces. She bit her lip and prayed for Tatul's safe return, and wondered if love could flower where hatred grew thick as thistles.

It was after one o'clock when she heard him enter, walking softly so as not to wake her. Through slitted eyes she watched him.

He did not remove his coat but took a bit of bread, cheese, and milk to the table and had barely sat before the food was gone. He sighed dejectedly, rose, and came into the bedroom to stare at her still form.

Tatul went to the window, lifted the blind, and stared out. For a long while he did not move, and finally Adrine opened her eyes a crack and studied him.

He was disheveled, sweating, knees caked in road dust as if he'd been kneeling in dirt. No less handsome than when he'd ridden down out of the mountain heights, he did possess a newly acquired rigidity of shoulders and chest. A watchfulness that was unlike the natural alertness of the Fedayeen— more a city wariness born of betrayal. Trust no one, it said. Beware father, mother, friend, and lover.

From the bed, she held her arms out to him. Most of the citizens of Istanbul reclined on pillows and slept on floor mats, but with money from her enterprise at the Grand Bazaar, Adrine had surprised him with western luxury: a four-poster with goose-down mattress.

"Come, my mountain lion," she called to him now, "tell me what you have learned of Constantinople this Sabbath morn."

He pulled the blind again and filled her arms, careworn and rueful, and she breathed in the muskiness of trail and campfire imbedded forever in his pores. But this day there was something else, something heavier, biting, more metallic in his skin and clothes.

Gunpowder.

She did not ask. She did not want to lose his gentle hands, nor the lips that hungrily sought hers. She did not want to talk of heated debate, the halls of power, or the streets of treachery. He was with her now, lavishing her with himself, and it was all that mattered.

"Guess how the sultan used to announce the births of his children," he mumbled into her neck.

She laughed merrily at his antics. "Colored fireworks?" she guessed.

"Nearly right." He fixed her eyes with the sparkle in his own. "A seven-cannon salute from the seawalls for a boy, three cannon blasts for a mere girl. Repeated five times in twenty-four hours, followed by a royal procession of the jeweled infant cradle through the streets of Constantinople right into the royal birthing chamber of the imperial palace. I think that's how we should announce the birth of the first little Sarafian, don't you?"

When he caressed her cheek, the bite of gunpowder was heaviest on his hand. She looked away, not wanting to give news of the growing certainty that God had heard their prayers. Not yet.

"I thought you were too sore from your mauling to entertain such vigorous romantic thoughts?"

"Oh, I am," he said, kissing her about the ears. "I most certainly am!"

Tatul removed his coat before kissing her again and falling more deeply into her arms.

She pretended that the smell of gunpowder was no longer as strong.

———

How long she watched the midafternoon sun light the pillowy cloud of canopy she could not guess. Long enough for the light to shift from high and bright to thin oblique shafts

fragmented by the buildings to the west. The somber, late afternoon city light going down took her joy with it.

He cradled in her arms on the edge of wakefulness, his fine
chiseled nose nestled against her skin, the steady stream of his
breathing stirring the fine, invisible hairs of her shoulder and
neck.

She loved him there, loved that this restless soldier of Ararat could sleep at all, loved that he seemed most at peace in
the crook of her arm, in the bend of her neck, in the uncon-
ditional acceptance of her embrace.

But the quiet room held something other than a man and
woman in love. Something from outside had slipped through
the door with him, something that filled the room unseen and
now hid among his clothes and rode the tiny dust motes drift-
ing on the shafts of light dividing canopy, bed, and the bodies
of man and wife.

Something threatening.

"Why do you smell of gunpowder?" She feared the truth,
but it was better to give the intruder a name, to haul it from
the shadows and give it a good shake, than to allow it to dwell
with them unconfronted.

The answer took its time, which meant it would not be the
whole truth. She would be reassured, placated, diverted with
another exotic nugget of fact from ancient Istanbul. The war
had made storytellers of them all.

"Weapons drill," Tatul said with a yawn and a kiss to her
neck. "Our weapons must be cleaned and fired with as much
regularity as limited munitions will allow. We will not be
taken again without a shot." The few thousand male Armenian survivors of the extermination chafed bitterly from the
ease with which the Turks had rounded up their fathers,
brothers, uncles, and sons, had summarily disarmed them,
and then executed them en masse on the flimsiest of charges.
With frightening speed, the emasculation of Armenia left
hundreds of thousands of women, children, and old men in
the hands of zealots who had been taught from birth that to
kill infidels would earn them a quick pass into paradise.

Adrine stiffened. They had plowed this ground many

times, she trying to teach him the mercies of God, he trying to educate her in the realities of personal honor and national security.

"A man is required of God to protect his family, to defend his people. I would be no man of honor, my jewel, if I did not learn from yesterday's horrors. The jackal Turks would laugh at such a surrender."

She pushed him away, stood, and snatched the pocket watch from the nightstand. Click! Snap! Click! Snap! Open and shut. Open and shut. Over and over she worked the time-piece lid, an angry habit he teased her about when there was not something unholy and uninvited in the room.

"Private weapons aren't permitted, Tatul! Yet you have them in the house, carry them wherever you go." She stormed over to the smooth ebony dresser top—another concession to western influences—and traded the watch for a pincushion and hair ribbon box, which she began to rearrange. "What you are doing is illegal and will result in all of us being shot or deported, and all our efforts at restoration will be ruined!"

He leapt from the bed, grabbed her shoulders, and whirled her about to face him. His handsome features were as dark as an Ararat storm. "Private weapons are not permitted in the hands of Armenians, you mean! The Turks understand just one thing, and that one thing is force!" The muscles along Tatul's jaw knotted furiously. "Our nation has been flattened, our finest thinkers, craftsmen, and statesmen destroyed, and our gentle people reduced to a mountain of empty, sun-bleached skulls! The pride of Armenia, even were it only to be found in one last man, is all that remains to protect. I will defend that pride to my dying breath!"

Adrine did the unthinkable. She laughed. His stern gaze foundered. He was hurt. She hadn't meant to wound him, yet she harbored a rage of her own at the gross injustice visited on her people. But deep within she knew that God would not be mocked. He would judge and His judgment would be sure.

So righteous a judge as He would not want the People of the Book, the ancient Christian Armenians, to return horror for horror.

She plunged on, the fire building in her breast. "Armenia's pride? It is your pride—yours, Tatul—that endangers your ability to negotiate with Constantinople. The possibility for peace is precarious at best. President Wilson has refused to send American troops to help in the occupation of Turkey, despite our friend Frank Davidson's most persuasive efforts. I know that disappoints you terribly, as it does me, but you know how passionate Frank is for us, for Armenia. In spite of his position as a neutral American observer, he risked his own life and career to get us to safety, all the while trusting that we would use our heads, not our hatred, to bring sanity and accord out of chaos.

"But we must face reality, my fine Fedayee." She reached for him, but this time he stiffened, and she dropped her hand. "America will accept no responsibility in the Near East. Americans themselves don't want it."

Tatul leaned against the window frame, face buried in one arm. His muffled voice came thick and discouraged. "And so you have proved my point and the reason why I must defend the homeland the way I choose. No one loves the Armenians except the Armen—"

"Stop it!" she cried, dropping to her knees on the Persian blue carpet, tears flooding the flashing brown eyes. "*God* loves the Armenians. *He* will fight our battles!"

Silence reigned between them for a while. When Tatul spoke again, his voice was low and tinged with deadly resolve. "You have seen the naked Armenian mothers covered in the tattoo markings of their Turkish owners. You have seen the severed Armenian heads hanging from Turkish clotheslines. You have read the pashas' goal to annihilate all Armenians, keeping aside just one man and one woman for display in a museum as historical oddities. You have been in the orphanages and seen the little children, utterly alone, who will never again know a living relative, nor do they dare go outside the dark little warehouses where they are kept like mice in a woodpile. Where is God in that, my love? Where is He?"

The question rang like a bitter gong against the only other sound in the room—Adrine's soft weeping. "God is faithful," she whispered, then louder, defiant. "He is always faithful!"

It was her husband's turn to laugh, but there was no humor in it. "I have learned that God does not cure all ills at the first sign of prayer. When we are done with praying and have at last leaned our shoulders to the problem, He will lend His. I have done that—the brothers have done that. All our wits and meager resources are His. You speak of God's faithfulness. I say that He expects us to join ours to His, and so the Armenian Committee for a Restored Homeland believes in its motto, *ad mortem fidelis*. Faithful until death. Our faithfulness. His. Inseparable."

Adrine looked up at him, wanting to believe every word but knowing too much. She got quickly to her feet, crossed the room before Tatul could stop her, and pulled a pistol from his coat draped across a chair. "Is this your idea of faithfulness?" she mocked, waving the gun in the air. "Is this how you love?" She threw the gun onto the bed and wished she hadn't. It lay on the soft gold coverlet like a fat black toad, evil and violent. It gave off a warning that divided them in a way that background, temperament, and a world war could not.

A loud pounding rattled the front door. Startled, the Sarafians reacted a second too slow, and the pounding thundered again. Adrine shook her head with an expression that begged him not to answer. She sensed from its insistence that it was not happy news.

Her husband gave her a reassuring smile and brushed against her back with a hand of apology. On the third pounding of the door, he wrenched it open, and a gasping, burly brother Andranik nearly fell into Tatul's arms.

"What?! What is it?" Tatul shouted, holding the excited little man firmly by his stout shoulders and giving a shake.

"It's all . . . all over the city!" Andranik sputtered breathlessly, bulbous eyes darting about his head quickly as a lizard's searching for flies. "Haven't you heard? The Judas is dead! Not three hours ago. Shot through the head in midtoast, wine all down the front of that expensively tailored jacket, his blood all over the fine crystal the Turks gave him. Executed in front of his guests! I tell you, he was shot dead before his wife and son. The Judas is dead!"

Adrine, lips trembling, locked eyes with Tatul, but asked the question of Andranik. "Mugurditchian? Dead? Who did this thing? Who?"

"They do not know, good Adrine," Andranik burbled, his joy unmistakable. "The gendarmes have spread over the city in search of a lone gunman. Strange, but none of the Armenians in the area saw much. They're talking to the priest now. I say it was the angel Gabriel!" At the look on Adrine's face, the little man visibly lost some of his enthusiasm.

"Do they know the weapon that was used?" she asked steadily, searching her husband's eyes for the flicker of guile, the expediency that came with the politics of nationalism. She doubted neither his love for her, nor for Armenia. But sometimes the latter meant a kind of compromise she doubted a great deal.

Andranik looked uncertainly between Adrine and Tatul.

"Andranik, the weapon?" Her tone bore a warning. No prevarication or he would lose all rights and privileges to her stuffed mackerel and chicken pudding.

"A . . . an automatic pistol, good lady, if the effusive new police administrator is to be believed."

Adrine caught Tatul's desperate look at Andranik, but it was too late, and the Fox let out a slow, defeated sigh. Andranik gulped and looked as if he'd consumed bad fish.

"What more?" Adrine insisted. "What more did the talkative captain of the gendarmerie have to say?"

Andranik hung his head and mumbled the rest. "They've seen the like countless times in the wounds of war. German Mauser, Model 1910 most likely, one of the best-finished pistols ever . . . made. . . ." He trailed off.

No one else said a thing, and Andranik cleared his throat. "Good day, friends. I have other rounds to make. I . . . I just thought you should know."

Adrine nodded, the tears beginning again, and walked slowly back toward the bedroom. Tatul said nothing but opened the door and stood aside. As the flustered Andranik brushed past, unwelcome for the second time in twenty-four hours, a strong, reassuring hand pressed on his elbow.

"*Ad mortem fidelis!*" Sarafian whispered in his ear.

A radiant smile of relief wreathed the sweating round face. "*Ad mortem fidelis!*" came the return whisper, followed by a wink in salute.

The door closed on one man, but the house felt empty of all life.

Tatul found Adrine staring down at the gun on the gold coverlet, her shoulders trembling along with her hands.

"It's a common weapon, used extensively by most of the German forces in the war," Tatul said, knowing it would do little good. "Many were collected from the dead by Armenian and Kurd civilians and have found their way into the general population. Anyone could have—"

She stopped him with an upraised hand, the skin forever scarred by neglect and slavery.

The smell of gunpowder in the room had strangely intensified.

CHAPTER 4

She dodged the scurrying *hamals*, men bent low to the ground beneath their impossibly high bales of cloth, straw, and matting bound for storekeepers in the Grand Bazaar. The pull of duty was strong and a part of her wanted to run alongside them to her own food stall on Produce Street, where the bright fruits and nutritious nuts of the Anatolia penetrated the sunless bowels of the greatest market on earth. God's good gifts of light, water, and soil always made her feel right again.

Adrine's enterprise, A Taste of the Homeland, offered a wonderful mix of fresh fruit and vegetables, preserves and jams, shipped by rail from the fertile farms of Hamit Batu, a wealthy and sympathetic Turk. Eventually they would export to foreign markets from the port of Stambul and fetch a fine price from war-weary Europeans. Until those markets opened up, Adrine's coveted retail location in the Grand Bazaar was always one of the most crowded stops in the ancient, teeming marketplace.

But duty took precedence this morning. She was on her way to the orphanage, where the orphan boys were in constant danger from Tekir Pasha, the head of the Istanbul security force, and his disdain for impoverished foreigners. The boys took hope in her visits. First Cheyrek, the mute one. It would be good to see him. He channeled her misgivings, gave her somewhere to direct her rage against Turkey. Yesterday's frustrations; Tatul's beating; the growing suspicion of an agenda he kept secret from her; the slaying of Mugurditchian; the smell of gunpowder on her husband's hands and clothing,

43

and still strong in her nostrils; the pain of childlessness—yes, Cheyrek was exactly what she needed today.

The outstretched arm of a toothless beggar reached for the hem of her dress. She jumped aside, snatching the garment away from the trembling reach of three fingers and two festering stumps. She fished in a pocket for a coin and tossed it into a worn basket at the man's bony knees.

"Father God is good," she said and smiled at him.

"Allah the Avenger is better!" he croaked, high-pitched and slurred, anger and contempt for her in the suspicious squint of watery eyes.

She hurried on, chastising herself for not paying closer attention and for being so casual with her outlawed faith. Adrine Sarafian would not be the first Christian infidel to be tripped by a stick and pulled into a side street to receive her final correction.

Tatul did not like her coming here to Sulukule. He had offered to come with her today, but she was still reeling from the news of Mugurditchian's assassination. She didn't want Tatul beside her now, not when her heart was so stormy and conflicted.

The gloomy, ramshackle Gypsy district clung unwanted as a boil to the massive land walls of the Old City that had protected the capital of Byzantium for more than one thousand years. The churning tumble of humanity numbered several hundred Gypsies, who, if it were possible, were the most despised of all people who drew breath in Istanbul—worse, even, than Armenians, most of whom did not trust them either.

Packs of ravenous dogs ran wild through the seams and furrows of Sulukule. They fed on the high ridges of refuse that marked the decaying boundaries of the evil place. Whole families burrowed into the crumbling fortifications of old and built their patchwork dwellings from the city's castoffs. Woodburning stoves sent a thick pall of semidarkness over winding cobblestones and decrepit dens of gamblers and fortune-tellers.

But the beauty of Sulukule was that it formed an effective buffer between the little orphanage full of destitute Armenian boys and the rest of Istanbul. The sympathetic Gypsies gave Adrine a free pass through their quarters, and gladly she tramped the gloom, the quicker to leave prying Turkish eyes behind.

"I wouldn't go there!"

Adrine started at the snarl spoken from the shadows of a darkened doorway. She could see no face, only the vague shape of scuffed, torn shoes and what looked like some sort of cane. She hurried faster.

"They are born of incest, and their women command the invisible spirits!" The voice rose and the cane thumped out a warning. "Allah told the people of the world to write their creeds in stone. All obeyed but the Gypsies, who wrote theirs on a cabbage leaf at once devoured by a donkey. They are not human; they have no souls. Don't . . ."

Adrine ran, gasping prayers against the powers of the air and old wives' tales. She turned to look back, tripped on a cobblestone, and fell hard against a mountain of rank fur.

She cried out, scrambling back from the musty, heaving sides of a brown bear. A short, stout Gypsy with a bulging sack over one shoulder, a pole over the other, and pockets spilling rags threw back his bald head and crowed delightedly.

"Shik Shik seeks female companionship. He dance, you dance, and I return to my castle stinking of money! Beautiful is the plan, yes, woman?"

Jesus, my Savior! My Protector! Adrine shrank back from the bear master's proffered hand and felt wooden bars grind against her shoulder blades. *I am a fool for coming here. . . .*

A beastly roar at her ear turned her blood to ice. She fought to scramble forward, but enormous claws hooked the hem of her dress and pinned her to the pavement. She turned her head and, wild-eyed, saw that she had backed against a cage crammed with bears. All were muzzled but one. The bear attached to her dress stretched through the bars with its other paw and caught her in a double grip. With a tearing of cloth, a toss of the great head, and a roar from between glistening teeth and slavering jaws, it began pulling her toward the cage.

Adrine yelled and kicked to get free. She gave the bear master a pleading look. He remained where he was but did add a crooked grin to a sweaty, grizzled mouth.

The bear flicked its head, shedding strings of spittle like slivers of glass, looking for all the world as if it wanted to toss Adrine in the air like the ball it balanced on its snout for laughing children. She could smell its breath, hot and rancid, and felt panic rising in her stomach.

Suddenly, with a command that sounded like he'd cleared his throat and was prepared to spit, the bear man waved an arm. His performing pet released its hold and sat back to whine and roar its disapproval.

"You are handsome woman! My wife is old and ugly with the world's fattest nose and one eye that sags to here," the man said, indicating his knee, then offered Adrine the end of the pole. They both pulled, and she regained her feet, brushing street filth from the heavy gown meant to conceal her femininity. The plain brown garment was less constricting than the hated *chador*, the head-to-toe covering that Muhammadan men liked to encase their women in for public appearances. Adrine had one for disguise and wished she'd worn it now, but the thought of peering out through its narrow eye slits like some jailed criminal made her furious.

The man leered, assessing her as if imagining the many ways he could benefit from her addition to his menagerie. "You got belly?" He smacked his stomach to show he meant one that was flat, suitable for belly dancing. "Perhaps you can see the future or play the strings. Maybe sell the goods I pick from the pockets my Shik Shik attracts? The taverns of Stambul drip with French and English officers in much need of companionship." He drew imaginary lines in the air before her face. "We redden the lips so, lay a touch of rouge here and here, take you from those heavy coverings, and dress you in a single belt of gold—ahhh! My tambourine will break from the weight of your earnings!"

"Leave her, Barg. Get away, stupid man!" From out of the smoky gloom rose a tall woman in stained pantaloons of faded blue, a long-sleeved brown quilted blouse, and a yellow head covering looped about the chin and tied to the side. Her large thin feet were dirty and bare.

Before her commanding blue eyes and stern, narrow-faced countenance, the loutish bear master visibly shrank. "Yes, *Myrig*," he mumbled, shuffling over to the cage to still the agitated Shik Shik. "A little business, nothing more," Barg pouted, as if hurt by their accusing stares.

"Come, child," Mother Agop said to Adrine, scanning the underfed bears and their chastened keeper with searing disapproval. "Let us leave these creatures and go for soup."

Adrine, only too glad to leave, picked up the tattered hem of the dress and hurried off after her protector angel with a fervent prayer of thanks.

The nameless orphanage materialized from the acrid gloom as poor and shabby as the scavenger land around it. Square and lumpy like the old warehouse that it was, it housed eighty boys aged five to thirteen, who were looked after by four myrigs, or mothers—three Armenians and the head mother, Arpi Agop. Though her name was Armenian, Adrine guessed she was Swiss. One's past and politics were forbidden subjects.

By war's end, scores of orphanages run by foreign missionaries had sprung up in southern Turkey in abandoned schools, warehouses, and military barracks. Thousands of Armenian offspring were gathered by the Allied troops from the deportation camps in the Syrian desert and from private Turkish, Kurdish, and Arabic homes where they had been "adopted." Often, the children were eager to go but had to be forcibly removed from their substitute parents.

In the hope that the children would eventually be reunited with their real families, they were brought to what were often smelly, diseased-filled holding stations like the nameless orphanage at Sulukule. It might be months or years before any were claimed, if ever, by surviving relatives.

Adrine and Mother Agop walked through an unpainted archway, climbed twelve steps, and entered a large open hall that smelled of urine and unwashed bodies. Two grimy windows near the ceiling shed the only outside light; three kerosene lamps smoked and sputtered scant illumination inside.

The boys were on the floor, leaning on their right arms, dipping little tin cups into steaming pots of cracked wheat and water with their left. A low murmur of childish voices, not as loud as eighty boys normally would generate, echoed below the clank of metal on metal. The thin sleeping mattresses, upon which two and sometimes three boys were required to sleep in the large hall and three adjoining rooms, had been taken to the roof to air out.

Mother Agop wrinkled her nose. "We do what we can. I teach them where and how to relieve themselves, but they are so nervous and stunned by all the atrocities they have witnessed that they forget, or cease to care." The words were heavy with sadness. "They know their names, but half have forgotten their day of birth. We guess at their age from their size, but many are stunted from lack of nutrition. We give them new birthdays, usually the day they arrived at the orphanage. Coming here, poor as it is, is a rebirth for my *yavrums*, my little sons." She frowned and tucked an errant strand of auburn hair back beneath the yellow head covering. "It is so difficult to carry the water from the fountain down the street. We try to keep them clean. We really do!"

Adrine tried to smile reassuringly, but Mother Agop and her few helpers were exhausted and riddled with guilt from the condition of their charges. Many boys had itchy rashes, rickets, and open sores; others, suffering from forced marches, limped and were missing nails from their fingers and toes; still others had the sticky eye, a disease that glued their eyelids shut overnight. They would rub their eyes for relief, then touch their neighbors and bedmates, spreading the germs on contact.

Mother Agop brightened. "Since you began delivering fresh vegetables and fruit, the boys' spirits are noticeably better. The older ones are willing now to teach the younger, and we manage some school every day. You watch when they come to the bottom of their cups and discover a chunk of sweet vegetable!"

Several were there now. Dirty fingers wiped the cups free of anything solid. Little exclamations of delight peppered the hollow interior of the spare, furnitureless room.

"Look! Look there! A bit of tomato big as my finger!" shouted a little lad in too short trousers held together by string and patched scraps.

"That *is* your finger!" snorted a bigger boy, rough and brutish in manner. "It fell right off because of all the lies you tell!"

"Meat! Meat!" shrieked another dirty-faced urchin, obviously a foil for his brutish friend. He crammed a hand into the little boy's cup and fished up the piece of tomato. "What'll you give me if I share this finger with you?" he sneered at the frightened younger boy.

Adrine started to intervene, but Mother Agop stopped her. "Watch," she said. "They've got to learn on their own to be human again."

Another boy, about the same age as the two bullies, quietly grabbed the dirty one's wrist, extracted the tomato, and dangled it over the little boy's open mouth like a mother bird with a worm. The tomato piece disappeared with a contented slurp.

"Garouj, you are to eat your food, not draw attention to it," the protector gently admonished the fledgling. "Now get ready to be painted." With great dignity, the bigger boy guided Garouj past the glares of the two who had been thwarted and over to the side of the room. There he began to remove his meager clothes and fold them carefully. The smaller boy followed suit.

Adrine averted her eyes and looked at Mother Agop questioningly.

"Help me paint the boys and then you may visit with Cheyrek. He has missed you," Mother Agop said.

Adrine nodded and followed the myrig to a stool situated in a pool of gray light that trickled from the windows above. The other women were at three other stools, each with a pail of putrid-smelling yellow sulphurous liquid.

The naked boys lined up before each stool. The first in Mother Agop's line was little Garouj, his guardian defender close behind. It was obviously not the first time they had submitted to the treatment. All seemed eager and not the least bit self-conscious to stand there naked.

Mother took a clean cloth and dipped it in the foul mixture, then gently smeared the boy from top to bottom with great care, all the while quietly murmuring words of endearing encouragement. The liquid cooled the torment and relieved the itch of bitten and diseased skin.

"You'd better hope that little monkey of yours doesn't wet on you tonight," the bullies in the next line taunted Garouj's champion. "When was the last time you slept in a dry bed?"

Adrine stung for the boy and felt like taking the bullies back to visit Shik Shik the bear.

But with all the humility of one three times his age, the taunted one placed a reassuring hand on Garouj's bare yellow shoulder and steered him toward the stairs to the roof. "You'd wet the bed, too, if you'd watched your mother finished in front of your eyes. He's my friend, and if no one comes for him, he will be my brother." With that they ascended the stairs to lie on the roof and dry in the sun.

Boy after boy received the treatment, some with smiles and chatter, others sober faced and not uttering a word. In shifts they dried out, then returned downstairs to dress and rest before the evening meal of gruel. A few of the more restless, feeling refreshed, ran to one particularly productive crack in the plaster of the big hall, where swarms of bedbugs of all sizes hopped and wriggled, awaiting the night and another feast of boy flesh. Some came the size of a pinhead; others were fat with the blood ingested the previous night. The bloated ones were seized and flung against the wall in a burst of blood to the accompaniment of boyish glee.

By the time the last boy had disappeared up the stairs to the roof, his emaciated anatomy painted like some strange and newly discovered creation, Adrine looked anxiously toward the room on the far right.

"He does not take the treatment," Mother Agop answered Adrine's unspoken concern. "Cheyrek does not remove his clothes. Go see him. Talk to him. That is his medicine."

Adrine swallowed but did not trust herself with more. What terrible horror had Cheyrek suffered? What had man done to him to steal his speech? What would become of him?

She found him rocking on the edge of his mattress, clothes dirty and smelly, one shoe on, the other nowhere in the immediate area. His bedmate lay on his back on the mattress, eyes closed, hands folded, still, but breathing contentedly. Only a dull yellow face and hands, scabs on both, and one patch of yellow-painted rib cage showed through his scraps of clothing, donated by Near East Relief. The boy was seven or eight years old, most likely.

Adrine guessed Cheyrek's age at ten or eleven. She'd taken a special liking to him from the first day she'd visited the orphanage. He was a handsome boy but pinched and bony from too long without good food, his skin flaky and bumpy from neglect. Big hands, long fingers. A pianist? At some point she would like to place him at a keyboard and see what he might do. The language of music could find the lost.

"Hello, Cheyrek." He kept rocking but looked up, and she saw the spark of recognition in his large dark eyes. She cupped his chin in her hand, sorry for the rough, sulphur-stained fingers, alarmed by the angry red infection spreading down his neck and beneath his shirt. She could tell he liked the feel of her skin normally. Did it remind him of his mother's touch? "I brought you soap. It's scented." She extracted the small white bar from her dress. Cheyrek snatched it from her and held it to his nose, rocking and sniffing, rocking and sniffing.

She gently unwrapped his fingers from the soap and took it back. The rocking never stopped, but his eyes hardened and his body stiffened. Adrine put her face close to his and smiled. "I just want you to be a caring boy, respectful of me. You may have the soap, but please take it from me in a calm, caring manner."

For several seconds, nothing changed. Then slowly, deliberately, with no slowing of the rocking, Cheyrek's hand lifted, palm up and open to receive the soap. Adrine looked deep into those distant eyes and laid the soap softly in his palm. Instantly youthful fingers curled closed around the soap and her hand, holding both to his cheek. She planted her other hand firmly on Cheyrek's shoulder and halted the rocking. She felt the familiar stiffening as if he resented the interruption of an established pattern, took solace in the steady movement. She wondered if the motions approximated the pace of marching, when bayonets and whips had kept the refugees moving long after their brains had ceased to comprehend what they were doing.

Adrine kissed the sweet face damaged by ill treatment and weeping sores. Cheyrek raised his face, his nose close to her neck, and breathed deeply. She felt him relax like a child reassured that the monsters of the night are not real.

The tears on his cheek were hers.

"I saw them drown my sister," the boy next to Cheyrek said without opening his eyes. "That's why he won't take his clothes off. They made the people in the caravans do that just before they killed them; then they sold the clothes at the next village. The Turk soldiers were drunk and ordered my sister to take off her clothes and dance for them. She took off her dress but refused to dance so they brought me up to her and told me to watch while they taught her a lesson."

To that point, he had told the story without emotion. Now his lower lip began to quiver, and he covered his eyes with both hands. "My sister . . . was good. She gave me candy and told me not to look. . . ." The boy's chest started to heave, and sobs tore from his throat.

Adrine took his hand and pulled him to her, hugging one boy in each arm. "Shh, shh," she comforted, "your dear sister is with God."

The sobbing boy clung tightly to her neck. Cheyrek remained quiet. "I . . . I think so too," the other boy said, "but I'm afraid there were too many for God to care. . . ."

"No, no," Adrine soothed. "God knows each one and cares very much."

"Then why won't God help me remember?" the boy cried, his face contorted with guilt.

Confused, Adrine asked, "Remember what, my *yavrum*?"

"My sister's name," he said, the desolation thick in his throat.

Adrine held the boys a long while, craving to restore a small part of their great loss while deeply feeling hers and Tatul's as well. To date, the Sarafians had found only two distant cousins, the remainder of their families unaccounted for. Mother, father, baby brother ... It was an incomprehensible loss, and daily they prayed for word from the deportation camps that someone close to them had survived.

A few thousand others prayed the same prayer.

Eventually, the heaving of the weeping boy's chest subsided to an occasional sob, then stopped altogether. "Would you let me smell the soap?" he asked timidly.

She left it with him and led Cheyrek to the roof. Mother saw them go and followed at a distance with a pail.

Carefully, gently, Adrine undressed the boy, telling him how much better he would feel from the medicine, how he could not allow the Turks to continue to terrorize him because of what they had done in the past.

Mother Agop began to paint Cheyrek, and between the two women they were able to complete the task.

Though he still would not speak, Cheyrek Effendi ceased to rock back and forth. Painted and dressed in clean rags for the first time since he'd come to the orphanage, he went to bed and slept for twelve hours.

The noise of the exploding bullet; the spray of shattered glass; the horrified stares of Istanbul's elite; the dumbstruck collapse of their host's wine-soaked demeanor; the sudden ugly appearance of a hole black with blood in the center of his forehead—the harsh details of yesterday's act of justice unreeled in the assassin's mind like a silent film, complete with flickering brought on by nausea, uncertainty, the ease with which a man's life could be yanked from him.

He refused to think of himself as the villain in the piece. He so wanted to be the hero, and intellectually he was the gory conqueror worthy of a ride through a sea of adoring people waving palm branches and shouting his glory.

But what of the lingering tremor in the hands, the ringing, the diminished hearing in the right ear, the night sweats and dreams of his mother weeping over the remains of her executed son? Were these the rewards of an act of honor?

The ferry horns cleared their metallic throats, and the gulls swooped low for a handout. Finding none about the lone man, they wheeled skyward and flew off, chattering in scolding tones.

The assassin clenched and unclenched fists slick with perspiration. He tugged at the sleeves of a coat suddenly too small. His body felt swollen, someone else's onto which his head and limbs had been poorly sewn. He wanted out of his body, out of Istanbul, out of the small tasks that gave his people the appearance of normality but were the mere movements of a vanquished people trying not to go mad.

He should go after the woman he loved, not leave her without a man's shelter and a lover's touch. But how could he give himself to her fully without first completing the job he was sworn to do? The Turk pashas responsible for the rape of his people must be brought to account in the same manner the Judas had died—publicly, suddenly, decisively. Once they lay forever silenced, only then could he give his love what she wanted and be the husband that she had every right to expect.

Without that, the job was incomplete.

The assassin thudded unsteady fists against hardened thighs and filled tight lungs with the tang of the sea. He prayed down the strength of a hundred Samsons for what he had yet to do and started walking briskly away from the bridge and its disgruntled gulls.

CHAPTER 5

"They are leaving, I tell you, leaving in droves!" Artin Chazarian shouted above the tumult of the assembly. His father and his father before him had been proud members of the outlawed Hunchakian Party, Marxist Armenian agitators with a fierce hatred for the sultan and any Armenians who served him.

It was no secret that the equally volatile Chazarian the Younger slept with live grenades under his pillow.

Cries for silence peppered the hall, but Artin's passionate hatred for anything Ottoman shouted them down. "It is written that a Turk is a Turk, and neither God nor the devil can make a human being of him! You have smelled Turk justice, tasted it, witnessed the blood-soaked lie of it, my brothers, and now you must not shrink from duty. Ararat, our mother, demands that you take action before all of the Armenian citizens of Stambul have disappeared or fled the city!"

Here he took a deep breath, raised up on his tiptoes, leaned out over the dais, and pointed an accusing finger at the moderates led by Tatul Sarafian. "There are more Christians buried in the ground of Istanbul than walk upon it! Our people are afraid. To use the streets is to be raped or shot. To call a sudden meeting like this is more a criminal act than to set fire to a mosque. Our brave brother Martin assumes a terrible risk giving us his auction hall for our use." A man of five decades was thrust to the center of the room by his fellows and accorded a rumble of grateful respect from those gathered. He quickly leapt back into the crowd, growling protest at the recognition.

"Little children spend their lives in the dark, prevented from playing in the sun," Chazarian hurried on. "And if they did, they would soon be snatched away, suffocated, and fed to the wild dogs that roam at will and are more revered by their cousins the Turks than God's own children the Armenians! Though once we lived as trusted confidants in the palaces of Constantinople, kept the royal treasury, taught the royal military, and kissed the royal rump when expedient, today we are human waste. I say, brothers, let us stand on our own hind limbs and help the sick man of Europe along to his well-deserved death!"

The assembly erupted in a din of conflicting shouts and angry pronouncements. Two men came to blows. Four more attempted to wedge them apart, then joined the fray. Tatul Sarafian, grim faced, eyes squeezed tightly shut, gripped the railing that separated him from the dais and listened to the roar. Despite the broil of emotions in his own chest, he smiled to himself. The Hunchak was in rare form, his language as colorful and incendiary as usual. Abuse the long-suffering Armenians, and though devoted to God and family and peaceful industry, they became impossible to contain. Sadly, it was as true for reformers as for insurrectionists. Unsanctioned meetings like these risked police retribution but were necessary to release steam from the dangerously creaking pressure valve of Armenian grievance.

Tatul said a quick prayer and brought his hands together in a loud clap. Again and again, two beats apart. The bruised and blackened fighters dropped their fists. Gradually, the warring factions ceased their shouting and turned their attention to the one man more persuasive than the voice of violence. The man from Erzurum. The legendary Fedayee. The favorite son of Kevork Chavoush, the Black Wolf.

Tatul Sarafian, the Fox.

"Was it your finger on the trigger, my brother?" Tatul asked, looking steadily at Chazarian. "Do you honestly believe that killing the Armenian servant of the pashas, little human that he was, in any way strengthens our claim for a sovereign homeland?" Tatul was on exceedingly dangerous ground, and he knew it. No one had witnessed the execution. None in the room, be they rebels or moderates, mourned the loss of Mugurditchian the Judas. Not even Tatul. But the killing had been ill-advised if the return of Armenia was the ultimate desire.

The sinister buzz in the room indicated just how thin was the support for a critic of the Judas execution.

At first Chazarian swelled like an indignant cat. But quickly it dawned on him that so reckless a statement on Tatul's part might actually be a clever chess move in disguise. He warily examined Sarafian's face for clues of intent.

"Yes, I do think selective retribution is effective," Chazarian said at last, careful to avoid the first of the moderate's questions. "Assassination, precisely targeted, can demoralize the Turk nationalists to the point where each is feeling his own throat for blood. They will soon realize that driven underground, we are far deadlier than if allowed to peaceably farm and govern our own territory."

Tatul nodded. "I empathize with the heartfelt need we each feel to extract a tub of flesh—nay, a barrel, a wagonload! But to expect total capitulation in response to murder, selective or otherwise, is folly. Did we capitulate after all of our leaders were killed and dumped in mass graves? No! Armenia preserved the faith, though our people are but a faded memory. We refused to die entirely. We refused to abandon our fight for the homeland. The Turks failed to annihilate us, and we refused to become like them!

"But now you propose a counterattack built on a systematic program of bloodshed—fighting slaughter with slaughter. When has that ever worked? What did your Hunchak forbears gain twenty years ago by assassinating the Armenians in the sultan's service? Mistrust is all, police gunfire, the suspension of the Armenian Constitution. Muhammadans permitted to beat Armenians to death in the streets—these streets! We are fools if that is our glorious proposal for the restoration of Armenia!"

Many in the assembly looked doubtful. Others appeared convicted by what Tatul said and the strength by which he said it. Chazarian saw their hesitancy and threw his arms wide.

"You are the fool, Sarafian! Where is the Balian family who built the sultan's palaces? Or the Dadian family who made his gunpowder? The Armenian doctors who closed his children's wounds? His printers, photographers, rugmakers? All were Armenians, all swallowed by the lion when he tired of them and decided they were full of evil intent after all. Just like every demented, inbred sultan that ever lived, he blamed the immigrant, the foreigner, the infidel because he had grown too fat and lazy to crawl from his silken bed and relieve himself without the aid of twenty footmen!"

A raucous cheer of approval swept the hall. Chazarian turned and acknowledged their applause, which only encouraged the thunder of stomping feet and a piercing cascade of whistles. The Hunchak had them very much where he wanted them.

Sarafian held up both hands and motioned for quiet. Because of his stature among them, they submitted one last time.

But before he could say a word, Chazarian grabbed the silence for himself. "How is your health today, Tatul my brother? It must be difficult to stand this long on legs so terribly beaten by your friends, the Ottomans!"

Tatul felt his composure slide and could do nothing to stop it. Trembling, both index fingers pointed accusingly at his Marxist opponent, he shouted, "*Your* friends, Artin, your *Armenian* thugs attacked me in the dark like the traitorous snakes they are! Cowards!" He looked about him, one by one at the men surrounding him, molten fire in his gaze. "Are you here, cowards? Dare you face me in the light? You'll not persuade me with your cudgels! Can't you see how ambush and dissent and unauthorized murder play into the hands of the enemy? We have no voice in postwar Turkey because we trample our own wonderful arguments. We are seen as little more than rabble here and in the rest of Europe. The Americans think of us as pathetic peasants, mindless as infants, and with good reason!"

Tatul saw the knowing look and wink Chazarian gave the crowd before turning to him with a gaze of mock sympathy.

"That sounds a great deal like that good wife of yours talking. Is it true Adrine Sarafian conducts trade with the Turks?"

Tatul felt a stab of regret. Sweet Adrine should not be dragged onto this battlefield. This was not about her. It was about the need to find the surest way for Armenia to either rise again or necessarily step from the world stage forever. But give Chazarian his due. He had no equal in a verbal duel.

"Excuse me, dear Artin, I mistakenly assumed we were here to debate matters of great import, such as the salvation of Armenia. But you have come to discuss kitchen matters. So be it. Is it true that no one consents to become your wife because all you have to offer is wind and pipe smoke?" Tatul's face was the picture of patience and concern for Artin's domestic shortcomings, and it was a picture he made certain everyone in the hall could see. A smattering of laughter indicated that the ploy had worked, and the tables were on the turn.

For a moment Chazarian said nothing. Like the consummate actor he was, he brushed away the rude laughter and formed a dark, troubled cloud over the folds and jowls of the cracked and expressive face that had incited the passions of a people on many like occasions. His shoulders sagged ever so slightly, and his voice, when he finally spoke, was heavy with regret. "Does your wife continue to frequent the dark dens of Sulukule, my friend?" The assembly gave a collective, knowing gasp. "How can you allow her to roam so freely, to do business with those who so thoroughly despise man and religion? The Gypsies have no god, and Adrine Sarafian has no sense." He said it regretfully, as one comforts another whose spouse has only recently sunk into madness.

Sarafian's fists clenched and unclenched. The cords of his neck strained. Those men close by, who had borne Tatul's battered body home, hoped that he would leap the railing, storm the dais, and pummel the smirk from the Marxist's face.

Instead, Tatul Sarafian's reply came with deadly calm.

"You know she ministers to the orphans, Artin. It is beneath even you to imply otherwise."

Chazarian saw that Sarafian's admirable restraint had won him valuable points with the brothers. He nodded agreeably. "To be sure, Tatul, to be sure. But Sulukule is a place of whores and scavengers who cast spells with the rattle of their tambourines. Adrine's senses would not be the first to fly from her. I am just anxious that she not meet with any injury or suffer an indignity from which neither of you might recover. Her business in the Grand Bazaar is going so well. . . ." Again their eyes met and danger flashed on both sides.

"I accept the caution and thank you for it," Tatul said with a slight bow toward Artin. "I also recognize it for what it is in its fullness—a thinly veiled warning that may come from a genuine concern for the safety of my household, but more likely, it is a threat that more of your Marxist persuaders could visit me in the shadow of a Stambul night or in the dirty gloom of a Sulukule day."

Chazarian wore his indignation like a thick winter coat.

Tatul turned to the assembly, raised his hands palms outward, and lifted his voice to the far rafters. "Hear me, brothers, and mark this moment well. You have heard Artin Chazarian deliver his caution to me. I admonish you each to hold our Hunchak brother personally responsible for my well-being, and the well-being of my wife. This is only reasonable, for each of us ought to place the highest price on the other's welfare. To the degree that we are united as one and that the world shall know our allegiance to Jesus Christ by our love, to that degree only will we succeed in again living and worshiping at the foot of blessed Mother Ararat!"

This time the tumult that erupted was all for Tatul. Thumps and claps on the back, though painful on his sore muscles, were as welcome as spring rain to his heart.

It was Artin's turn to grip the dais in an effort to steady baser inclinations. All he could do was allow the uproar to go on while he sorted out his options. He had been soundly, albeit momentarily, outfoxed.

When the noise began to die at last, Chazarian smiled

guilelessly at his worthy opponent. "A pretty speech! So peace filled, so Christian! Astounding that it would come from the mouth of a once mighty Fedayee. A man who bribed his way across northeastern Turkey, using money and threats to secure the loyalty of Kurd chieftains. True, it was a loyalty founded on sand, but it allowed Armenian freedom fighters the room to maneuver. Because of it, the Turks never did have a firm grip on that part of the empire. That allowed us to aid the Russians, and they us. You experienced those benefits firsthand, Tatul, when you and your wife were smuggled into Russia with the help of border priests. Eventually, the hundred Armenian women of Hekim Khan and their children that you so bravely rescued made their way to safety by those same priests. They could not have operated so effectively without the cunning arrangements made by the Fedayeen with the Kurdish tribes."

Chazarian sensed that the room would soon be his again. By touching on the much revered saga of the daring rescue of military camp slaves from the clutches of the evil Turk, Captain Ozal, the Hunchak gained instant credibility. Praise the work of the courageous Fedayeen, and one could get elected provincial governor.

But mutual admiration was not Artin's goal. For his plan of selective assassination to succeed, he must possess sole leadership of the assembly. For that, he would now take the greatest risk of his career and show the Fox for the tentative eunuch he had become.

The Hunchak pointed at Tatul but spoke to the assembly with a measured amount of sorrow and contempt. "Before you stands a once bright knight of the fighting Fedayeen, who in weakness now hammers his sword into a plowshare before the fight is finished. Once a phantom to be feared, today he is a politician to be scorned. Proud Tatul Sarafian hides behind the skirts of a woman. She is his chief advisor, and because he sleeps with her, she withholds her love if he even hints at the only justice a Turk understands—hot lead and cold steel! We have seen the harvest that capitulation brings. We have counted the ribs of our dying children. Europe denies us.

America denies us. Let us not, good brothers, deny ourselves!"

Slowly at first, then building in deep-voiced intensity, a chant of "Victory! Victory!" cannonaded between the walls of the narrow hall. In a fevered antiphonal response, Artin's men interjected with "Hunchak! Hunchak!" and soon it seemed everyone but Sarafian and his core of faithful supporters had joined the disturbing fury of the Marxist chant.

The sound, the heat, and the stink of agitated, closely packed bodies made Tatul's head spin. The beating had cost him much blood and the physical strength that went with it. Down to his knees he sank, hands clasped, heart thudding rapidly, head bowed as if in prayer.

Short, burly brother Andranik had all he could take and jumped down to the floor before the dais. Eyes bulging, he whirled like a dervish and shouted for attention.

"Hunchak! Hunchak!" the assembly roared, beginning now to crowd the dais and lift Artin Chazarian to their shoulders.

"Stop! Stop, you fools," Andranik sputtered, barely heard in the front row. He ran from railing to railing like a trapped rat, his bald head glistening with sweat. "Did Father Noah plot against the wicked giants of his day? Did . . . did he stockpile weapons against the betrayers of God? Or did he bow humbly before the Father's command to build an Ark and save the few righteous ones? Listen to Tatul, the brave one who listens to Christ's command to love our enemies, to revile not when we are reviled—"

"Hunchak! Hunchak!" The mob tore the dais aside and poured onto the central entry of the hall, knocking Andranik into the raised walkway that encircled three sides of the room. He fell, sobbing, against the rough wood flooring. "Holy God, stop them. Please stop them. . . ."

But nothing did, and like a black wave of crazed ants, they bore their new hero on into the streets of Istanbul.

From the windows and rooftop across the street, Turkish police soldiers watched the noisy Armenians loft their hero of the moment and proceed away from the auction hall. Tatul and his followers turned to face the police. He saw hands slowly seek pistols concealed in waistbands.

"No!" he spit through gritted teeth. His men hesitated.

Empty hands dropped to their sides.

Eight soldiers leveled rifles on chipped windowsills, and Tatul fully expected to hear the signal to fire on the mob.

"Hold fire!" ordered the commanding police officer who stood in the street, a slight man with slick black hair and narrow shoulders. The men withdrew their weapons from the open windows and stole quizzical looks at one another.

Their commander first looked at Sarafian's band warily watching back, then turned and stared at the jostling knot of humanity moving swiftly up the street until they were but a distant, indistinguishable blot.

Tatul and his men did not move.

A second officer stepped smartly into the street from inside the vacant building. He was younger, ambition in the straight set of jaw and spine. Crisp was his inquiry. "Commander?"

"Yes, Lieutenant?" came the reply, loud enough for all to hear.

"The auction hall?"

His commander spat in the street. "Torch it."

Andranik moaned.

Tatul felt every rifle barrel aimed at their hearts. Bitter frustration flooded head and belly, almost more than he could bear. Far ahead, Martin Matossian stupidly roared adoration for the Marxist orator. Soon he would return to find his livelihood burned to ashes. It would finish him. He would throw himself into the sea.

Finding barely enough breath to speak, Tatul hoarsely whispered, "Leave, brothers! Just turn around and leave."

He did not wait; nor did he return the police commander's curt nod of recognition. Neither wanted a bloodbath.

Sarafian turned and forced his feet to move away. He sensed the others reluctantly begin to follow.

The German Mauser beneath Tatul's shirt felt cold against his flesh.

CHAPTER 6

Adrine Sarafian drew the wrap more tightly about her shoulders and hurried toward the Grand Bazaar. She felt a dark premonition of trouble and wanted to look in on her produce stall. Perhaps apprehension was her just reward for keeping the stall open on the Christian Sabbath. But to leave A Taste of the Homeland shuttered and unguarded, for even a day, would invite mischief she did not need. To the shrewd merchants of the bazaar, a closed stall meant death in the family, a business failure, or an infidel at worship, any one of which could kill business by agitating those with a superstitious or hateful bent.

A chill fall wind blew off the Bosporus and made her heart beat faster. Every blast of a ship's horn seemed to push another frigid draft ahead of it.

Her one trip to Constantinople as a child had been in the fall. She rode the wind then, trying to outdistance each gust, laughing breathlessly every time Grandmother called in that far-reaching voice of hers to *"halt your tail feathers until the old legs catch up."* Every time they did, the little goose was off on another puff of wind, her flying feet barely grazing the surface of the ancient streets. *"Collide with the butcher, and you'll be sausage before I get there!"* Grandmother huffed. *"Goose sausage you'll be—sweet, mild, and full of squawk!"*

How light and lovely that journey had been.

How different today.

She hurried past the incredible grandeur of the Mosque of Sultan Suleyman the Magnificent. Muhammadan males washed their feet at large stone fountains in the courtyard in preparation for prayer. She heard the splash of cold water on bare feet but averted her eyes.

If only they would avert theirs.

She felt the eyes of young men appraising her, estimating the beauty beneath the heavy yet revealing garments—by Muslim standards—of the infidel. Centuries of tradition allowed them to hold Christian women in contempt as pagan daughters of evil. It also permitted them to beat their Muslim women in private yet pursue a public piety with great zeal. The Allah they served was as capricious and permissive as the Greek gods.

Stambul contained five hundred mosques, but none finer than Suleyman's. The "Lord of His Age" had for his architect the Christian Sinan, from whose mind and fingertips came an imperial splendor unmatched.

Adrine felt as small as an insect beside the mosque's immense domes and buttresses of stone, layered to a distant towering height like stepping-stones to heaven. Inside: tiles, stained glass, fields of rich carpeting. Outside: six schools of religion, a medical college, an asylum, a Turkish bath, and a caravansary, or inn, for the weary camel trains from the East.

She skirted the sultan's tall octagonal tomb and said a prayer for courage as she rushed past the daintier nearby tomb of Roxelana. She, of all the concubines, had captured Suleyman's heart and become his sole consort. The measure of her influence over the smitten sovereign was evident in the fact that he had married her, which sultans almost never did, and that he had allowed her tomb so close to his. And, most horribly, that she had caused Suleyman to execute his firstborn son. Royal rivals often fared poorly at the hands of their parents.

Suddenly from behind the tomb raced three ugly shadows.

Dogs. Adrine froze. The wild curs of Istanbul were another ancient curse the Muslims brought upon themselves. For nearly four hundred years, thousands of dogs had roamed the city at will, fed stale bread, calves' liver, and sheep spleen by the Muhammadans who considered them an omen of good fortune, a strange symbol of Muslim logic: "To have so many dogs means we have an abundance of garbage to give them. To have an abundance of garbage to give them means we have more than enough food to eat ourselves. To have an abundance of dogs to eat the garbage from the food we eat means we do not have to step in it." Muslim logic did not address the corresponding abundance of dog droppings on the streets of Istanbul, nor the increased fleas, disease, and dog attacks that kept Stambullus ever on the defensive.

To Adrine, the dirty, shiftless dogs were no more than despised Turks on four legs. Packs of them divided the city into territories, each controlled by one leader. They fought and killed trespassers and rivals. Some dogs became so aggressive that residents would walk miles out of their way to avoid them. Other dogs had to be beaten off the tram tracks with sticks to allow the trains to pass. At night, the curs joined in a ferocious hail of yelping, growling, and snarling that would begin in one quarter and soon roll over the entire city in waves of barks and bayings. The dogs of Istanbul defied the sultan himself.

Short and feral, their brown fur patchy with mange, the three dogs of the tomb eyed Adrine with slanted, darting glances. They licked their snouts and sidled toward her, squirming submissively for a handout.

The eerie wail of *muezzins* sounded loud and insistent from the four minarets of Suleyman's Mosque, calling all Muslim faithful to the fourth prayer of the day. Muezzins from one end of Istanbul to the other echoed the command to cease everything and fall down before Allah the All-Glorious as evening drew nigh.

The dogs, older and more grizzled than most who barely survived the streets, dropped to their bellies and began to howl their protest with necks stretched upward, eyes shut in torment. Perhaps they remembered the Great Collection nine years before when hundreds of strays were gathered into boats and dumped on Sivriada Island in the Sea of Marmara. A gruesome bedlam of bawling could be heard from the mainland for several nights, until the dogs died of starvation or turned to cannibalism and tore one another apart. The Stambullus still spoke in hushed voices of that terrible sound and the speed with which stray survivors and their puppies rushed into the city from outlying villages to fill the void and begin the cycle anew. Adrine was grateful she'd not been there.

She shivered now, fled around a corner away from the howling curs, and disturbed a cloud of pigeons who startled her. She stopped, waited until her breathing grew calm again, and berated herself. "You are a stupid goose! God blesses your life, and you wonder what He's up to. Superstition is for pagans!"

If only the sultan had spared his son.

Maybe she could adopt one of the orphans, just to be assured a child.

Cheyrek? Yesterday, when she had gotten beyond his outward defenses and reached a small, tender place inside, her heart had filled like . . . like what? A mother's?

"Is that what this apprehension is all about?" she said aloud. "You have so long been without child that the world tilts, water runs uphill, and dogs are evil?" She sniffed angrily and looked about to make certain no one heard her talking to herself. There was a new sensation in her belly now. Could the strange newness inside be anything other than the pulse of life? She waited respectfully for the prayers to end, said her own to Jehovah God, then continued on her way.

At the street corner a sheep auction was in full shout. Two men wrestled a lively purchase into the back of a rocking wagon. The big ram had other ideas and kicked one man flat beneath the wagon and butted the other in the shins with tightly curled horns. Their chances did not look good for getting the sacrifice home in time to commemorate Abraham's offering of his son, Isaac.

" 'Let us rejoice and shout for joy.' " Adrine recited the psalm of David to calm herself. What was she so nervous about? She hoped the two young women she had hired to run the produce stall were managing. Today was their first day without constant supervision. "Spread your protection over them, Father, that those who love your name may rejoice in you." She would rather have had Sosi Emre, or one of the other sisters smuggled away from the horrid military encampment at Hekim Khan, work with the unseasoned ones—girls, really—but they had their own children and other meager jobs to attend to. Sosi, the kindhearted Turk who had helped Adrine and become a follower of Christ, had married a good Turk who ran a popular bakery near the Grand Bazaar called The Scratching Chicken. He loved Sosi and her son Kenan and permitted them to practice their Christianity while he practiced Islam. It was not unusual to enter the bakery and find Sosi's husband on the floor facing Mecca, forehead to the ground, and Sosi behind the counter, arms white with flour, slapping dough and humming "What a Friend We Have in Jesus." That is, when her customers did not include a bold-eyed gendarme with sharp ears.

The psalm and the warm thoughts of friends calmed Adrine a little, but the tumult of the city, the memory of the deadly bear claws and bursting bedbugs, the constant threat of violence, and yes, she supposed, her own misgivings about Tatul and the tensions between them weighed heavily upon her. Andranik's news that morning of the assassination and Tatul's evasive strangeness had not helped. How ironic that she would struggle against fear now after—what did the world powers call it?—the "ceasing of hostilities." Well, maybe they had ceased elsewhere in the world, but in Turkey they were as hostile as ever, just not so open that the world could see.

The Grand Bazaar was a sensual, sprawling maze of three thousand merchandise shops and two thousand workshops spread over seventy streets and countless dark little connecting warrens. Older children loved to be blindfolded and taken deep within the teeming marketplace to a mystery location, then released to find their way out again. The blind could negotiate their way from corner to corner of the city-within-a-city without help, guided solely by the smells and sounds of commerce. Though victim of multiple fires over the ages, the fifteenth-century emporium remained the grandest market of them all.

Drawn to the familiar cacophany of barter and craftsmanship as a camel to water, Adrine instantly felt apprehension drain from her. Despite war shortages, the bazaar bulged again with goods of every kind and every color, so much so that there was no room for nagging worries. It was as if through some strange alchemy, merchants pulled brass and copper and jade from thin air. Among the Turks and their compatriots, there was no war so savage as to dam the flow of commerce.

The fishmongers held the outer edge of the market, where ocean breezes diluted the aroma of fin and gill. Adrine liked the smell of the sea and the silvery shimmer of the varied food that came from it. Bass and mackerel, herring and flounder, shrimp and squid, dredged from beneath the waves in nets of plenty. She marveled at the speed and accuracy with which the fishmongers hacked and gutted the harvest. Nothing wasted, nothing despised. The castoffs were swept into a huge slimy drum for fertilizer.

"Be aware!" came a shout from behind. She whirled about and threw her hands up in reflex just in time to receive a wiggling bundle of slippery bluefish.

Fevzi the Fisher smiled with every tooth he had—seven in all. "You needn't hold it so far from you, Sarafian's lady. The last woman swallowed by a bluefish has seventeen grandchildren and a small villa in Galata!"

Not all Turks were animals. Fevzi wouldn't give an anchovy for what anyone thought of his kind treatment of Armenians. His fishing partner, whom he loved like a brother, was a Greek-Armenian from Mersin on the south coast near Tarsus. Fevzi believed the best test of a man's mettle was not his ethnic origins, but the number of sardines he could eat at one sitting.

"I caught this one escaping," she said, tossing the bluefish back. It felt good to laugh. "Maybe if you paid your workers a decent wage, they wouldn't always be swimming over to the competition!"

"Fevzi has no competition!" huffed the fishmonger good-naturedly. He also didn't believe in keeping women in a box. Once when he ran out of paper in which to package a Muslim woman's purchase, he wrapped her fresh turbot in the startled woman's veil.

Fevzi gave Adrine a damp cloth, and she wiped her hands. He looked at her slyly and lowered his voice. "I'm sorry my friend was so slimy. I did not know he was a Turk!"

She laughed again and marveled at Fevzi's self-deprecating humor. "Keep the bluefish for me, fish mangler. I shall return for it in a couple of hours."

She paid him, and he took an exaggerated bite of the coin to make certain it was genuine. "Come back again when you can stay longer. We shall have that swordfish fight, I promise you!"

Adrine placed her hands in front of her chest, palms together, and bowed respectfully. "I shall bring my husband and a portion of mutton tripe soup to thaw that cold heart of yours."

Fevzi smacked appreciative lips and laid the bluefish aside. "Corn on the cob, good woman. Bring me six ears, and the gentleman bluefish is yours."

"Done!"

As the smell of salt water and fish faded behind, the aromas of lathed wood, new leather, and incense intensified. Cigarette vendors, comb sellers, black-market money changers, and beverage pourers converged in a swell of personal enterprise. She stopped a man with a silver samovar strapped to his back and was poured a small glass of squeezed orchid root.

Though her stall was farther down on Produce Street, Adrine wandered inside the bazaar, entering through one of its eleven gates, soaking up its fabulous excesses. It was as if her apprehensions had been anesthetized in a glorious swirl of sounds and smells and flashes of color. Goldsmiths' Street was ablaze in yellow riches. There were streets, too, for carpet makers, hand-beaten copper and brassware merchants, flower growers, embroiderers, and haberdashers. Vaulted ceilings covered a dizzying array of ceramic, crystal, and porcelain;

vases of green onyx and pipes expertly carved from soft white meerschaum stone; intricately inlaid weaponry and solid silver clocks; and a den of antiques at the very center of the bazaar.

A thousand whispered prices and as many indignant shouts of "final offer" formed a rushing current of commerce that left the newcomer pale and damp from the exertion of escaping with enough money for the evening meal.

"You like fine worship stone, lady?" a sweating vendor asked. She had worked the bazaar long enough to know the genuine article. The fine weathered inscription on the stone as long as his forearm was the real thing. The carvings were pictorial with a kind of ancient writing. His business was clearly black-market antiquities.

She shook her head and worked her way steadily back to the gate, where she once again emerged into the fading day. It always felt as though she had visited another world.

Adrine resumed her journey along the outer wall of the bazaar to Produce Street. It was not far now. The nagging anxiety returned, but she refused to rush headlong toward her business like a beginner. She knew the people who ran adjacent stalls, and they knew her. Most looked out for one another; many had had their same shops for years, handed down through the family for decades. Adrine and A Taste of the Homeland were newcomers but had quickly earned the respect of most of the other shopkeepers in the bazaar. A few resented that she was Armenian. A few more begrudged her the success she experienced. Her produce gained a well-deserved reputation for its size, color, flavor, and variety. Customers long loyal to other stalls switched allegiance to hers.

So Adrine personally went from stall to stall on Produce Street and greeted the owners. She presented them with bright jars of her special tomato, pepper, and aubergine pickles. Though hers grew to be the largest selection of fruits and vegetables in the market, she deliberately did not stock some items so that she could refer her customers to others along the street. Slowly, she was winning them over.

"Some of today's nice fresh cheese, Mrs. Sarafian?" barked Tansu Bir, the cheese merchant. Hairy goat hides hung headless from his stall, slit from throat to hindquarters like monstrous purses. Inside, protected from heat, cold, and flies, great yellow, white, and brown chunks of cheese stored up ripe pungency for the moment they were released from their dead hides.

"Nice young goat, not too sharp," promised Tansu and quoted her a price for one large square.

Adrine wrinkled her nose and looked as if she might run away from so ridiculous a proposal. "It's not worth a dog's ear," she said. "I can smell it from out here. It's spoiled."

Tansu dropped his price a fifth but looked deeply wounded. "I prepared it myself, and in twenty-five years of cheese making, never have I seen a more handsome goat square. If you'll move out of the way, I can sell it for twice the price."

"It is because I feel sorry for you that I will not move. It would embarrass us both for others to see that I'm even considering buying what anyone else would bury for fear of being poisoned." She countered with a price reduced by another fifth from the original asking.

Tansu sighed, and for the benefit of the other shoppers—and a few imaginary ones—he rolled his eyes at the sky.

"I wouldn't look there," Adrine huffed. "Heaven won't help you rob me."

Tansu gave a frown that said he must be insane to be talking to a woman as unstable as this. "I think I'll keep my prize cheese for the sultan."

Adrine shrugged. "I don't even like cheese."

Tansu reached inside the goat hide and withdrew the fine white cheese with care, as if it were his newborn grandson. He lowered the price again. "I will give it to the flies before I sell it for any less."

Adrine sniffed disinterestedly and crossed the street to inspect aromatic open sacks of mint, thyme, cinnamon, and allspice. She continued down the row to feel the pretty lace flowers sewn to the edges of the *yemeni*, or head scarves, traditionally worn by the women of Anatolia, her people. Next, she crossed back to the stall beside Tansu's and breathed the fiery aromas from strings of spicy sausage and slabs of cured beef covered with red pepper and smelling of garlic. "Finest meat I have seen today." She complimented the vendor but did not buy.

Without turning her head and still studying a slab of beef, she shouted, "I can buy much more cattle flesh for the price of Tansu Bir's cheese, and it is better for me."

"My pretty, handsome goat cheese is the best in the bazaar!" he shouted back and dropped halfway to her last quoted price.

"Then the Grand Bazaar has fallen on desperate times!" she countered, raising her bid halfway to his.

"Done!" Tansu closed the deal. He slapped the precious block of the finest goat cheese down on a piece of heavy paper and began to wrap. "I give it away just so that you will leave and not infect my sensible customers with your lunacy!" How Tansu Bir the Elder, and now the Younger, loved to bargain.

Adrine smiled, thanked the cheese man, told him she would be back to collect the cheese in a half hour, and handed him the agreed payment plus an extra fifth. She did not wait for the change.

Adrine continued to wander her way toward her own stall until she heard a loud commotion and looked up. The old nervousness came flooding back. She craned to see and saw there was the beginnings of a crowd—around her produce stall. The closer she came, the bigger the crowd, until she had to shove her way through to see.

She wished she hadn't. Someone had kicked the legs from beneath the tables that supported her colorful, neatly arranged displays of emerald green cucumbers, rosy yellow pears, ruby red cherries, and wonderfully large hazelnuts, almonds, and pistachios. They had stomped their way through the squash, the melons, the tomatoes, handpicked and lovingly packed by Hamit Batu and his family to prevent bruising. Crates of produce waiting to be put out had been split open, their contents crushed. Lettuce, carrots, eggplant, and plums in all their vivid colors helped turn the splintered stall into the garish, knee-deep creation of a demon-possessed sculptor.

Over the top of the disastrous stew, the destroyers had smashed the wooden frames, fresh from the hives, dripping with liquid gold gathered by thousands of bees. The smell of all the wild flowers of Anatolia joined with the ripe, musky aroma of mounds of garden pulp.

Numb, barely able to think, Adrine stepped over beans and corn and felt everything beneath her feet squish sickeningly with each step. She put her arms around the sobbing girls. "Hush, now, hush," she soothed, too shocked to say more.

"Can we help, Mrs. Sarafian? We are sorry for your misfortune and would stay to help you take the damage away to the outskirts. The . . . the dogs there, they . . ." The man speaking trailed off, as if suddenly realizing how maddening his words sounded. A handful of other sober-faced customers sifted through the mushy, dirty carnage from which juice leaked into the street but could think of nothing to do with it. Some—those who had witnessed what happened—could not look the owner of A Taste of the Homeland in the eye. The fear was too great in their own. Others who saw had already left rather than be implicated.

Adrine stared as if she did not comprehend. "No . . . no, thank you," she said vaguely, still in a state of shock. "I—we will manage. We . . . are closed now . . . until further notice."

The crowd began to disperse, murmuring to one another.

"Wait!" Adrine stood in the midst of the disaster, her dress wet with juice, her face twitching with hurt and disbelief. "Can you tell me who did this? Why they did this?" Her voice began to rise, anger mingled with grief. "Did any of you try to stop them? Did you, stupid girls? Did you just stand here while they destroyed everything?" She shook one and then the other of the wailing employees, but they would not look at her, nor answer her accusing questions.

"I saw the men come without warning," said an old bent woman, a cucumber-shaped bulge in her shawl. "Five or six of them, with sacks over their heads, slits cut for eyes, but otherwise dressed like everyone dresses. Silent they came and quick. It was over in minutes. The girls could do nothing. No one did anything." She covered the bulge in the shawl with a hand, as if she could hide what she had done.

"I see." Adrine gathered her thoughts and, without praying, spoke to them. "Who among you would want to defend the property of an Armenian? It is far too risky to protect Armenian melons and beans from marauders. You could get killed for pears." She wept, but they were hot tears of rage. "I charged you a fair price for the best in all Turkey. I helped you plan your meals and gave your babies fruit to suck. If you could not pay today, then I let you pay tomorrow. I brought you God's basket and poured it at your feet and . . . now . . . this.

"Please go now . . . all of you go. We are closed until we in this country again find . . . find our minds." Adrine clamped a trembling hand over her mouth and stifled a groan. They would not defeat her like this. They would not split her open like they had her tomatoes. She would rebuild, restock, regain the high ground.

Jesus the Christ gained the high hill of Golgotha . . . where He was crucified.

Satan was a mocker.

"Stop that crying!" she ordered the girls gruffly. "Help me gather what is still whole for the orphanage. The rest we will put into the wagon and take to the Turkish military encampment at the corner of the Seraglio Wall where we will cook such a feast as they have never had, certainly not on government wages. A vegetable and fruit soup so fine that it may well bring peace in our time. Hurry, now, we've nearly lost the sun!"

A goodly mound of things usable for the orphanage grew quickly. Then came the backbreaking work of scraping the smelly rest into the wagon for transport to the military site. A couple of workers from neighboring stalls, eyes downcast, worked silently alongside, and she thanked them.

"But, good lady," said one of the tear-streaked girls.

"Yes?"

"There are rock bits and nuts in their shells. . . ."

"Yes?"

"And pieces of the wood when the stall broke."

"Yes, I know."

"And mud . . ."

"Yes, yes."

"And places where people have stepped and dogs have been, and birds . . ."

Adrine smiled at the girls for the first time since she had arrived on the scene. "All of it, good girls, all of it into the wagon!"

At last the horse-drawn vehicle, bearing its sticky, stinking load and trailing a stream of liquid produce, pulled into the street and turned toward the Cannon Gate Palace on Seraglio Point, one of the seven hills of New Rome. Those who watched thought perhaps she was unhinged from the vandalism.

Though a bit cold, Adrine Sarafian clucked at the horse, snapped the reins, and warmed at the thought of what a perfectly lovely night it was to return a favor.

Tatul Sarafian let the curtain fall back on the inky darkness. He snapped open the gold casing of the fine pocket watch given Adrine by the brave American.

She was never this late. They had an agreement.

He felt supremely uneasy. He knew too much. "God, be with her. Let no harm come to her," he prayed aloud.

He studied the angry lumbering elephant painted on the watch casing, the wild attacking lion, the East Indian taking careful aim with a rifle.

Tatul didn't like the looks of the lion, the elephant, or the rifle.

Not one bit.

CHAPTER 7

The bicycle rattled and squeaked over the uneven roadway. Tatul Sarafian gripped the bucking handlebars and steered down the narrow side street. Sometimes, given the news of the day and the temperament of various political factions ascending and descending in power, it was safer to skirt the main thoroughfares and take the small side streets. At other times, the thin, darkened byways between buildings, spaces scarcely wide enough for two wagons to pass, were hiding places for malcontents and desperate men awaiting their next victims.

Tonight, Istanbul's mood was a guessing game. Guess wrong and . . .

An autumn moon hung starkly bright at the far end of the street like a huge celestial streetlamp wedged tight between the wooden walls of people's homes.

Howls and yips carried on the harvest air, boosted in volume by the slender canyons between buildings. At times the snarling grew so fierce and ricocheted about so wildly that it sounded as if mortal combat raged from rooftop to coal bin.

A darkened doorway; a wet snuffling; a shift of shadows. The hair at the nape of Sarafian's neck stiffened.

He sniffed the crisp night air and searched his memory for Adrine's exact words that morning before they parted. It meant pushing aside the treachery, the uncertainty, the dangers with which he dealt every day. It meant blanking out the beating suffered at the hands of Artin Chazarian and his Marxist thugs, the sting of being outfoxed at the assembly meeting, the sight of Andranik bleeding, sobbing for the mob to stop and listen to the words of peace.

Overhead, a clothesline, heavy with laundered underwear, drooped from the third-story home on the right side of the street to the third-story home on the left side of the street. The dark squares and rectangles of cloth cut the looming moon in two, leaving a jagged fragment of moon shining above, another below.

The Sarafians had awakened with the strain of the assassination and Tatul's gun still in the room. As they dressed for the day, Adrine's eyes had darkened to a coffee brown.

"I must go, Tatul! I know how you despise my going to Sulukule alone, but no more than I despise your having to go toe to toe with the Turks and the radical Armenians." She did not mention the topics of the previous evening, but he heard them by their absence nevertheless.

"Then I will go with you. The sisters at the orphanage could use another pair of hands."

She had shaken her head. "No! I mean, it's a gallant gesture, and I thank you for it, but not today." At his annoyed look she had quickly added, "The boys are still tender and easily frightened. Your dark countenance and bold moustache could set them back several days." She had smiled clumsily, clearly hoping he would see it as a small joke.

"Not today!" he repeated aloud to the moon, exasperation drawing out each word. Tatul steered around the torn carcass of a dead rat, itself the size of one of the smaller canines whose kingdom it had invaded. The fact that the vermin was mostly whole indicated it had been slowed by disease, and even the scurvy dogs of Istanbul knew not to eat certain flesh.

Though the discussion of her visit to the orphanage rankled most, Tatul did not aim the bicycle in the direction of Sulukule. At the end of the street he turned left, west toward the Grand Bazaar. He was certain she had said she would go there from the orphanage to shop for the evening meal and to check on Aida and Adelina, the two young women hired to operate the produce stand. Her stand was Adrine's pride and joy, and Tatul was glad she had it. Not only did it satisfy her business ambition, but also it provided them with a steady source of income much of the year. Tatul had his own dreams, but for now they must wait, and he would content himself with doing what he could for the homeland.

He rode into Binbirdirek Square. Nearing the fountain, a number of shadows separated themselves from the one huge blob of blackness that was the fountain itself. Tatul stopped, placed his feet on the ground, and still straddling the bicycle, waited, a steely resolve hardening his every muscle. A string of six cigarette butts glowed orange in the dark before him. One lowered to point at the ground, followed by an exhalation of smoke. The man behind it spoke.

"State your sympathies." The order was crisply given and brooked no other reply.

Sarafian did not doubt that there was a gun behind the authority. Without any sudden motion, he cautiously pressed an elbow against his waist and was reassured by the hard contours of his own weapon. "Ararat, my mother; Noah, my father; Christ, my king!" He replied as crisply as he'd been addressed.

"Are you prepared to die and take ten Turks with you?" the voice in the darkness demanded.

"And their forty wives!" Tatul answered and spit on the ground to his left.

"And their concubines?" the voice insisted.

"Nothing is to be done for them!" Tatul snapped. "So great will be their joy at the death of the tyrant masters, they will die from sheer happiness!" Having said this, he spit on the ground to his right.

Sarafian felt slightly silly reciting the rebel code of allegiance, but there were those who put great faith in it and would not hesitate to behead anyone who belittled it.

"State your name and purpose, Turk hater!"

"I am Tatul Sarafian the Fox, adopted son of the Fedayeen. I go for a night ride as those born free are permitted to do. Because Christ has taught us to love our enemies, I strive not to hate but to overcome evil with good. Turks, although it pains me to say it, are created in the image of God as you and I. What they need more than a bullet in the head is the Holy

Redeemer in their souls!" He slowly slid a hand into his waist-band and felt for the reassuring pistol grip.

"A noble and Christian sentiment worthy of a priest," the voice responded, thick with sarcasm. "Greetings, brave Fox. The very paving stones of this square turn to gold at your passing."

"As rebel stomachs turn at the passing of my opinions?" Tatul retorted. He allowed five seconds of uneasy silence, then chuckled. The others quickly joined him in strained joviality.

"It is said you have been untimely tamed by beauty and soft skin," the leader ventured. "What says the cunning Fox to that?"

"I say I have been tempered by a superior intellect, something we will all need before we can again eat *achot* in peace and sing the glories of the homeland."

"Then look to the west, good citizen of Armenia. From there approach the brothers of freedom, who this night will again strike fear in traitors to the homeland and those infidels whose boots they lick!"

Suddenly, the dark and hidden buildings bordering the street on the far side of the square sprang to a flickering yellow gleaming. From the mouth of the street poured a shouting, chanting stream of humanity, torches and lanterns in hand, striding noisily toward the fountain.

They arrived in loud procession, some drunk and clutching bottles of wine by the neck, others simply inebriated with the thought of helping the political process along by catching and dispatching whatever hapless Turk citizen might foolishly be out alone after dark.

The mob quickly surrounded the little knot of Tatul Sarafian and his interrogators, shouting and cursing their love of women and drink, and hatred of Turk despots. A ragged effigy of Talaat Pasha, the interior minister who had ordered the deportation of the Armenians, was hoisted high on a pole and sent into flaming oblivion with a rabid bawl of human frustration.

On and on they poured into the square, mostly older lined faces, forever embittered by the horrors they had endured. So many of the young were dead. This sweating, angry, jostling clot of survivors, united by resentment and thirsty for the gall of retribution, was all the family most of them had left. They kissed and embraced and shook fists at the shuttered Turk shops and residences lining the square. And they sang in dazed disharmony of the ancient fall of Constantinople.

Gardens on gardens, domes on domes, arise
And endless beauties tire the wandering eyes.
In distant views see Asian mountains rise
And lose their snowy summits in the skies.

Those marble mosques once the Christian boast,
Those altars bright gold, sculpture graced,
By barbarous zeal of savage foes defaced.
Vain monuments of men that once were great,
Sunk, undistinguished, by one common fate!

Tatul wondered how long before Turkish gendarmes and their rifles would surround the mob, how long before sharpened bayonets would meet with crude cudgels and a handful of pistols. Part of Tatul could not blame his countrymen. What other forum did they have for expressing their shame, for letting out the disappointment and futility they felt at the thorough and brutal way they had been set upon by the nation in whose good graces they had lived and prospered so long?

Many had survived the war only to die of heartbreak.

Then, when it seemed that not another body could possibly squeeze into Binbirdirek Square, four rough-clad burly men, walking shoulder to shoulder like pallbearers, stumbled forward. Above their heads they bore a burlap sack, the wriggling contents of which squirmed and kicked to be free.

The sack bearers stopped in front of Tatul and the men behind the glowing cigarettes. The lead voice turned to the new arrivals. "Whatever you have captured and brought for our inspection, you may now lay at the feet of the Fox himself!"

The sack bearers, however, did not lower their struggling burden but punched the sack with their fists and struck it with stout branches cut into clubs. A high, youthful voice from within the sack cried out in pain, fighting and kicking all the more.

One of the men beneath the uncooperative bundle beat against the top of the sack and swore mightily against heaven, earth, and creatures of the sea. "The monster in this sack deserves to die! It is spawn of hell and must be killed before it can spread again!"

The crowd, hearing this, swelled up and in one collective voice pronounced sentence. "Burn him! Burn him! Burn the spawn of hell!"

The bearers hurled the sack to the street, and three others rushed forward to touch their torches to the burlap.

Tatul leapt from the bicycle and threw it aside. "No! Stop this murder! Stop!" He beat at the flaming burlap and smothered the fire with his body.

From inside the sack came choking sobs, coughing, and screams for help.

"Get back!" Tatul ordered, brandishing his pistol. "Get back!"

He sliced at the ties of the sack with a dagger, the acrid smell of smoldering burlap sharp in his nostrils. The ties came free. He wrenched the neck of the sack open and pulled it back to reveal the person within.

Tatul let the sack drop and stared. His heart burned. Perhaps they were right. Perhaps this one should die.

———

Adrine's wagon pulled away from Fevzi the Fishmonger's, its load now leaking a steady stream of fruit and vegetable juice. With all the rain, it had been a particularly fine year for melons and squash, and now their smashed hulls were giving all that sweet juice back to the earth from which it had been taken.

Adrine fought against a numbness that threatened to take over her entire body. About the only part of her that still felt alive was her head. Night had fallen and with it descended a frostiness that tingled her scalp, heightened her senses, and forced her to wrap the shawl tightly around her face and tie it off beneath her chin.

The rest of her responded dumbly to whatever stimuli came along.

Aida and Adelina had ceased their sobbing and were functional enough to retrieve the goat cheese from Tansu Bir so that Adrine did not have to leave the wagon seat. She was afraid to stand for fear her legs would give out and she would pitch right off into the street.

It was not until she was within sight of the fish stall that Adrine looked down at the cheese wrap on the seat beside her and discovered that Tansu had returned all of her money, including the fifth extra. She turned and looked at the silent girls. They had new tears in their eyes.

"Take it," she told them, tucking the cheese money into Aida's pocket. "It's not a lot, but for now consider it a down payment on your first day's wages. It may be a while before I am again in a position to pay the remainder. But I will. You are not unemployed. Do you hear me? Tell no one you are. You keep account of your daily wages and help me build again, and you shall have full pay whether the shop is open or closed."

They appeared afraid to protest.

Then, with a sudden, unexpected change of subject, Adrine asked, "Did God make the cheese?" When they did not answer, she insisted. "Did He?"

They nodded.

"I can't hear you!"

"Yes—yes, good lady, He did make the cheese."

"And the melons?"

"Yes."

"The eggplant? Did God make eggplant?"

"He did, good lady."

Adrine breathed deeply, willing herself to relax. "Yes, He did. Contrary to what some of the higher society cooks will tell you, eggplant was God's idea."

For fifteen seconds, no one spoke. "The fish?" Adrine prodded, like a schoolteacher on the scent of an enlightened truth. "Did God make the fish?"

"Yes, Mrs. Sarafian, God made fish." The girls looked bewildered and uncertain as to where the discussion was headed, if anywhere.

"Now, think carefully. Did God make Armenians?"

"Of course. Armenians came from the dust, as did Adam."

"From the selfsame dust as the English and Germans, Kurds and Ethiopians?"

"True," said Aida with a long-suffering sigh. "The same."

"From the selfsame dust as Turks?"

Now Aida was stumped. She well knew her catechism, and no race, no nationality was excluded from God's taking the dust of the ground and breathing into it the breath of His own nostrils. But if she said yes that from the selfsame dust the terrible Turks did come and to the selfsame dust the terrible Turks would return, her employer might, in her current frame of mind, throw Aida off the wagon to find her way in the Istanbul night all alone. But if she said no, that Turks were of Satan, she would be lying. Satan did not create. It would be the right answer, but would it be the safest?

"I will let Adelina answer that question, good lady. She has not had a turn."

"That's fair, Aida. Adelina? Please answer the question."

Adelina dug her nails into the back of Aida's hand. She gave her a silent, frantic look of "What should I say?" Aida shrugged and held onto the wagon bed for dear life. She didn't want to be knocked out by Mrs. Sarafian's response to Adelina's reply.

"Come, little goose, the answer please."

Adelina perked up at the use of the endearing term Adrine had said her grandmother had used with her. She'd told them that story, and it was a sign to Adelina that absolute truth was called for. "Yes, Mrs. Sarafian," came her tiny, high-pitched answer. "Turks were created from the selfsame dust as you and I."

Involuntarily, Adelina and Aida cringed behind their employer, hoping to escape a swing of her arm or a backlash from the reins. None came. Only "Hmmm ... I sometimes wonder ..."

The wagon turned right. Ahead was Binbirdirek Square. The foot traffic was unusually thick for the time of night, and as they drew ever closer to the entrance to the square, the crush became unruly and threatening.

Adrine's first thought was *I hope Tatul's not here.* She knew he would be worried about her, and it wasn't truly safe for women to be on the streets after dark. No matter what her business, a woman outside in the night was thought to be a prostitute. She had considered stopping by the house and getting Tatul before continuing on to the Cannon Gate Palace. But she was certain he would try to prevent her from cooking the special meal for the Turk troops.

She did not want to be prevented.

The wagon's pace slowed, the horse being unable to negotiate the heavy crowd. Pera snorted and shied from the torches, flames illuminating the horse's wide eyes, chestnut coat, and ebony mane. The atmosphere was palpable with rebellion, and Adrine could feel it skitter along her spine like a demon's claw. She shuddered. Shouts and drunken threats grew louder. Ahead, near the center of the square, what appeared to be a body engulfed in flames was thrust into the night sky, and an ugly cheer burst from the agitated hive of humanity on every side.

" 'What a Friend We Have in Jesus,' girls. Sing it! Here, I'll teach it to you." Adrine led off the first verse, loud and breathless with anxiety. Tentatively, the girls joined in the second time. By the middle of the second round of the second verse, they were stronger, and the trio's lovely soprano gained in fullness.

> *Can we find a friend so faithful,*
> *Who will all our sorrows share?*
> *Jesus knows our every weakness,*
> *Take it to the Lord in prayer.*

A half-drunk man, his face blackened with soot, held a lantern up to the wagon seat and hooted them down. "Nice singing, sisters of Armenia, but you're one war too late! Jesus himself would cast the jackal Turks into the sea!" He growled and took a swing at the front wheel with his lantern. It shattered against the rim, the coal oil igniting, causing the horse to buck and rear.

Adrine yanked the bottom of her dress away from the flames and fought for control of the horse. "Down, Pera, steady, good girl! Whoa, now!" Others grabbed the reins at the horse's head and kept it steady. "Douse the fire with the slop from the wagon!" Adrine yelled. Aida and Adelina scooped the pulp over the side as fast as they could, and the fire soon fizzled out.

Adrine chewed her lip and tried to think. There was just one course of action that came to her. "Lord God," she prayed aloud, "surround us with your angels and let not Pharaoh's armies overtake us. And if you'd like to put wings on Pera's hooves, that would be a good idea too!" She rose on cold, numb feet, which felt as separate as detached stumps. She wavered a moment, then steadied. "Hold on to something solid, girls. We're going through!"

Adrine Sarafian clucked to the horse, snapped the reins, and the wagon lurched into the deadly mob.

———

Tatul stared at the curly black head of the handsome son of the murdered traitor Mugurditchian.

The boy kicked free of the smoking sack, and Sarafian pulled him to his feet. The frightened child flung trembling arms around Tatul. He pressed so hard against his rescuer's legs, it was as if he was attempting to find a way inside in order to place someone else's flesh and blood between him and his tormentors.

Despite the fact he was a mere child, son of the Judas through no fault of his own, Tatul felt involuntary revulsion for the boy. But he shielded him all the same.

"Now, that's a sight!" the ringleader with the cigarette exclaimed. "The son of Judas hides behind the son of Black Wolf, God's captain of the Fedayeen! We grant you the honor, great

Fox, of plunging your dagger deep within the black heart of the child traitor before he, too, becomes an informant for the Istanbul police!"

The boy whirled to face his accusers. "You don't even know me! I'm not like my father!" he yelled.

The ringleader laughed. "Ah, so now the whelp turns on the sire and bites the memory of his own beloved parent. Judas breed!"

The boy burst into tears. Tatul buried his fingers in the child's thick hair and pulled back, the hand with the dagger dangling by his side.

"Cut his throat! Cut his throat!" the mob chanted, pressing forward all the better to see.

But Tatul turned the boy to face him and whispered in his ear, "Take my bicycle and peddle south as if Satan himself were crawling up your pants. You can outpeddle them. Now go!"

The boy, face stricken, looked behind Sarafian but did not move.

"What, lad, what?" said Tatul frantically.

The child swallowed hard. "I think, sir, your bicycle has been stolen."

Man and boy braced against the mob with little more than their wits about them, and less than half of those.

The gathering grew denser and wilder by the minute. The wagon was getting nowhere, and Adrine was afraid she would trample someone deranged by drink.

But the more the rebels raged, the clearer Adrine's thinking became. She had driven Aida and Adelina into mortal danger; she was responsible for getting them out.

The wagon wrenched to the left, then to the right. The girls squealed in fear as the wagon bed was rocked from side to side. Shoulders leaned into the task. Hands reached to snatch the reins from Adrine's grasp. A man fumbled with Pera's harness. What did he want? To unhitch her? To steal her?

With a groan and a slosh, the wagon and its contents tipped up on two wheels. The girls fell screaming against the side. A wave of reeking slop smashed against them and they held on to keep from falling off. Adrine struggled to keep her seat.

The wagon teetered a moment, felt as if it would go over, paused, then crashed back onto all four wheels, sending girls and slop careening to the opposite side.

Adrine prayed for God's mercy, secured the reins again, and yanked them to the right. She kept yanking and turning, yanking and turning. Pera snorted, pawed the paving, and, bless her reliable lineage, kept her head.

Curses and shouts rent the air, men trying to keep clear of wagon wheels and thudding horse's hooves. A thunder of heavy clubs pounded the wagon's frame, many taking a swing at the imaginary head of a Turk soldier. Adrine heard the splinter of cracking wood. A stone, then another, whistled past her ear.

"Look at her and the little babes she keeps in the bed of the wagon!" came a lascivious shout. "Didn't know Gypsy prostitutes rode out to their customers! Phew, you can smell the nasty things from here!" Men laughed and whistled suggestively.

Over the heads of the teeming mass, Adrine caught sight of a tiny opening on the outer perimeter of the square, barely a street at all. Mentally she grabbed God's hand. Snapping the reins, she hawed, "On, Pera! On, girl! Haw!"

With a mighty gathering of horseflesh, Pera all but vaulted forward and made straight for the opening. None stood in her way, and soon they clattered into the lane.

The moon did not go with them.

Adrine eased back on the reins, slowed the wagon, and discovered they could not have entered a darker, less traveled route than this. The towering walls of the buildings were but a long jump apart, the street barely wider than the wagon. Light, sound, warmth were shut out. The sun did not reach here; the cobblestones conserved no midday heat. No candles or lamps burned in any of the windows. A foul, dank odor overpowered even the mess in the wagon. Aida and Adelina held each other despite the rank coating of mush they now wore.

" 'Jesus knows our every weakness . . .' " Adrine sang shakily under her breath. She had difficulty getting any volume.

The lane wound deeper and deeper into a district Adrine had never seen. Would she find a way out? A way back? Tatul would be half crazed with worry.

The wagon pitched down a steep incline, turned a corner, and came to a sudden halt entirely at Pera's discretion.

The blank wall immediately ahead took them all by surprise. The air was still and wet, and in the women's minds it was as if the evil chill seeped from bottomless holes in the broken pavement and dropped in a fine mist from the rickety balconies and sightless windows above.

" 'Take it to the Lord in prayer . . .' " Adrine mumbled, urging the patient Pera to turn the wagon slowly in the tight confines at the end of the black lane. In the back, Aida and Adelina held each other tightly, eyes screwed shut, shivering against the damp.

The wagon turned to face the steep incline. Adrine halted Pera and gave them all a chance to calm down. As scary as it was, the lane was a quiet place to restore nerves jittery from the mob.

The only sound for a long while was the whooshing of Pera's great lungs settling down, punctuated every so often by a soft nickering and snuffling of her nostrils.

How long they dozed there in the dead well of the lane was uncertain. Later they would say that a strange sixth sense told them that something else, something alive, approached from up the lane, or maybe from out of the cracks and under the steps of the lifeless buildings.

Wherever they originated, the living things came on silent paws, at first just darker shadows moving along the ground like spirit thieves, mere darts across the vision of half-closed eyes. Who saw them first was also a matter of later debate. Probably Pera, who shifted nervously and made the wagon move.

Before the wary shapes took definite form, a bloodcurdling snarl began deep within one thin chest, soon joined by others, and rose until it expelled from them in a torrent of snaps and growls.

"Easy, girls. No sudden moves, please." Adrine pulled her feet and legs beneath her and sat on them. "Let us take a moment to ask God to bless our situation, then another time or two of 'What a Friend.'"

They all held hands and bowed to pray.

Teeth bared, heads low to the ground, the hounds of Istanbul crept closer to the kill.

———————

"What is your name, boy?" asked Tatul kindly, praying to do the right thing, one eye on the men with their glowing cigarettes.

"David, sir." The boy's voice cracked.

"Well, David, do you believe in God?"

"God the Faithful, God the Provider, God the Source," the boy intoned. "Yes, sir, I do believe in God."

"Cut his throat! Cut his throat!" The mob pressed forward, held back only by the five smokers who had linked arms, their leader staring curiously at Tatul Sarafian and the son of Judas as if they were on display in a curio shop.

"I'm thinking of God the Savior, the one who spared King David of the Israelites from death on occasions as frightening as this."

"Are you planning to cut my throat, sir?" asked the boy.

"No, I have no such plans," Tatul answered.

"Then, sir, God has already spared me from two deaths— one by burning and one by having my throat slit. Is it not true that he likes to work in threes and sevens?"

Tatul marveled at the lad's pluck and asked God for more of his own.

Tatul would take the risk.

He raised his voice and shouted, "Only those possessed of the devil and a generous portion of stupidity would want this boy dead! We know the Turks are child killers. Hardly a one of us here has not lost a brother or sister, a child of our own, a grandchild, a niece or nephew to the butchers of Byzantium. Are we to become like them? If we sink a knife in this one, we risk being hunted down and finished off, our one final hope for a restored homeland lost forever—"

Off to the right, someone was hoisted to the railing of the fountain and supported there. He rose to his full height, and the familiar, persuasive voice of Artin Chazarian carried on the night.

"I am told that Tatul Sarafian defends the seed of Judas! I do not know whether to be insulted, incredulous, or incensed. What do we care what the men of slaughter think of us? I think the Fox has lost his cunning. Can he believe the Turks will seek revenge for the killing of this perversion of an Armenian child?"

He paused and the crowd at the foot of the fountain cheered his words. Tatul motioned to the leader of the men with the cigarettes, the only protection between Sarafian and the fury of the mob. "Raise me onto your shoulders," he said. The man hesitated, studying the earnest face of the Fedayee. Then he nodded, threw down his cigarette, bent a knee, and hoisted Sarafian into the air.

"Brothers!" Tatul said, arms raised for attention. "Hear me and hear me well. You know me, and you know that I risked my life for the cause of Armenia and every one of you brothers! I do not say this lightly, but our humanity, our very blessing from God, depends on how we treat this boy right here. David Mugurditchian's blood is Armenian. His flesh is Armenian. His faith, like any good Armenian's, is in God alone. If you allow yourselves to murder one of our own Armenian children, a son of Ararat, a Child of the Book, then you are guilty of cannibalism, of shedding innocent blood. From such as David will spring the new Armenia!"

Disputes arose at the controversial words, but many held their tongues, weighing instead the sobering impact of what was said. Chazarian, as was his style, filled the breach.

"Hear me, brothers! Sarafian is brought low by the responsibilities of wife and home. He no longer possesses the necessary vigor and audacity to stand up to the Turks. We must show the bloody Ottomans that we are no longer dumb sheep easily led to slaughter. We who are left are lions who will trade eye for eye and are unwilling to harbor betrayers no matter the color of their blood!"

"We are lions without claws!" Tatul countered immediately. "We cannot fight cannons with sticks and stones! Our strongest defense is our reason, our conduct, our righteous cause. God honors valiant men but chokes on men who shed innocent blood."

He was stopped by distant cries of pain and angry shouts. The substance of what was happening on the perimeter of the crowd traveled back and forth across the square like breaking waves. Those close to Tatul jeered at the news. "We are joined by those who dash the brains of infants and rape our mothers and daughters! Look to your weapons, brothers, for here come the bloody Turks!"

Rifle fire, screams. Gray uniforms waded in with bullets and clubs. Tatul heard a rifle go off from behind, felt the man on whose shoulders he sat grunt, spin, then stagger to his knees. Tatul fell into the boy, who struggled to keep his savior from going down.

The rebel leader lay glassy eyed on the cobblestones, blood seeping from a hole in his neck, a smoking cigarette stub still pinched between his thumb and index finger. He looked dead already but still breathed. The jostling, panicked crowd threatened to finish the job beneath trampling feet.

"Grab his legs!" Tatul shouted, and the boy jumped to do so while Sarafian grabbed the wounded man under the arms and dragged him back out of the main crush.

"You!" Sarafian bellowed at the nearest man. "Get help for this patriot!"

A mumbled assent and a gnarled veteran of the street wars dropped down and listened to the wounded man's chest. "No help for this one," he pronounced.

"Look out!" yelled another, who, with his shirt nearly stripped from his back was pointing insanely into the confusion.

Tatul heard it before he actually saw anything. Rabid barks and snarls. Nerve-shattering shrieks of terrified women answered back the alarmed cries of men. The mad clatter of stampeding hooves.

From out of the mob, parted in two like the waters of the Red Sea painted on the wall of the Armenian cathedral, careened a swaying horse-drawn wagon. Standing Roman–chariot–style high atop the wagon seat, wild hair streaming, reins clutched in one fist, flying whip gripped in the other, rode Adrine Sarafian. "Haw! Hiyaw!" she ordered with every slash, her eyes ablaze. At her feet two young girls with knives, feverishly trying to keep their balance and avoid being flung from the vehicle to the pavement, cut pieces of flesh from a large bluefish and tossed them to four mangy curs running inside the length of the wagon bed, lunging and snapping at the charging, unrestrained mob. Ugly and menacing, the Gypsy hounds voraciously gulped down the fish bits without missing a single vicious lunge.

The wagon rumbled and rocked past Adrine's husband and David Mugurditchian. Stunned by the sight, they froze where they stood. "Run!" they shouted in sudden unison, heels flying after the wagon, enraged men with torches in close pursuit. Turk gendarmes burst in from the side and attacked the pursuers, knocking their torches flying. Heavy wooden clubs met with bone, and the moans of the beaten mingled with the dying gasps of those shot and bayoneted.

David and Tatul gained on the wagon, but the shorter boy lagged behind. Tatul reached out, grasped David by the collar and the seat of the pants, and, ignoring the stream of putrid leakage out the back of the wagon and the froth and fangs of the big black mongrel roaring over the rear gate, launched the boy up into the wagon bed.

Without questioning David's fate, Sarafian reached forward, grabbed hold of the rear gate with first one hand, then the other, and hurled his own body up and over.

The landing was the juiciest, smelliest, and loudest he could ever remember.

"What in the name of all that is Ararat were you doing out after dark with these girls and a wagon full of ... of ... of whatever this wagon's full of?" Tatul's sharp tone set the curs on edge again. They growled low in their throats and warily circled where he sat in a corner of the wagon on the shore of the now greatly reduced sea of sludge, wiping with futility at his ripe, scum-coated clothes.

They were home, the wagon tucked out of sight of prying eyes in a narrow little space at the back of the building. Tatul felt great relief that Adrine was safe and great heaviness at the riot in the square. He could still feel the weight of the man with the cigarette and see the ragged wound that ended his life so senselessly.

"Good Pera, good nag. Breathe easy, now. Aida, would you be kind enough to bring Mr. Sarafian current on the evening's events?" Adrine, with her hair stuck sweatily to her forehead and her dress a sodden mix of perspiration and produce paste was shaking from nerves and cold. She picked up the slimy fish skeleton with its head and tail still intact and flung it far out into the lane. With threatening yelps and softer yips of anxiety, the four dogs of Istanbul leapt to the ground and fell on the remains of the bluefish. Within seconds, it was but an oily memory. The curs dashed about, noses to the ground, looking for more. Thwarted, they licked the remaining scales and flecks of fish from one another's muzzles.

The more he heard from Aida's small, weepy telling of what had transpired at and since the Grand Bazaar, the more Tatul Sarafian wanted to exact justice from the guilty. But who were the guilty? Popular assumption would place the blame on the heads of the Turks. But the vandals had said nothing, revealed nothing of their loyalties or their identities, and stomped away as quickly as they had struck. If Turks, why would they not have seized the opportunity to sneer their open contempt of the Armenian remnant? It would not do to say so, but they could have been Chazarian's men as easily as Turks. Given the scene at the Armenian assembly that morning, it was probably more likely.

"Thank you, Aida," he said kindly, when she had finished her story. He did not look at his wife. "You and Adelina were very brave to stay with the stall despite what happened. We are glad you were not harmed. God has not promised us the absence of trials in this life, and at times our hardest work is reduced to ashes. But we have much to be thankful for. All we have truly lost is a few pickles, a bowl of applesauce, and"—he surveyed the disheveled lot—"a bit of dignity. We will send word to Hamit Batu on the farm, and within a week we will be back in business!"

The girls nodded and smiled bravely.

Adrine was dangerously silent.

Tatul slipped an arm around the boy, who looked about to fall asleep where he sat. "This, good sisters of the Book, is David Mugurditchian. He will need sanctuary for a time, at least until all this latest mistrust comes to an end."

He gave his wife a look that warned her not to ask further questions within hearing of the youths. She wiped at her ruined dress, but it was beyond smoothing. "Then he will never go home." The bitterness in Adrine's voice frightened Tatul. The boy, too, caught the defeat in the words, and his shoulders sagged.

"No, sweet pigeon," Tatul replied. "Like fog off the Golden Horn, this confusing mist that envelops us will soon evaporate. You'll see."

Body hard and uncomforted, Adrine's eyes followed the dogs in their frantic search for more fish. "You weren't there, Tatul. I bring you all that remains of A Taste of the Homeland."

"Nonsense!" her husband cried, jumping from the wagon and helping everyone down but Adrine. "Your business, your reputation, your assets are built on far more than a few onions and leeks. Hamit will supply you again, with payment deferred. Meantime, I will deal with local suppliers, and even if we display nothing but roots and bark for a week, news of your return will travel, and you will soon be the wealthiest roots and bark merchant on Produce Street!" As soon as he said it, he wished he hadn't. So many of their people had been forced to eat grass and roots just to survive the horrors of Ottoman governance.

Adrine said nothing but looked into the bed of the wagon as if assessing the meager pool of pulp yet left. She straightened, turned to face Pera's rump, and picked up the reins. "Good, then, my sweet. Resourceful as you are, you can help with the evening meal." The words were oddly distant and strained of affection.

Hastily, Tatul ran to the front of the wagon and grabbed Pera's halter. "Talk to me, Adrine. Where are you going? We should go inside now, prepare sleeping places for the children, and once things are quieter, we can discuss the details." His words were wary, exploratory, feeling their way around his wife's sudden strangeness.

"No," she said softly. "First we must go to the military encampment at Cannon Gate Palace and make soup for the men. Why let so rich and nutritious a stock as this go to complete waste? Plus they will be quite weary from a night's work of assaulting Armenians. It will be our way of redeeming the day for them and us by feeding them what their boots have crushed. They could lie on their blankets and would not have to lift a finger." She licked her lips and made a wet smacking sound. "We can feed them, and when they've had the last of it, we can take their spoons and choke them to death!" She broke then, her shoulders shaking with deep, mournful sobs.

The children pressed against the back of the house, sad faces reflecting fear and misery.

Tatul climbed into the wagon, pulled the reins from Adrine's hands, and gathered her into his arms. He feared for her but was proud of her daring. "Shoosh, shoosh, my darling," he comforted. "We have come through worse. We are home. The children must be allowed to sleep, and I could not let you serve this slop to your worst enemy. Shoosh . . ."

She sank against him and seemed to breathe easier at last, but it was as if he could feel a decisive, racing torrent of independence and conviction rise to the surface and take possession of her.

"All my life I have believed," she whispered, tears streaming silver in the moonlight. "I have come through flood and flame, survived horrors that so many have not. Yet only now after some hateful persons have stepped on my lovely peaches and my prize tomatoes do I at last understand that all that I own—surely, eternally own—is my God. I have access to His power, assurance of His favor, the bounty of His table, the guarantee of His grace, the fountain of His forgiveness, the healing of His touch, and the salvation of His Son. No matter how much I hurt or despair or rail against injustice, I cannot exhaust His treasures or come to the end of His love.

"Oh, Tatul," she pushed back and looked far inside him. "I can finally say with the prophet, 'Hear oh Israel, the Lord your God is one' and know that it is enough. He is our inheritance, and all we or our children will ever need. The rest is just so much—"

"—mashed carrots?" Tatul finished for her. He was glad when she laughed. God help them when the laughter stopped.

He wished he could say he had found that same surrender to God, that he had come to the same irreversible conclusion. But he hadn't. Not yet.

He buried his mouth in her ear and whispered, "I must say, my mountain flower"—he flicked a squash seed from her neck—"you are in no condition to be seen in public. I will get wood to heat the bath water. Did I hear you say 'children'?"

She slipped deftly from his arms and hopped nimbly down from the wagon. "Yes, you did," she said, her movements brisk and all business again. "And since we each brought some home, I think I need to hear more about how you spent your evening!"

CHAPTER 8

The old fishing vessel bobbed like a giant's float toy on the shimmering waters of the Bosporus. Normally thick with freighters and a bustling commercial fishery, much of the usual boat traffic was idled by postwar embargo and uncertainty. But the beauty of the legendary waters and the shadow play of towers, domes, and minarets along their shores provided chilly autumn relief from the density of confliction that inflamed those on land.

Tatul and Adrine sat huddled together on a tackle cabinet alone with their thoughts. They had to get away from the tensions in Stambul, if even for a few hours on the water in the gentle rock and sway of an odorous fishing boat. They had nowhere to go but aimlessly about the harbor, a rare and welcome relief nonetheless.

Asleep on a nest of nets and big wooden floats at their feet lay David Mugurditchian, blessedly oblivious to the swirl of controversy that placed so high a price on his twelve-year-old head. He had chattered away the first hour or two of their excursion but was now making up for lost sleep. They'd spent a fitful night, including more than an hour just watching the dancing reflection of flames on their wall from two torched buildings in Binbirdirek Square and listening to the clang of distant fire bells.

In the morning, they had taken Aida and Adelina home to their weeping and much relieved invalid father. David was in a more difficult situation. He said his widowed mother, fatherless brothers and sisters, and a legion of spiteful cousins would not allow the approach of any Armenians. Nor was it certain if the mansion from which the Mugurditchians had not yet been evicted was under police surveillance. Better, the Sarafians felt, to allow things among the gendarmes and the militant Armenians to cool down for a couple of days, then drop David off near his home for a quick dash inside to the safety of his family.

A fat steamer listing to starboard with too many passengers collected from villages along both shores of the Bosporus sounded its horn at Fevzi's little fishing boat. Fevzi the Fisher, busily wrenching and abusing the boat's balky engine back to life, shook a greasy fist at the rusty steamer that passed too close to port and set the *Little Seagrass* to bouncing from side to side.

"You sons of Gypsies!" he yelled, then said to the Sarafians, "Their mothers are heifers. Pardon my language, young lady; pardon my dogfish of a mouth. You saw how close they came to my little camel of the sea. . . ."

He cast a curious look at the sleeping boy and went right back to the engine, muttering under his breath, and would probably that evening drink *raki* in convivial unity with the captain of the offending steamer. After dark, water men stuck together, no matter the offenses of the day.

"Gray mullet and silver palamut are so thick there you could spear them from shore," said Fevzi to no one in particular, staring out to sea, the engine momentarily forgotten. "Mackerel, sea bream, lobsters, oysters, and mussels more plentiful than a harem's complaints. Too bad the pasha didn't banish your people to the sea. They could have lived forever out there."

The engine roared to life, as if fueled by the fisher's stories. They pulled alongside a waterfront café, and a rough, unshaven waiter in gold frock coat served them tea in glasses. David roused from his sleep to drink half a glass, then promptly curled back into his nest for more rest from the harrowing escapades of the previous night.

Fevzi sipped long and appreciatively of the thick, hot beverage. They took it *sekar*, sweetened with sugar. He stared at the boy for a moment, then spoke from the steam streaming over the sides of his glass. "Did I tell you how I used to stand on the rocks of Uskudar and catch tunny with my hands? Near there was one of the most dangerous capes on the Horn. It became so violent at times that the crabs would abandon the sea altogether and walk across the headlands. To this day you can see the path they wore in the rocks." He held out as long as he could, then gave a wide grin.

This trip out onto the waters of a faithful God was good for them. Good to leave the alarms and the rancor and the subterfuge behind. Good to breathe God's wind, to clear the senses, to feel the spray. Adrine ran her tongue over her upper lip, enjoying the saltiness. When she looked at Tatul, he was studying her, deep black eyes full of love and concern.

She reached for his hand and kissed the backs of his slender fingers and rubbed her cheek against strong knuckles. Brown, rough, and leathery from his days on farm and mountain. He was not best suited for the great, sprawling "city of the world's desire."

Had he submitted to settling in Istanbul less because it was the last battlefront of Armenian nationalism and more because she needed it for the fulfillment of her childhood dream? She thought of last night, safe in his arms, confessing that God at last was sufficient for her every need. But now, here, in the light of day, away from the terrors of the night, did she really believe she could walk away from all that she had built and from that which remained to be done before she secured a truly international mercantile operation?

She did not yet travel by private railcar to conduct her business and oversee her operations. That was a lifelong ambition and one that she fervently believed would come with time and the increased ease of postwar travel. It still was not safe to be an Armenian. Nor was it necessarily prudent to be a woman in commerce. She felt the constant need to prove herself. Centuries of female subjugation would die hard, even under a more progressive secular Turk government.

She turned and looked at the sea, lips pursed in a rueful

smirk. To suggest that Turks could govern was a bitter Armenian joke.

How impossible for her to think thoughts of prosperity in a city rocked by so much hatred. She understood that Istanbul had endured more warfare than any other city on earth. It was the capital of three world empires and the only city to span two continents. Some called it the belly button of the world because it had been central to so many of the world's growing pains.

And this was where she wanted to make a home and raise her family? Was it what Tatul wanted? She smiled shyly at him.

"What?" he asked, passing her a wedge of orange.

She did not answer but looked mysteriously away to the horizon, sucking pensively on the orange.

Tatul shook his head at her. "You agreed not to hold back thoughts and the meanings behind your expressions so that I wouldn't assume you are hiding the fact you are carrying Tatul the Magnificent around inside you. You're not, are you?"

She pretended to ignore him. Something made her hold back the news she wanted to shout from the tallest minaret.

"Adrine the Infuriating?"

She laughed the most unburdened laugh she'd released since the day they'd first smelled the sanctified air of Russia. It had been to them both the snow-fresh fragrance of freedom.

They looked at the slumbering David, as curly haired, long lashed, and cherub mouthed as they would dare hope for in a child of their own, and sighed. In another cruel irony—ironies in Stambul being plentiful as fleas—David's mother had been jailed on suspicion of having plotted her husband's murder. The rest of his relatives were in hiding to avoid a similar fate. David himself was probably wanted for questioning. They warily spied each passing boat, half expecting the police to send a boarding party.

Tatul suddenly brightened, groped in his coat pocket a moment, and pulled forth a folded white envelope. "I almost forgot," he said, unfolding a thin sheaf of onionskin. "We've received a letter from Frank Davidson!"

Adrine's excitement matched Tatul's. Every six months or so they heard from Davidson, the neutral American consul who had been stationed at Harput in eastern Turkey. Responsible for smuggling many Armenian refugees out of harm's way, Davidson had also recorded his eyewitness account of the atrocities committed against unarmed Armenian civilians during the war. He had personally observed the mass graves and ravaged bodies of thousands upon thousands of slaughtered men, women, and children and had worked diligently at getting those reports into the hands of diplomats and men of great power such as American President Woodrow Wilson. He was also responsible for aiding the Sarafians' successful escape into the arms of "Uncle Christian," the Russian bear.

Frank was now back in the United States with his wife, Catharine, where he was preparing to retire from public service. Adrine noted that the return address was for an alias, J. Stanley Cromer, with a post office box on Long Island. Censorship had ended as an official Turk policy, but high-profile Armenian insurgents like Tatul were still being watched and their mail in danger of being snatched.

It was unlikely, however. With the war settlement negotiations in the delicate phase they were, even the acerbic Turks were loath to risk an international incident with the American consulate over sovereign U.S.A. mail. Timing, Frank was fond of saying, was everything.

Davidson's neat, regimented script was as welcome as a warm coat in a storm. Adrine began to read the letter eagerly.

My dear Sarafians,

Cat and I are facing another New York winter in which we shall be frozen solid as a brick for three months. But it suits us. (The Turk might say *evet, evet, evet*! It is very good! I regret that I don't know the Armenian equivalent for it, as, sad to say, I never lived among you in happier times.) Anyway, we are most glad when the air is full of frost crystals and the shouts of children and we are able to skate on the pond together.

Do you have any shouting children of your own to report? Cat's looking over my shoulder and that question earned me a rebuke. Sorry to be so blunt. I just feel that the two of you will have strong, beautiful children and will be very fine parents. Please forgive the ramblings of an aging diplomat, but I feel as something of an uncle to your future offspring. You know that we never had children of our own, so this gives us a delightful excuse to look for miniature ice skates for yours. (That is, if the Young Turks permit the water to freeze over there. Any official word on that?)

Adrine smiled. Frank's jokes about Turkey's politics were almost Armenian. She read on.

I was, of course, interested in what you had to say about the continuing work of independence. I agree that you should be at the Ninth Assembly of the Armenian Revolutionary Federation in December, but don't take any more chances than necessary. The fact it is outlawed by the Turks and as of now you will have to meet in secret troubles us both. Be doubly careful.

You wrote of your misgivings about the establishment of a permanent homeland. I say to you, do not speak of failure. Failure is not to be entertained in the least. Do not even call it failure. As gut-wrenchingly disappointing as these setbacks can be, as soon as you name it failure, so shall you fail.

No, as God is our witness, speak only of victory and let God shape the way. I am as disappointed as you in Wilson's inability to hasten an American mandate for an Armenian state under the League of Nations. I fear it may now be too late. His health is not the best, and Americans simply do not want to embroil, sorry, *involve* themselves in European affairs, the Treaty of Versailles notwithstanding. If I could just get Woodrow out on the ice, I think he'd see more clearly, but he prefers dry land. As large a man as he is—I can see why.

As soon as I post this, I'm off to Washington again to see how close I can get to the president this time. Probably no closer than Undersecretary of Shoe Blacking, but perhaps as near as a tour guide at the Library of Congress. Forgive my cynicism.

Pray for me. As time wears on, the number of listening ears dwindles. My source at the *New York Times*, upon whom I could always rely for a couple of inches in the international section, has become a speech writer for a New Jersey senator. I shall have to cultivate a new contact. The son of a Turk Armenian family who worked for me in the consulate in Harput—and for whom I helped arrange a "tour" of America—is a passable journalist and quite egalitarian in his thinking. If I can find him a suit that fits, he might land a job at the *Times*. Think of that! Five years ago he was dodging a firing squad; today he has a chance at writing for the world's greatest newspaper. God bless America!

When should we expect the Sarafians in New York Harbor? Please consider it. There may come a point at which you would be more effective solidifying the American Armenian community and working for reparations from this side of the planet. I know how difficult it is to leave home and be forced by duty to live elsewhere. However, it might prove more beneficial to remove some of the wagging fingers from the face of Turkey and apply a more subtle pressure from abroad. Show the world how successful you can be in another setting, how much poorer the Ottoman society is without the People of the Book, and wonder of wonders, the Turks themselves might soon appreciate the magnitude of their folly. We westerners have a colorful saying that what the Turks have done is to "cut off their nose to spite their face." You were their scapegoat but may yet prove to be their salvation. Stranger things have happened over there.

The letter clutched tightly in one fist, Adrine bent and stroked the sleeping boy's curly head, damp with sea spray. Her beautiful face was somber, the warm brown eyes swimming with hope and heartache. A buoy bell clanged in the distance. Fevzi adjusted the wheel and muttered a Muslim axiom.

Day quickly faded as *Little Seagrass* chugged toward a weathered pier and its humble berth alongside, but it was several minutes before Adrine read the haunting words of Davidson's closing paragraph.

Cat has gone to the kitchen to prepare supper. Though I promised her I would try to keep these ramblings conversational, I feel I must honestly confide in you. I've been seeing a doctor for night terrors and a slight tremor down my left side that gives every indication of staying. Please, for your own sakes and for the sake of your children, give serious thought to leaving Turkey. A sword hangs over you in my dreams. I fear for your safety. Come stay with us in freedom, and we will do all within our power to help you fight for the homeland from here.

Affectionately,
Frank and Catharine

Fevzi, eyes shut in prayer, guided the fishing boat from instinct. *Little Seagrass* bumped softly along the dock and settled contentedly into its moorings, with Fevzi clucking encouragement. "Like a good wife!" the fisher exclaimed, opening one eye to admire his unerring steersmanship. "Without a word she does your bidding. Without complaint she takes you home after the party and puts you to bed!"

The thick, briny smell of a thousand catches wafted over the harbor. Fish heads and their fleshless spines lapped against the wharf. Shriveled entrails, fins, and silvery scales littered the dock in oily patches and piles. Fevzi, bow rope in hand, jumped nimbly from deck to dock and gave the hemp a swift wrap around a piling. He held out his hands for the stern rope, caught it from Tatul, and in a blur of practiced motion secured it to a second piling.

The fishmonger stretched a thick, rough hand to his passengers. He knew better than to ask questions, but as the Sarafians gently awoke the sleeping boy and helped him to his feet, the curiosity in Fevzi's eyes burned brighter, and he could stand it no longer. "Children," he ventured, "such a blessing. They say that by the second born, the parents are sure never to divorce. I have to speak of my surprise at the handsome young man in your care. A nephew? Cousin perhaps?"

The Sarafians knew that Fevzi knew of the evening's events in the square. Who in all of Stambul did not know? Thus he knew the true identity of the boy but was attempting to maintain some semblance of politeness. It was the Muslim way of asking without asking.

"Go ask your wife's mother," Tatul replied with a dismissive chuckle, an arm around David's shoulders. Fevzi had married and divorced two women and was currently without a wife. Tatul's words meant that the boatman would have as much chance of getting a straight answer from his ex-mother-in-law as he would from Tatul.

Fevzi's gaze narrowed, and the smile vanished from his face. He spoke low, eyes roaming the pier and dilapidated buildings close by with suspicion. "The boy is not safe with you, or you with him. His death is desired by many, and yours would be ruled only a slightly lesser pity were you to be found with him. Leave him with me until you have made other arrangements. We will stay aboard the *Seagrass* and fish far out in daylight." He read the hesitation in their faces. "You know me. You know my partner. If I could drain the Turkish blood from my veins, I would. I may be your staunchest ally—frightening thought—and I, too, want a Turkey where all may breathe free. I will guard each hair of his head, good friends. Death stops here!"

They studied the earnest seaman, the leathery lines and creases obtained in an honest life at sea, and quickly understood that he was right. They were foolish to think they could walk the streets or sleep unmolested with the son of a traitor in tow. Together, the three were at risk. Fevzi's offer of asylum was a great kindness.

Tatul looked at Adrine, and reluctantly she nodded.

"Thank you, old friend," Tatul said. "We will find a safe house and return for him as swiftly as God allows." He knelt on the wooden dock and spoke eye to eye with the boy, who was beginning to cry. "David, be strong! We know this man, and you can trust him. Do what he says, and we will come for you within a day or two. Can you do that for us?"

David snuffled loudly but replied with courage. "Yes, Mr. Sarafian, I guess I can. You saved me from the mob, so I have to believe you." He looked skeptically at weathered old Fevzi, who was smiling reassuringly. David swallowed hard. "Please hurry," he whispered in Adrine's ear.

She hugged and kissed the boy and looked the fishmonger in the eye. "Armenia's hope," she said, putting David's hand in the fisherman's. "Guard it well."

CHAPTER 9

Adrine and Tatul stood in the full moonlight and stared a long time at the paper tacked to their back entry, reading its contents by matchlight.

My good Sarafians:

Condemn these perilous times! Civilized people ought to take tea and discuss their differences in a neutral atmosphere without fear of harm. I offer you just that. This evening, seven o'clock, please join me in my home for a small refreshment and civilized talk. Neva, my constant wife, will join us. As all our conveyances in this city of unrest are on patrol, I regret not to be able to bear you here in the proper manner. I will, however, send an escort to walk with you. I trust this meets with your approval, as it does with Allah's.

Tekir Pasha
Chief of Military Police
Istanbul Gendarmerie

Adrine's hand gripped her husband's arm. "Why?" The hand that held him and the voice that formed the word were hard as iron. "What does he want of us?"

When "he" was Tekir Pasha, there was no answer to the question. So ruthless was the Istanbul constabulary that Armenian mothers invoked them to strike fear in the hearts of their children. "You have misbehaved. What if this matter comes to the ears of Tekir Pasha and his police?"

Tekir Pasha and his police. It was spoken as a curse and brought the most terrible images to mind. Cruel beatings.

111

Marathon interrogations. Men, women, and children taken, missing, "lost" in a bureaucracy that didn't want them found. Tekir Pasha—judge, jury, and firing squad.

Tatul gripped Adrine's hand in his own. It could be one of a hundred possibilities, or all of them: the secret meeting of the Armenian Revolutionary Federation in December; the attack on the produce stand; Adrine's forays into Sulukule; the incident in the square; the harboring of the Mugurditchian boy, easily labeled an abduction or obstruction of the law. How could he have been so stupid as to think he could just act without there being certain consequences? These were not the mountains of Ararat, where a rebel could vanish without trace. This was steamy, treacherous Stambul, where danger crouched behind every lamppost and door.

Worst of all, his beloved Adrine was a constant target for retribution. To wed her to a Fedayee had done her no favor. And now—*this* night—they would walk into the jaws of death. Whether they would walk out again was up to God and a Turk with hands so bloody, they were said to glow red in the dark.

"We won't go." Her words came out high, nervous. "We are free people. We have choice. He cannot order us about like the mindless gendarmes, who spring into action every time he clears his throat. No, we are free citizens, and we choose not to go."

He turned her to face him and drew her close to his chest. His heart thundered too.

"We must go, sweet melon." She started to protest, but he shushed her still. "We must. Tekir Pasha has not stormed our home and removed us at gunpoint in his usual way. I believe that shows some respect for the Armenian Committee. This grants us an audience with perhaps the most powerful man in Stambul." He held her at arm's length, and the sparks in his eyes flew between them like wind-whipped embers. "I think God is telling us that this is an opportunity that will not repeat itself!" His face fell at the resistance in her eyes.

"I see," she said. "Tekir invokes Allah; you invoke God. I think the one cancels the other, and that is a sign we should not go. Listen to the language he uses, Tatul! All oily and sweet. When has anyone ever accused him of sweetness? To me, it echoes of the serpent in Eden. 'Come, eat. Why not? What harm could it do?' I tell you, dear husband, if nothing else, the Marxist Chazarian and his Armenian bullies will have you in bed with the pashas and the traitors of the homeland before the breaking of the dawn! Tomorrow's newspapers will tell of your 'treachery.' I beg you, Tatul, do not go. I, at least, cannot."

His shoulders slumped, but he nodded in understanding. He would not insist that she violate her own conscience. And with her at his side, he might be forced to hold back in his appeal to Tekir Pasha. They must speak frankly, as men. The less Adrine was exposed to the likes of the chief of police, the better. He might try to gain greater knowledge of her affairs, and that could place a number of innocent people at risk. He could see no other reason that so calculating an official as Tekir should invite a man *and* his wife to what was certain to be a raw-edged discussion.

"All right," Tatul said, kissing her cheek. "You stay and I'll go. Draw up a replacement inventory for Hamit Batu, and I will see that he has it within twenty-four hours. A day after that, and you shall be back in business, all new cabbages in a row!"

She sighed and placed a hand on the door latch. "Very well, your stubbornness, but take the gun with you. It may afford you the time needed to dodge Tekir's fangs and gain the street. I'd much rather it was with you than with me. And take that motley pack of yours. They've done little to protect you of late, but if the police chief knows they are hovering about outside, he may be less inclined to keep you for his collection."

Tatul smiled and kissed her lips.

"Do me one favor?" she asked.

"Yes?"

"When appropriate, look at his shoes. If they are caked with fruit pulp and vegetable bits, excuse yourself and come get me."

He smiled and hugged her close. She was God's own blessing and as resilient as Moses covered in frogs.

The door opened into a darkened combination washing room and scullery. Adrine waited in the doorway while Tatul lit the lamp, then another in the hall beyond.

Adrine closed the door and locked it, hanging her wrap on a hook by the door. She turned and Tatul could see by her expression that she felt the same odd sensation he did, a chill that had nothing to do with the temperature in the room.

She stood still in the middle of the scullery floor while Tatul lit the other lamps in the house. He rejoined her. Their eyes darted over the familiar shelves and cooking utensils, the little heating furnace and large porcelain bowl of dried fruit and nuts covered with a linen cloth.

All was in its place. All but the air.

Dust from the coal bins of Istanbul that had settled on every surface was in the air, recently disturbed. They could smell it.

Tatul stepped beyond the kitchen, turning slowly, taking stock. "Adrine," he called, drawing out her name as if uncertain of that which called for her attention. He did not have to say more.

Someone had been in the house while they were away on the *Little Seagrass*. That someone had only just left.

Slowly she approached the archway from which she could see the dining room, sitting room, and bedroom at a glance. Back to back they turned, and with each step, something else had disappeared.

The dining room table.

The tableware cabinet.

The ebony dresser.

The Persian blue carpet from off the bedroom floor.

The pale gossamer canopy.

The goose-down mattress.

The bed.

All gone. The front door had been forced.

Tatul faced her, his jaw clenched in a grim line. He started to speak, but her arm shot straight out, her index finger upraised for silence, her face an expressionless mask. Gradually, deliberately, as if dreamwalking in molasses, Adrine's eyes traced the interior of the house. Whenever she came to the space where a treasured piece of missing furniture had stood that morning, she carefully stepped around the emptiness of it as if its ghost still presided.

"Adrine, don't do this." His voice was tinged with sorrow and rage but more with a fear of what the theft would do to her. "They want to break us, to destroy us from within."

She stopped at the foot of the space that had contained their marriage bed, their most intimate moments, their fragile hopes of children and a shining future. Tatul watched her and knew she imagined the laughter of love and felt his arms around her, snuggled in down.

For several moments she said nothing. He waited, wanting to enfold her in his embrace and weave for her the wistful tapestry of what could be if only they got past the hatred and violation of trust that stabbed at them from every corner of this pestilent city.

Instead, he waited and wove the tapestry as antidote for his own cynical thoughts.

Adrine folded her hands in prayer and raised the knuckles to silently moving lips. In a few moments, as if having reached a conclusion, she crossed to the mahogany wardrobe, which remained, and withdrew her finest green brocaded gown. She laid it over Tatul's arm, undressed, laid her dress of the day over his other arm, and slipped into the gown. She looked at her husband as if seeing him for the first time in a long while. "You had better change, darling. Tekir's man will soon be here. We can't keep the chief of police waiting."

He buttoned her and watched while she fixed her hair high on her head in the western style he adored. "You're . . . you're going after all," he said to the image in the wall mirror, one piece of furniture that had been left behind.

"Why, yes, my fine Fox," she said, fastening the thicket of hair in place with a pin. "I have a theft to report."

The entrance to the home of the chief of military police resembled the front of a foreign embassy, with a curved drive,

wrought-iron fencing, and carved lions roaring in silent warning from the gateposts. The edifice itself was three stories of
pale pink marble with a showy entryway more spacious than
the Sarafians' entire home. It was but a short walk from there
to the Pera Palace Hotel, the opulent meeting place of princes,
spies, and international couriers of every stripe.

The stone-faced gendarme who had collected them depos-
ited them without ceremony on pink marble steps amidst a
flourish of flags that hung from the ramparts in billowing
clouds of Islamic stars and crescents. A blocky black automobile sat idle on the drive. As they passed, Adrine placed a
furtive hand on the metal hood, felt its coolness, and wondered that there was no available police vehicle to fetch them.
Were Armenians a waste of petroleum?

Vahram, Ephraim, and the ever faithful, burly Andranik
accompanied the Sarafians and remained alert at the foot of
the steps, studying every vein of the marble edifice for signs
of an ambush.

Inside, the home was strangely understated, as if everything had been put into its exterior, all that the vast majority
of Stambullus would ever see. The Sarafians were invited by a
towering Turk in crisp military tunic into Tekir's living quarters, a closed-off section of four rooms to the right of a sweeping marble staircase that encircled the entire entry.

The Turkish officer searched Tatul's coat and pants pockets for a weapon. "My apologies," the Turk said in a voice cold
and resentful. "Assassination is becoming an increasingly
popular career choice. Mrs. Sarafian, your wrap?" He held out
his hand for what he must have regarded as a means of stran-
gling the host.

Adrine pulled the jade green shawl more tightly about her
shoulders. "No, thank you. I find large estates such as this
sometimes drafty. I'd like to keep it."

He studied her lovely features with glacial distrust, gave a
slight nod, and turned his back to lead them to their hosts.
Tatul and Adrine exchanged a hasty glance.

In the Turkish style, the chief of police and his wife, Neva,
who was bundled from head to toe in heavy religious gar-

ments of sable and brown, sat on the floor among a sea of handsomely woven pillows in blues and saffron. Neva's eyes, like two jumbo black olives, lashes caked together in a dozen spikes, peeked curiously from between the excess of cloth that enshrouded her. Tekir Pasha, resplendent in a tan uniform ripe with medals, yellow fringe, and gold trim, looked small, as if tucked into a pocket of pillows like a toy soldier in a child's ornate diorama. He had taken a tall wife.

Three attendants, hovering about on the edge of the room, were dismissed with a diffident flick of Tekir's hand.

"Welcome, my friends!" the police chief said with an expansive wave. He gave a disapproving stare at Adrine's western coif, but behind the eyes of official reproof flashed an unmistakable interest. "Come," he motioned without rising, "come and sit with us. Neva and I are pleased that you accepted our invitation. First talk, then tea!" They bowed slightly, hands together in front of them in the Muslim way. The Sarafians followed suit.

Adrine settled herself uncomfortably opposite Neva and looked up to see that Tatul had stopped at a magnificently hand-carved table, which held an enormous volume as thick as the distance of a man's arm from elbow to wrist. She did not miss Tekir's scowl that she had taken her seat before her husband.

"You know of Ibn Sina's great work?" Tekir Pasha quickly recovered from Adrine's social blunder and seemed genuinely eager to make a show of the book.

Tatul looked suitably impressed by the Latin translation of *The Canon of Medicine*. More than a million words long, it was a monumental summary of medical practice and history in the first thousand years after the birth of Christ. "The observations of the greatest Muhammadan physician of all time," he marveled. "It was the basic text in the medical schools of Europe for five centuries."

"Yes!" Tekir exclaimed, rubbing small, fine hands in delight. "By the age of ten he had memorized the entire Qur'an of Muhammad's teachings. At the age of seventeen, he cured a sultan's digestive discomfort and was granted any reward his heart desired. That was how he gained access to the sultan's massive library, which he consumed in large quantities."

"And such wisdom led to the discovery of herbal treatments, hot baths, and major surgeries that restored many a suffering person to full health," said Tatul, his words thick with appreciation. "He wrote two hundred seventy different works of medicine and philosophy, some of which were composed on horseback as he rode into battle."

Tekir nodded. "You are a learned man," he said. "Not at all the reactionary wilderness beast you might have been had you remained longer with the Fedayeen." His eyes were narrow, probing, as if to see into Tatul's mind.

Tatul replied in an even, congenial tone. "There is much to be admired by all men in the singular intellect of one like Ibn Sina. With you, I mourn the loss of so many great Muslim thinkers and innovators to barbarians—"

"—and Christian Crusaders!" Tekir interrupted.

"And Christian Crusaders," Tatul conceded. "The use of antiseptics, the blessing of anesthetics ... Only in the last hundred years have western scientists and doctors rediscovered what your wise men knew a millennium ago."

Conscious of how exposed she was compared to the heavily bundled Neva, Adrine pulled the hem of her gown as straight as she could, arranged a pillow over her legs, and hid a smile. She suddenly understood a very practical use for her husband's penchant for little-known facts.

The police chief, elbows resting on his knees, rubbed his temples with the middle finger of each hand and continued. "You can appreciate, then, the chasm between ancient practices and modern medicine that was bridged by our blessed scientific minds."

"Indeed. They were the preservers of an enormous amount of scientific lore, collected and cultivated by the fine minds of Greece, India, Persia, and beyond. Muslim experimentation and observation of the natural world have increased man's longevity and made the impossible possible. Pity they were unable to discover the key to the one thing man wants above all others."

Tekir no longer held the upper hand in the conversation, and his sour expression showed that it pained him greatly. Adrine enjoyed his discomfort. For him to not say the thing that would allow Tatul to make his new and most likely unwelcome point would be to open a premature void in the conversation into which all manner of unpleasantries could slide.

And so he asked the obvious, a question thick with irritation. "Oh, and what might that be, good guest?"

Tatul's reply came without hesitation. "Why, peace, of course." His look was focused on *The Canon of Medicine*, and he rubbed the fine leather binding of the specially commissioned book.

"Something I suppose your Christian scholars have found and safely locked away in a subterranean urn deep beneath the Holy Land." The pasha's countenance darkened to match the sarcasm of his words.

Neva's large, expressive eyes flashed fear, and the silent woman squirmed among the pillows as if to burrow to a safer depth.

Adrine stole a look at the policeman's shoes. They were soft gold slippers that walked only on carpet.

"No," Tatul replied. "The peace that Christ brings is a peace of the heart and mind. An end to the hostility of spirit and character that drives men to war. A cure for the bitterness, greed, and depravity that plague us all from the first rock of the cradle. Your Ibn Sina spoke of this peace in medicinal terms. But just as God created medicines and cures for ailments of the flesh and mind"—Tatul ran a hand over the pages of the huge book—"so He gave His one and only Son as medicine and cure for the pain and death of sin. It ought to be our starting place, but so often we reach first for the gun."

Adrine shifted uncomfortably. Was he thinking of the German Mauser tucked inside the waistband of her gown? They had gambled she would not be searched. The shawl concealed it well, but Adrine sat rigid as if the weapon jabbed. She prayed it would not be needed.

Tekir sucked in his cheeks, his look sardonic. "Why do you bait me, Sarafian? You have inconvenienced a number of lesser Turkish officials throughout Istanbul, so I know you are aware that it is blasphemy to speak in a Muslim's presence of the Almighty One as having a son. God is indivisible. There is no God but God. This Christ peace of which you speak is a mere prophet's peace and cannot atone for anything. The way of atonement in this life is to rid the earth of all who blaspheme against Allah the Only! And sit down when I am seated!"

Tatul settled quickly into the cushions. Adrine saw how careful he was to keep her between himself and Tekir's wife. She knew he had taken note of the servants and guards hovering at a distance. They must have heard the rising inflection in Tekir's voice, for they moved in closer, keeping taut the protective net around the chief of police.

Adrine kept her eyes carefully averted, not wanting to look at Tekir's eyes or betray the alarm in her own. *Walk softly, dear Fox. Stay calm as a pond.*

"Forgive me," Tatul said, arms wide, head bowed. "I meant not to offend, which I would most certainly have done had I rationed my words and spoke without passion of the Messiah I serve. You would have been as insulted and suspicious of such guile as I would have been if your reply had been any less heated and passionate than it was. Besides, your government is moving away from religious fundamentalism to embrace a more secular rule. I recognize that, and in my speech I celebrate the religious freedom that I see coming under so enlightened a new system."

The pasha nodded and chuckled, conceding the point. He must respect an opponent's cunning, Adrine knew.

"The Fox a diplomat. How refreshing!" Tekir laughed. At the sound, his sentinels faded farther from the room.

Tatul placed a hand on each knee. "But you are well aware, my host, that by simply entering your home as guests, the report has by now reached the ears of the city's Armenians that

Tatul the Fox and his lady do consort with the enemy, pardon the harshness of the word. Instantly, for many, we bear the label of traitors, and others now speak of us and Mugurditchian the Judas in the same breath."

Adrine stiffened and Tatul raised a hand to stop her words before they burst into the room.

"Please, do satisfy my curiosity, then. Why did you accept my invitation with so much at stake?" Tekir asked. It was a rare moment when the pasha's mind and Adrine's wondered the same thing. But unlike her worried countenance, his wide smile betrayed the amusement he must feel over the complications he had caused the great Armenian freedom fighter. He apparently marveled at how the mighty fell with such a loud thud.

"We came to tell you that perhaps at no other time since the end of the war has your life been in the danger it's in now."

In a blur, six men instantly materialized in the room, pistols drawn, cocked, and pointed at Tatul's head. Adrine gasped, but her husband smiled disarmingly and slowly raised empty hands. "Would I speak of Christ's peace, then shoot you in your own home?"

"You shot Mugurditchian in his." The words were harsh, but Tekir seemed to enjoy the tableau and allowed the room and its inhabitants to remain frozen where they were. He pulled a cigarette from a jeweled case, lit it with a match from a similarly jeweled box, and settled back against his cushions. After two long draws on the cigarette, he picked a bit of tobacco from his tongue and waved the sentinels at ease.

"Tekir Pasha, you must believe me." Tatul lowered his arms and folded them to keep his hands in sight at all times. "I had nothing to do with that man's death."

Adrine studied her husband, asking God for confidence that Tatul's words were true.

"But you must remember that he was a man who reported three hundred of our poets, writers, clergymen," Tatul continued, "the civic, spiritual, and intellectual Armenian leaders of Constantinople. They died because he singled them out. He was, you could say, their executioner. Is it so surprising that he would in turn be executed by his own?"

"Perhaps not." Tekir drew another lungful of smoke and sent smoke rings in the direction of his wife.

The acrid gift made spiky lashes flutter, but not before her wide eyes flowed with obvious devotion. Only Adrine saw how ragged were Neva's nails, how nervously her fingers had tapped without once being still since her guests had arrived.

Tekir coughed, then continued. "But what he did under the articles of war was to serve his country, right or wrong. To feed his family, right or wrong. To obey the constituted authorities. For that he should have been decorated, not gunned down at dinner before family and guests. I can still smell the blood!" The police chief's cigarette hand shook as he stubbed the smoke into a silver ashtray.

"The smell of rotting flesh is with us every day." Tatul's sadness covered him like a mask. "Our people were killed and left to disintegrate in the sun like so much spoiled meat. Your Turkish youth died by the thousands at the Russian front. All for what, Tekir Pasha? All for what?"

The chief of military police appeared not to like the direction of the conversation and changed it. "What business did you have last evening in Binbirdirek Square?"

"My wife was overdue from the bazaar, and I went in search of her."

The pasha's eyes strayed to the cameo brooch at Adrine's neck, and there they remained. "I shouldn't wonder. She is a captivating woman, for an Armenian. That unfortunate business at the produce stand did not escape my notice. I ordered the patrols in that area doubled.

"What has me curious is why you allow her to frequent Sulukule. Don't you know that Gypsies are not human? Does anyone ever count the children at the orphanage to see if they're being eaten? I'm under a great deal of pressure to level that pit of fortune-tellers and prostitutes, and I would hate for Mrs. Sarafian to be caught up in so sordid a business."

She felt his gaze and gathered the shawl together, clutching it at her throat.

"The condition of Armenian orphans is appalling," Tatul

leaned forward, blocking Tekir's view. "Without adequate housing and care, we are forced to find quarters for them where we can. If you, sir, were to open a dry warehouse or two and free just a small amount of supplies with which to feed them and treat their illnesses, I feel that such goodwill would begin to turn the tides of animosity and would demonstrate winds of real change. Allow our assemblies to meet openly and our people to go about unmolested on the streets of Constantinople, and I can assure you that the threats of assassination and mob violence will cease."

The face of law enforcement in Turkey's largest city again looked amused. "Tides of animosity? Winds of change? You did not come equipped with anything with which to bargain, my empty-handed guest, but rather to deliver a weather report! I fear we shall have to shutter the windows against so stormy an opposition!" He gave a mocking laugh. Neva matched it in a high, gulping soprano that made the veil across her mouth puff out with each titillated gust of air.

Against her better judgment, Adrine spoke. "You are the chief of military police, Tekir Pasha, and I appeal to your understanding. Before this terrible war, Armenians lived peaceably and industriously, applying their skills for the good of the country, raising their families to be God-fearing, respectable citizens of Turkey. Torture, killings, destruction, hatred—these things were as foreign to them as to Muslim Turks. These things are unnatural to them now and utterly forbidden by their faith. It is just that what is right has been blurred by the need to survive and the will to prevail. They would abandon retribution overnight if they were shown by you that the time for us to be adversaries is done, that the only way to heal Turkey is to bury the sword and begin again."

Tekir nodded, a sober, pensive expression replacing the ridicule of moments before. He stood and paced the area in front of the lounging cushions, hands clasped behind his back, medals glinting lamplight.

Tatul gave Adrine a look of pure admiration. It appeared that her words had found their mark.

"*I* set the example. *I* make the first move. Without admitting fault, *I* demonstrate mercy by caring for the lost children of Armenia," Tekir said, his voice rising. "What a novel approach! Yes, yes, that could work. Let me think on it at tea." He paused, and a smug little smile toyed at the corners of his mouth. "Come, my guests. You prove yourselves more imaginative and stimulating than I would have thought possible. Please, follow my man to your seats."

The Sarafians rose, but a signal from Tekir kept Neva where she was until last. The four followed the tall, crisp Turk who had checked Tatul for weapons through an archway into the orangy glow of a dimly lit, low-ceilinged room. The table was exquisitely set with silver-etched tea glasses and blue china. Platters of flaky almond-filled pastries soaked in honey and pumpkin slices boiled in milk and sprinkled with grated hazelnuts, pistachios, and a dusting of sugar sparkled in reflected light.

"I invite you to sit and take your refreshment," Tekir said. He waited until his guests sat, then took his own seat, with Neva taking hers last. "Light!" he cried, with an insistent clap of hands. "It's darker than the insides of a camel's belly. I won't know if it's tea or poison!"

The lights came up, and Adrine dropped her spoon with a clatter.

Directly across the table, at Neva's back, was a familiar dark tableware cabinet. Adrine's eyes jumped from there to a hand-rubbed ebony dresser in the corner of the room. Suddenly, she jerked her head down in horror and knew with sinking heart that the very table upon which they took their tea was the Sarafians' dining table where her husband had so recently lain beaten and bleeding. She pushed back and looked at the floor beneath.

Their feet rested on a lovely blue Persian carpet—their carpet!

And Adrine knew—as surely as Tatul must know—that later that night in one of the other rooms nearby, the pasha and his wife would take their slumber in a beautiful four-poster bed with pale gossamer canopy and goose-down mattress.

Adrine stared at the wedge of pumpkin on her plate and saw a wagonful of stinking seeds and pulp.

"Try it, good woman," Tekir urged. "It is a sweet taste of the homeland."

She pushed the plate from her with a jerk.

The pasha was watching her carefully and looked as pleased as a cat full of canary. Neva's huge black eyes remained fastened on her lord and master.

The policeman's smile abruptly faded. Tekir wiped his mouth on a linen napkin and stood. "I have given your earnest entreaties the thought they deserve," he said in a hard and even voice. "Seven of my men are corpses tonight because of last evening's riot in the square. Their children will go to bed tonight without a father's kiss. Their wives lie awake tonight, arms empty, cold and alone.

"I am sick to death of Armenian demands. Here is what *I* demand. I demand that the Armenian orphans be relocated, somewhere outside the city where I cannot smell them, before I burn their diseased hides out of my city. I demand that not one wormy fig be supplied them from government coffers. I demand that every Armenian occupying a Turkish hospital bed within the city limits of Istanbul be immediately discharged. I demand that no more than three Armenians be found assembling together and that if they are, all but the three allowed are to be shot on sight. And last of all, I demand that within forty-eight hours you return David Mugurditchian to me upon suspicion of the murder of his father. Failing that, I will torch your precious orphanage and roast every one of those wretches alive!"

No one moved. Tatul strained to keep from springing across the table and fastening the police chief's neck in a death grip. Tekir Pasha was bent on erasing all trace of Armenia from his city and would stop at nothing to see it done. Why had they permitted themselves to be lured into thinking an invitation from this man could be anything but the proposition of a disturbed mind?

The ingratiating smile was bigger this time. "Of course I offer my guests protection. It would be rude of me not to. Two of my men are at your disposal, though I use the term advisedly. Please, I insist. Take them home with you. They do not mind sleeping on the floor." Tekir's enjoyment appeared immense.

Adrine stood to her feet, shoved the chair away, and dropped her napkin on top of the untouched pumpkin slice. Before Tatul could react, she rounded the table. Servants swarmed to stop her, but Tekir prevented them with a wave of his hand, apparently curious as to what she intended. Adrine yanked open the top drawer of the tableware cabinet, shoved aside the soup ladles, and grabbed the gold enamel pocket watch with the golden lion and charging elephant.

She whirled and faced Tekir, tightly squeezing the familiar hunt scene, as if by doing so she could choke the life from her tormentor. "We did not survive the slaughter to be mocked and subjugated by a little man with too much power," she shouted. "God have mercy on you, Tekir Pasha, and your soul. You can still escape the fires of hell, but not if you murder the innocents. I'm taking this watch as a sign to you that you have not won. You can steal it again, but it will be over my dead body!"

Tatul shot out a strong arm and encircled his wife's trembling shoulders. They moved to leave. No one stood in their way.

Tatul looked at the man in the tan uniform and gold braid. "Keep your men with you, Pasha. We have no need of them. The Fedayeen have a saying: '*Yehs Heesoos chem guhnar ooranall!* I cannot deny my Jesus! Nor will He deny His people. God the Father fights for us!'"

"Yours is a religion of myths!" Tekir called after them. "Remember the *Canon*, Sarafian, the learning of the ages. Muhammad the Prophet had a saying too: 'He who travels in search of knowledge travels along Allah's path to Paradise.' Come back under Turkish rule, Armenia, and we will teach you all that you need for salvation!"

CHAPTER 10

When they had turned a corner and were out of sight of Tekir Pasha's estate, Adrine began to weep. Tatul held her right arm the tighter, but she stumbled as if she would collapse and threw her left arm around a chipped and rusted lamppost. The three Armenian companions stopped at a respectful distance behind and averted their eyes as if hesitant to intrude on so private a grief.

In the feeble light of its grimy glass, Adrine gripped the lamppost and Tatul's neck with the strength of frustrated fury. "He is not human!" she sobbed. "It is how Satan governs! He intimidates, humiliates, and hires others to strip the weak of the little they have. He steals by right of conquest from beneath our noses and then forces us to watch while he . . . he . . ." She could not finish and bent beneath the weight of her sorrow, her breath coming in ragged gasps of lament. "Tekir Pasha is m-m-ore monster than man!"

Rage erupted from Tatul as from a long dormant volcano. "No, Adrine!" he bent and whispered fiercely into her ear. "Do not let them see how we twist and turn on the hot stove of his madness!"

He looked up at the windows of the apartments and shops lining the street. Curtains stirred; faces stared, mostly curious, but to his heated thoughts each was an arrogant sneer of those who occupied a city where the former war had not ended and would never end. Though still sometimes fought with clubs and guns, open combat had largely transfigured into a battle of wills and opposing ideologies. If the Turks could break

Armenian resolve, cast lasting doubt on their faith, fashion their people into objects of derision, then they could declare the ultimate victory.

Adrine tore her arm from his. "The hands that have strangled babies and old women now caress our belongings and mock us with our own food! The feet that have hastened to the destruction of others stand on our own carpet...." A mighty shudder passed through her. "And the body that orders a people brought low sleeps in our own bed! How can that woman stay with him? I would rather be a Gypsy slave!"

Tatul felt the hot lava of loathing deep in his loins. Christianity was impossible because it did not allow hatred, and at the moment, hatred was his most prized possession. He pulled at his hair, emotion running unchecked. "If you can indulge your rage in public, then I, too, can indulge mine!" Tatul snatched the pistol from the waistband of Adrine's gown and charged back the way they'd come.

Swiftly the three companions were upon him. They pressed Tatul against the wall of the closest building, wrestled away the Mauser, and held him while he cooled.

"Reckless fool!" Andranik remonstrated. "You draw unwanted attention. How can you be so careless?"

"Where is your discipline, Fedayee?" Vahram snarled, quickly sliding Tatul's pistol into the sleeve of his coat. "How did you think to get past Tekir's men? How could you risk another massive killing of our people? Have you the heart of an assassin?"

Tatul's chest slowed its heaving. He closed his eyes, composed himself, and nodded that he had regained his senses. "Forgive me, brothers. We found our stolen goods inside Tekir's home. He taunted us with that theft and with the food taken yesterday from Adrine's stand. He robbed us of what we have worked so long and hard for. Worse, he robbed us of our dignity." He knew the empty foolishness of the words as soon as they were spoken, but Andranik seized the moment.

"Tell the dead about your awful loss of dignity!" he sputtered, his disgust showing as he paced the walk and cast accusing looks at the man for whom his affection and admiration knew few bounds. "Tell our mothers and fathers who were cut in two for the valuables they swallowed rather than allow them to fall into the hands of the infidels! Tell the children who were starved and dashed against the rocks for sport at the evening's campfire." He stopped close to Tatul's face and spread open the lid covering his eyeless socket. Tatul turned away. "Tell *me*," Andranik said, voice low and bitter. "Tell me, whose eye is now the shriveled trophy of a Turk drover for whom the deportation had grown boring."

Suddenly Andranik hugged Tatul in an awkward embrace about the waist, tears of emotion streaking the again gentle features of the little man. "Forgive me for chastising you, great Fox. I know you have missing relatives of your own. But perhaps Chazarian is right in one respect." He looked quickly at Adrine, then away from her sorrow. He spoke low. "You seem caught these days between the swift and decisive actions of a rebel fighter convinced of his righteous cause and the uneasy world of a politician for whom compromise and agonizingly slow progress are the necessary tools of negotiation but in the end become too painful and unproductive for you to bear. I think you must choose—Fox or foxhole, which will it be?"

The others nodded their agreement, and Tatul felt both exhilaration and uncertainty at the truth. It was a difficult, if not impossible, path he was on. The Fedayeen knew no masters but God and freedom. Perhaps he was meant to ride forever with them. But living in rocks and eating whatever wild thing happened along was no life for a woman or her children. His children. *Their* children.

But how much more hospitable was life in Stambul? The Armenians remained the mistrusted scum of society, one rung above Gypsies, and a short rung at that. How much closer were they to establishing a legal ruling party? How much closer to regaining the homeland? Lips moved, words came out, fists beat the air, but as Tekir Pasha had so brazenly demonstrated, Armenians had gained little more than the rights of an ant.

He looked at Adrine still clinging to the lamppost, her cheeks damp in the murky light, her eyes closed, swaying slowly to and fro. He knew she was praying—for their safety, for his guidance, for their future.

For forgiveness.

They'd lost sight of their blessings. This city, for all its lawlessness and insult, was home to good people like Fevzi the Fishmonger and Mother Agop and the little homeless boys of Armenia in her care. People of many races and cultures—all caught up in the uncertainty, rumor, and prejudice of armed conflict—struggled to make a home and a life here. They were Adrine's customers, her workers, her cause.

He seemed unable to settle anywhere or form alliances of the heart, while she saw the growing possibilities, even a *vitality*, in Istanbul that often escaped him. Her strength came from the developing community, the vineyards, the productivity of a recovered people, where his gaze was more solidly fixed on the *idea* of Armenia the nation. National pride, sovereignty, and world stature were his meat. Collective dignity was much to be desired.

"You look near; I look far," he had once told her. Her reply had made him think. "For me," she said, her liquid brown eyes glowing, "the big painting is of the hereafter, the New Jerusalem; for you, it is heaven on earth, an Armenia unmolested, respected, even revered. Yet you know how flawed the kingdom of Israel was, how despised and enslaved they'd become, yet they are God's favored ones! Oh, Tatul, let us build the best kingdom we can right here in Stambul, with all the talents and abilities we've been given. Let us, God willing, pass our vision and our faith on to our children. We've been given a second chance. We must use it in the pursuit of the possible. That is how we will restore the homeland—by building our homes again. Hundreds, thousands, a multitude of homes where Christ is honored and the Father Almighty is worshiped!"

The memory of her words warmed him and calmed his racing blood. She was more than he deserved and possessed far more sense. Ignoring the three guardians, the public spectacle, the mental image of Tekir's smug smile, he went to her, pulled her close, and kissed the top of her head in the yellow gaslight glow. Let the curtains stir.

"To whatever you're telling God right now," he said in a voice husky with love and gratitude, "please add my amen."

"I am thanking Him that the boots that stomped my tomatoes belonged to my enemy and not my kinsman." Tatul felt Adrine relax against him, but his muscles tensed at her words. *Andranik is right*, he thought. *I am two people and of two minds.*

With a growing dread, the Fox knew that he soon would be forced to choose.

From the doorway to the public baths, a slender, neatly kept man, darkly dressed, watched their embrace and felt a stab of regret in his chest. There were two loves in his own life: the first woman, he loved for her farm-girl charm; the second, for her tireless devotion to justice. How would he ever pick between them? Would he ever have the chance? Their flashing eyes and sweet embrace seemed oceans away.

He felt a strong foreboding for the man and woman who struggled for answers in the dim night glow of a Stambul street. He didn't know the details of their ill-advised meeting with Tekir the Bloody, but it was obvious it had not gone well. Theirs was too open a fight for the homeland and one doomed to become a casualty of the current climate of animosity and fear.

Consorting with the enemy was not the answer. The Judas had come to that truth too late.

No, the treachery of the times called for secrecy, for lone operatives with no real ties, no permanent address. The times called for selective retribution delivered swiftly, unexpectedly, and without regret.

He would have to leave Istanbul soon. The primary target had been traced and his patterns of movement established. While the Germans publicly denounced the Turks' rabid handling of the Armenian situation, in private they were not at all reticent to harbor the evil man who had orchestrated it all. The American contacts had said now was the time for him to make the most telling move of all.

Talaat Pasha, former interior minister of Turkey, author

of the attempt to destroy all trace of Armenia from the face of the earth, had found sanctuary and acceptance in Berlin.

The slender man must therefore go to Berlin and do for Talaat what had been done for Mugurditchian the Judas. The fat whale of a traitor Judas had died in a mansion paid for by the blood of untold thousands of innocent Christians. The one small thing to be said in defense of so wicked a man was that he had not run to hide behind Germany's skirts. For that—and the near murder of a nation—Talaat deserved a slower and more agonizing end.

But before leaving Stambul, the dark man had one final task to perform. The request had come earlier that evening, anonymously, but the drama had played out as promised. He had watched as the Sarafians, dressed for dinner, had been ushered inside police headquarters, remained for some time, then had left remarkably alive. Evidence of conspiracy didn't come more damning than that.

The watcher said a quick prayer for the well-meaning couple across the way, then felt for the butt of his gun, familiar and necessary. He permitted himself one final twinge of regret. Their lives were ahead of them. They possessed vitality. They were not like the fat opportunist who toasted his benefactors with the blood of his own people. But they had transgressed as surely as he. And for what? Some empty promise of relaxed restrictions in the Armenian enclave, such as lower taxes or fewer beatings. Who knew what proprietary information they had given up in their visit with the police? They knew so many within the resistance, so many who strove for justice and a free Armenia. Before they could hand them over, before they could make a list of names, they would have to be silenced. One Judas was enough. The same mistake; the same devastating consequences. Intolerable. Armenia would not recover from another purge of leadership.

So it would be. He had one final task before his departure to Berlin.

Tomorrow . . . when he could get them alone.

The sea-moist air was less foul here away from the waterfront. The assassin filled his lungs with it, turned, and faded into a maze of backstairs and alleyways.

It had been a long day, made all the more tiring by ocean wind and the emotional shock of the theft and its aftermath. A heaviness lay over the city weighed down by fog from the Bosporus. The thick stench of open sewage along the waterfront at the foot of the Seven Hills was held close to the ground by a creeping mist and lapped sour against the senses.

Tatul and Adrine bid their friends a weary farewell at the street corner near their home. Andranik insisted on accompanying them to the door, but Tatul was just as insistent that they were fine and needed to be alone. At length, the passionate little man bowed to their wishes and was swallowed up, along with his two cohorts, by the deepening night.

"There goes a sweet, good man," Adrine said as they walked down the street alongside the house to the rear entrance. "He would make an excellent uncle for the children. May we adopt him?"

"Of course," Tatul responded, trying his best to match the lightness of her remark, "but wouldn't Uncle Andranik frighten them with his one all-seeing eye?"

Adrine slapped his arm. "What a terrible thing to say! My Uncle Saras had six toes on one foot, and once I felt reassured he would not eat me, we took a great liking to each other. He told funny stories and always had a sweetmeat in his pockets for good little nieces. Uncle Andranik would make a fine horse or cow upon which to ride."

"Reminds me more of a benevolent old monk," injected Tatul affectionately. "Put him in a cassock and point him toward Bethlehem, and I believe he could find his way, provided the star was not on his blind side."

They stopped and looked at their modest home for the second time that night. It was narrow and jammed against the dwelling next to it in typical Turkish construction. Another family lived above, and three men shared the tiny compartment above that, all connected by a precarious set of stairs, which for the moment was lost in the night fog. Tatul knew that Adrine hoped to move up, to be less accessible to the street. When she gave birth to their first child, though, Tatul would wager his right foot that she'd want to head back down again before the little one could walk or attempt to fly from the upper landing.

But now, for the first time since they'd moved there, he sensed that she did not want to enter her own home. He understood.

Tatul felt his vest pocket for the key and instantly felt foolish. They could simply walk in the broken front door. "At least they left us the dining room carpet," he said halfheartedly, "though the table did hide the wear. Thin as it is, with a few blankets and a coal fire, we should get enough sleep to satisfy the saints."

Adrine held back, and her husband knew she dreaded entering the house with its glaring empty places. But to seek shelter elsewhere was to admit defeat. They could not dwell on their loss. They had their lives, and that was blessing enough.

"Maybe we should invite a few of the street curs inside for the night," she said. "Their manners aren't the best, but they might provide a bit of heat." She laughed, but it sounded hollow.

"Their breath stinks of rotten fish," said Tatul, pushing the door open. "Besides, we have each other. Come, I have a new and utterly astonishing tale of the royal courts with which to regale you."

Suddenly, a menacing voice came from the darkness. "I wouldn't go in if I were you. You know what happens to traitors in their own homes."

Instinctively, Tatul shoved Adrine through the door, slammed it shut again, and whirled to face the shapeless threat.

A match was struck, and a torch flamed bright, followed by two more. The men behind the torches were not clear until Artin Chazarian stepped forward between two of them.

"Get away from the door," he said coldly. "Both of you must answer for consorting with the enemy."

Sarafian snorted his contempt. "I see that the Hunchaks

are gainfully occupied, as usual, interpreting their limited vision in ways most colorful and imaginary! Oh, I would invite you in, but there is nowhere to sit and nothing to eat, courtesy of the enemy with whom we have so recently consorted."

Chazarian's eyes narrowed. In the partial light his lean jaw and thin face looked almost wolfish. "If you suffered a loss, you should have sought help or refuge with the brothers, not from that renegade Tekir."

Tatul threw his hands in the air. "Can you ever forgive me, Artin? No sooner was I robbed than my first thought should have been the comfort and compassion of my local Marxist agitators. How thoughtless of me. How careless not to fall into your arms immediately!"

The leader of the Hunchaks was not deterred by Sarafian's sarcasm. "You and I have been long on the same side, though using vastly different approaches to reach the same end. But now you have crossed a line and must answer for your deception!"

Chazarian and the torchbearers started forward. Fast as a mountain cat, Tatul crouched low, snatched a dagger from his boot, and thrust it, blade raised, before their faces. "No mob takes us from our home. No Marxist touches my wife."

With a jerk of his head, Chazarian signaled to one of his men, who then reared back and threw his torch into the back of the Sarafian wagon parked next to the house and the lean-to stable that sheltered Pera the horse.

Flames leapt up the inside of the wagon, and Pera struggled to her feet, neighing in terror.

Chazarian nodded again, and a second man drew back his arm to throw a torch through the window.

The hurled dagger struck him in the forearm just below the elbow. The man screamed, dropped the torch in the dirt, and staggered back, staring wild-eyed at the blade buried deep in his flesh.

Tatul Sarafian crouched warily before his attackers with fingers itching to bury themselves in whatever throat drew near.

Artin Chazarian shook a fist at the wiry Fedayee. "Together, we could have done something!" He bellowed and cursed, less in control than Tatul had ever seen him. Chazarian snatched the torch off the ground and started for the house.

"I wouldn't!" The shout came from the street, where suddenly there were a dozen torches and chattered commands in Turkish. And above them all could be heard the unmistakable voice of the master seller of all things oceanic, the clarion sales cry of Fevzi, the gap-toothed fishmonger.

"Be aware! Step carefully there! You'll no longer be needing that torch, sir. Thank you. You, sir, please douse that fire." When the man hesitated, two of Fevzi's brother fishermen seized the Marxist sympathizer by his clothing and pitched him headfirst into the back of the flaming wagon. "Quickly, sir, quickly, or you and the fire will be as one!" yelled Fevzi jovially. The man frantically tore off his coat and beat the flames dead.

"Good! Good! Too bad about your coat, but it is replaceable. Men are not. Come work for me at my fish stand. Two, three days, and you will have earned enough to haggle for a fine new coat. Then you can go back to doing nothing again, Mr. Marxist, nothing at all! Do not bother to speak again, Mr. Chazarian. You use too much the mouth and too little the brain."

The Hunchak leader looked as if he would enjoy wrapping a tightly knotted rope around the fishmonger's neck. "This one thing the Fox needs to hear."

Tatul waved to Fevzi to let Chazarian speak.

The Marxist took a measured breath, clearly enjoying the ability to once again command an audience. "An edict has been issued. Either the Mugurditchian boy is found here by noon tomorrow, or an important Armenian resistance leader will suffer the unpleasant consequences."

Tatul quickly crossed the space separating him from his opponent and leaned into the man's face. "Who, Artin? Who issued the edict? Tekir just informed us we have forty-eight hours, and he mentioned nothing of a trade."

"Ah, my friend, you know by now that I do not reveal my

sources. Just have the boy here by midday tomorrow, or someone will pay a very high price for your disobedience."

Tatul fought to keep his hands off the Marxist's throat.
"Just tell me this, Artin, does this command come from Christian or infidel?"

Chazarian turned his back and walked slowly toward
Fevzi's men, as if doing them the great favor of surrendering
now that he had delivered the message. "It comes from God,
my fair Fedayee, and had better not be defied."

Most of Fevzi's crowd elected to escort Chazarian and
company to the far side of the Galata Bridge and to stand
guard there until it was certain they had dispersed for the
night. Quickly, they disappeared through a curtain of fog,
herding their glowering charges ahead of them.

Tatul watched them go, then looked at Fevzi. Despite the
Hunchak's threatening words, Sarafian could have hugged the
little Turk until the last of his seven teeth fell out. "Hail, good
fisher, and what brings you out on such a night?"

Fevzi stood soberly before Tatul, redolent of fish oil and
engine grease. A wide-eyed and very excited David Mugurditchian dashed from the shadows where he had stayed hidden
until now. He pressed against the wiry fisherman, clearly enamored of the man's combative style. A hand gnarled by rope,
line, and salt water came to rest softly on the boy's head.

Cautiously, Adrine looked out the window at the changed
scene to the rear of her home, then threw the door wide. "Fish
mangler!" she cried, "did you bring swordfish for the fight?"

He bowed low as if he had just put ten swordsmen and a
cannoneer to flight. "Ah, Sarafian's lady, what have you to
lessen the hunger of me and my men?"

"I believe mutton tripe soup should ease the sufferings of
battle. Come in, good men, come in!"

They did, but Adrine could instantly sense their uneasi-
ness. Fevzi stood in the middle of the dining room and looked
about.

"We heard of your misfortune," he said, "and now you
shall hear of mine. The *Little Seagrass* is no more. They burned
her to the water line. Thank Allah, I had the boy with me."

"Oh, Fevzi, when? How? We were with you all day!" Adrine felt tears well up. The hardworking little fishing boat had been Fevzi's life, more wife than any woman he'd ever married. What would become of his fish stand in the Grand Bazaar?

"It happened after you departed for the evening and I was at a favorite café having raki to wash the taste of tea from my mouth"—he paused, a pained expression on his face—"the offspring of a she-mongrel molested my child, my lover, and set her afire."

He must have bathed in raki the way he reeked of it. The wire whiskers of his lower lip began to quiver.

"She was too old and tired to resist." He swiped at a threatening tear. "All is right. All is right! Allah would not want us to cry over an ancient tub of bolts and fish guts. Lately she was more broken than fixed, and I spent so many hours with one hand on the tiller and one inside her greasy belly that the fish had to hook and clean themselves! She was too much trouble—I think it was her kidneys—and I am blessed of Allah that she is gone at last. . . ." His eyes nearly closed in his misery, and little David hugged the wiry sea leg tighter.

"I am worried for this lad," Fevzi said, stroking David's head. "He has done nothing wrong and should not have to fear for his life while in my care. He must be taken to a safe place."

"It shall be done," Adrine said, "for this son shall right the wrongs of his father."

Tatul looked at his wife sharply. She had spoken decisively. That often meant he would not be included in the deciding. He stared at her, but she acted as if she hadn't a thought for anything but serving her sudden guests.

Adrine made the tea extra strong that night and added water to stretch the mutton tripe soup. The Turkish fishermen stood in the dining room and kitchen, eating noisily, topping one another's sea tales, and discussing how each would give a portion of his catch to keep Fevzi's fish stand open. And they knew of an old abandoned vessel, tossed up on the point numerous storms ago, that with ingenuity and a little baling twine could be made seaworthy once again.

Tatul listened and watched the grizzled seamen make their plans. It had been a day of great loss, but here, before the ashes grew cold, a human salvage effort was under way to save a friend and keep a competitor afloat—made necessary because a Turk had shown compassion for an Armenian.

"Mesut says you can move onto his boat until yours is ready," someone proffered uproariously. "He cooks like a sea witch and smells like low tide, but he sings to the fish, and they enter his nets blindly and without complaint!"

Their laughter and salty imagery brought an unexpected peace amidst the injustice. And it covered the fact that they stood or sat on a barren floor.

"Thank you, God." Adrine breathed the words aloud as she added another pitcher of water to the remaining broth.

Tatul heard her and looked her way.

"I'm thanking God for taking my mind off myself," she told him and began to hum a hymn of praise.

Tatul breathed thanks of his own.

Once the steam rolled off the surface of the soup, Adrine Sarafian banged the ladle against the side of the pan and called out as lustily as if she had been a maiden of the sea all her life, "Sea swill, my hearty mariners? Who will brave another dollop of my stomach soup? Let not the cow have died in vain!"

Fevzi and his brother fishermen roared their approval and held out their bowls. Tatul came up behind, slid his arms around the slender waist, and gave her the fervent kiss of a Fedayee who had been too long in the mountains.

She smiled at him and, to their cheers, returned the favor.

Tatul felt such passion for her. He knew how much she loved her man, these rough seamen, this city. She was not yet defeated!

And they both knew the gossamer canopy had a tear in it. The dining room table legs were uneven, and the table wobbled. The top right drawer of the tableware cabinet would invariably stick.

And when the pasha and his wife climbed into the four-poster for the night's slumber, they had better do it just right, or the bed would buckle and the mattress would fall to the floor.

As if she read his thoughts, Adrine's smile widened, and the hymn she hummed rose noticeably in volume.

CHAPTER 11

Sulukule crackled with the news. Two male goats had wandered into the district, and the dogs had not yet found them. As if dropped from a cloud, the animals were dispatched with haste, their stringy flesh stripped of its tough membrane and chopped fine for the stewpot already aboil with onions and garlics.

Never mind that one of the animals had a bell around its neck. The gold trinket was thrown to a plump toddler, who promptly put it in his mouth. No one took notice. Ownership was relative.

Into the pungent brew an elderly Gypsy woman and an adolescent threw withered vegetables—eggplant, carrots, and okra—rice, and a handful of maggoty chicken, followed by a little sack of ground cinnamon bark, turmeric root, peppercorns, and mint.

Another few minutes and the ancient goat, on the boil for four hours, was declared tender enough to eat. The livers, a delicacy, were reserved for the Gypsy chiefs.

With an unearthly screech, followed by a low guttural clucking, the elder woman called her family and any other family within earshot to goat stew. A tumble of colorful humanity of all ages streamed to the pot: children and teenagers in flowered dresses, gold pendants, tight black pants, and silk shirts; older men in black coats and vests, embroidered skull caps, and flashing gold teeth; and older women in flowing print dresses, brightly colored shawls, and rosy makeup.

Pressing forward among the excited, chattering knot of

Gypsies were a woman and a boy, neither hungry nor Gypsy. Though the handsome young man, with features as dark and brooding as a nomad's, was bright with silks and neck encircled with shiny baubles of gold and brass, the woman holding tightly to his hand was encased in the thick drab browns of religious modesty. The beautiful expressive eyes above the cloth strip covering the lower portion of her face darted furtively about the crowd, the patch of stained earth that was the wanderer's kitchen, and beyond.

"You eat your share," Fatima the elder said, motioning to the stranger in brown.

"Thank you, but we'll wait until your family is fed," the woman replied, the energetic clatter of children making her sad for the family she had lost.

Fatima sniffed. "Don't wait too long." She eyed the stranger. "It smells, but there is strength in a lusty he-goat of many seasons. To hide your secrets in this city, you need the guile of a goat."

Beneath the heavy garments, Adrine Sarafian felt sweaty trickles of fear against her skin. She tightened her grip on David Mugurditchian's hand and felt the old woman's searching stare.

"Thank you, Fatima, for the loan of the clothing," Adrine whispered into the incredibly malformed ear of the old one. "We shall not forget you!"

Old Fatima snorted. "My people were despised long before yours. The only difference between us is that we are neither so pious nor so trusting. We have spent centuries building a wall of mystique for protection. You would do well to build one of your own." Gnarled fingers picked and pulled at David's costume. He fidgeted until she gave up. "This is a boy not yours, dressed as a false Gypsy. Either you are very stupid, or you have something in mind?"

Adrine swallowed. How far could she trust this one? "I intended to send him in here alone, but I feel we have been followed, and I feared for him. He—the Turks want him, and I can't let that happen."

Fatima pursed her lips. "Hmm. You have more to fear dressed like a false Muslim."

Adrine looked down and nodded.

The old woman nodded grimly. "Too bad. It's what comes of staying in one place too long. Ill feeling has time to take root and eventually bear harvest and we are forced to deceive to survive. That is our story. Bring food and come with us out on the open road. You are thin but sturdy and can easily learn to dance for money. We take what we can where we have to, but there is honor among us."

Adrine did not answer.

When it seemed that the parade to the stewpot would never end, Adrine shouted to Fatima above the clamor. "How many belong to you?"

"Twelve, thanks to my Kalo, who has recently given me my thirteenth." Fatima patted her already expanding belly. "I am glad when he goes from Stambul on the hunt!" She rolled her eyes in a universal gesture among women that needed no further explanation. "Only trouble is, he always returns! Come with us, and when I wear out, Kalo can start on you!" She laughed a kind of dry snuffle that made her nostrils—one impaled by a nose ring—flare out.

"How do you manage?" Adrine questioned, ignoring the ribald comment. She braced against the jostle and helped scoop the steamy broth into outstretched cups and bowls of cracked porcelain.

"By being grateful the other five did not survive," Fatima replied matter-of-factly.

Adrine stopped in midscoop and looked at the splayed, arthritic feet, then full into the wide, weary eyes of hard living.

"Stillborn," Fatima said.

The food disappeared as cleanly and completely as if in the path of locusts. Two of the children bouncing about the empty pot looked as if they would hop inside and lap the cauldron clean.

Adrine stared into a half cup of watery gray, squeezed her eyes tight, and gulped down the lot. David, more accustomed to rich delicacies, took three deep breaths, lowered the green scarf below his nose and mouth, and poured the brew straight down. A shudder passed between them, but the swill stayed in their stomachs.

On silent command, the entertainment began. Boys juggled and tumbled; men beat skin drums and sawed at fiddles; girls whirled and danced and spread their shawls in provocative interpretations. Gold ankle bracelets flashed, and print silk petticoats spun and billowed. What had been a dark patch of despised ground in an instant became the colorful stage of exuberant vagabonds.

In a dizzying blur of back flips a young man with a single gold earring and a dazzling show of snow-white teeth made a dramatic entrance. The other entertainers backed away, the drums rolled, and the young man flung a baton high into the air. In the time that it rose twisting and turning, reached the apex of its journey, and plunged back to earth, he juggled two balls, an apple, a carrot, and a rag doll while whistling a Gypsy melody. Just when it seemed he had waited too long, he rapidly collected the juggled objects to his breast, caught the descending baton with a flourish, and fell to his knees in a sweeping bow, arms outstretched to receive a burst of well-deserved applause.

A shower of gold coins rained down upon the virtuoso juggler, who quickly scooped them up and placed two in his pocket. He licked the rest one by one and stuck them to the foreheads of the laughing children.

Then he turned to the woman encased in brown cloth and, with a rakish grin, appraised her slowly from head to foot. The Gypsy throng melted away from around her, and suddenly Adrine felt cold and exposed, as if she and David stood alone at the summit of a snowy crag with night falling and no way down. She wanted to crawl away into a dark coal bin and bury herself, not become the unwitting shill of a Gypsy street performer.

Three women and a man began to sing in an eerie minor key, a lone piper accompanying them. The words were unintelligible to Adrine, but the plaintive melody and the Gypsy male's lovesick gestures conveyed the lyrics plain enough. The dancer, shirt open to the waist, long black hair flowing out behind, began to sway and whirl over the dusty ground in a nimble ballet. Halfway to where she stood, the rhythm abruptly changed and the tempo increased, drums joining in. The young man turned and twisted in a blurring combination of dips and leaps, his long hands knifing the air with grace and purpose.

"He likes you and believes that beneath your many layers of secrecy lies a soul that yearns to throw off the bonds of Muhammad," interpreted Fatima the elder. "He does not know you are an impostor."

Adrine started to protest, then bit her tongue. If the disguise worked on him, even in an unwelcome way, she had best keep silent.

Fatima appeared to read all in the visitor's brown and guileless eyes. "Survival makes storytellers of citizen and alien alike. I've decided that you are harmless and could benefit from some Gypsy heat. Tell him with your eyes that you invite his friendship."

Adrine's eyes shut tight.

The Gypsy dancer made an impossible stag leap above their heads. The drums reached a pounding crescendo midway through the jump, and he fell to the earth at Adrine's feet, light as thistledown.

Arms spread wide, face upraised in a beatific smile, the gymnast of dance knelt in the dirt. Suddenly, the only sound was his heavy breathing. The rest of the Gypsy band stood silent to see her reaction.

It was too still. Adrine opened her eyes and watched the rise and fall of the dancer's chest framed in a "V" of brightly embroidered red-and-silver threads. She laid an arm around David's shoulders and pulled him close.

"Tell our entertaining friend," she said to Fatima, "tell him that my husband thanks him for his concern but that I have attained full bloom and am in no need of expressing anything but my thanks for a fine athletic performance!"

The old woman smiled ruefully, bent down, and kissed the young man. He fell back in mock shock. Fatima loudly delivered Adrine's words in a rapid stream of Romani, the Gypsy language. The crowd laughed; the dancer groaned and rolled his eyes in disappointment. With a shout he threw his arms around the old woman's neck and kissed her passionately until she was forced to slap him away.

"Agh! That one!" Fatima exclaimed. "He has the charm to make cruel husbands kind and cold ones loving, because they do not want their wives falling into his arms. But as you can tell from the number of lovesick eyes that follow his every move, he has a charm bracelet full of choices to pick from. But always he has a tender heart for the worn ones like me. If I were twenty years and twelve—no, thirteen—babies younger, I might get in harness with that one!"

Adrine thanked Fatima for the goat broth. The Gypsy elder gripped Adrine's smooth hand in her rough and wrinkled one. Eyes closed, Fatima swayed, her thin lips moving in a silent reading. Without opening her eyes she spoke in a faraway, dreamy voice. "It is as if a dervish has whirled through your heart and thrown the furniture about. Your life is in disarray. As your business bears fruit, so shall your womb. You trust in the God of heaven, and He trusts in you. Good for you, Armenian. This child with you is not your own. He will be your death or your salvation. Guard him carefully. Now go, for a dark and evil dervish whirls in pursuit while we yet speak!"

Adrine dropped the woman's hands in alarm. Her thoughts collided. *God, protect me from fortune-tellers and those who tell the future through tea leaves and cow dung! I will trust in the Lord and lean not on my own understanding. God, spare me from dervishes, whirling or otherwise!*

Yet as she hurried away with David's hand grasped tightly in her own, the back of her head prickled from the fixed stare of bold Gypsy eyes. She could not shake the accuracy of the woman's words. Perhaps it was apparent from Adrine's clumsy attempt at concealment that her life was in disarray. But why had the woman chosen the image of "furniture"? Did she know of the theft? Were "fruitful" and "fruitless" meant to be a clever play on words, or was it a none-too-veiled reference to her means of livelihood? Her faith in God was easily determined from her nationality, but how could she be so certain David was not Adrine's child? And, dear God, what were the evil dervishes to come?

Immediately, she chastised her foolishness, so unwilling to put faith in a bad prediction, yet stupidly eager to embrace a pleasant one. Abomination! Heresy! *Our Father in heaven, holy is your name. Forgive me this day my flirtation with witchery. Protect us from the evil eyes of devilment and let me not drowse dumbly before wickedness in any form!*

Adrine hurried away, staying close to the tumble of Gypsy shanties and stone ramparts of the ancient battle wall that did little to protect Stambul from itself. Her head whipped side to side, alert to danger. She berated herself for allowing a skilled deceiver access to her thoughts. But that was surface matter. The key, the gateway to the deepest, most intimate places of her heart, belonged only to God and Tatul.

Tatul. Again she had taken things into her own hands. He was planning to take David with him to an emergency meeting of the Assembly before the noon ultimatum. He would walk right into Chazarian's lair and expect the more moderate brothers to protect the boy and overrule the Marxists. They weren't in the mountains now, and if the Hunchak thugs decided "the son of Judas" must die, it would take an army to stop them.

She had argued that David would be safer at the orphanage, where no one would think to look for him among Mother Agop's pitiful collection of waifs. Tatul was adamantly against it, fearful that if David's location were discovered, the other boys might pay with their lives.

So here she was in defiance of her husband, darting from doorway to gatepost, a fugitive harboring a fugitive.

Adrine stopped. This was wrong. She could not be so impulsive. She had married Tatul to build with him a life of trust and mutual respect. She needed to honor him whether she always agreed with him or not. To act without his blessing undermined his work and could well place his life in jeopardy. She had to stop thinking that she always knew better than he did.

David looked up at her quizzically. She crouched and looked him in the eye. "David, I know that adults have thrown your world into turmoil and that we are very difficult to understand, but I've made a mistake, and I need to fix it. I thought this would be best for you, but I can't make that decision on my own. I didn't even ask God to bless our journey today. Christ goes with us always, but it would be reckless to continue on. We must go back and talk with Tatul."

The boy nodded bravely and squeezed her hand. "That is fine, Mrs. Sarafian." He looked as if he might cry. "I love my mother and worry for her in prison. Whatever my father's crimes, I'll never believe she was involved in them nor in his death. I miss her. Will they treat her properly? She must be worried about me. I need to be a man for her."

Adrine felt the tears well up. She had no answers, only visions of Armenian prisoners of both sexes shot to death like rats. She kissed his forehead, and they turned around to go back.

And stopped dead still.

Blocking their way was a disapproving Artin Chazarian and six handpicked Hunchaks, grinning as if they had just made the catch of the day.

"I think the Gypsy male wants you in his caravan," the Hunchak leader sneered. "I've watched you since you left your home this morning, and I saw the way he looked at you. I wonder if your husband knows what you really do here among the Gypsy thieves of Sulukule?"

Adrine pushed David behind her. "My business here is honorable, sir, not that I answer to you."

Artin laughed coldly. "No, but an answer tart and swift is ever at the door to your lips for any occasion. I've urged your husband to tame that side of you before it led to complications, but it seems you are too difficult for him to handle. I think perhaps that we will have to do what Tatul Sarafian seems incapable of.

"But first, give us the boy."

Adrine braced herself and prayed that at least one of the thugs would lose a tooth in the fray. Only Chazarian had a gun stuffed in his waistband. The rest had their fists.

She pulled the heavy Muslim covering off over her head. The Hunchaks tensed, but she only smoothed the light woolen dress beneath, keeping her voice calm. "The boy remains with me."

Artin turned to the Hunchaks who flanked him. "My good men, hear the charges against this woman. She consorts with Gypsies, dines with Bloody Tekir, the gendarme, entertains Turkish fishermen in her home, and refuses to surrender the son of a traitor to the homeland when ordered to do so by a duly constituted leader of the Armenian resistance. Find you against this woman?"

The men did not hesitate to deliver their boisterous verdict. "Guilty!"

Adrine looked from one to the other. Only the youngest, a boy of no more than sixteen, faltered and dropped his eyes.

"Run, David!"

Her command caught them all by surprise, including David. He turned, tripped over his feet, got up, stumbled again, and was finally off like a frightened rabbit.

Adrine watched the gun come up in Chazarian's hand. Without hesitation, she extended her arm and flicked the chador around his wrist and jerked upward. The gun went off, firing harmlessly into the air. By then, David had disappeared around a corner.

Adrine took flight in the opposite direction, back toward the Gypsy camp. Five of the Hunchak underlings took after her, one after the boy.

A cursing Chazarian pulled free of the chador, saw his forces scattering, and fired two shots into the air. "Forget her, you fools! The boy! The boy!"

The five in pursuit of Adrine turned heel and ran pell-mell for the corner where David and the light-footed sixteen-year-old chasing him had last been seen.

With a wolfish grin, the man with the gun pointed it at the ground and started loping after the fleeing Adrine Sarafian. He knew exactly what would bring the Fox to his knees and end the moderate's hold over the Armenian Assembly. And with that happy thought, he cocked the pistol and took aim between the shoulders of the fleeing woman.

CHAPTER 12

To David Mugurditchian the terrifying sound of thudding feet close on his heels reverberated in the narrow streets like stampeding hooves of destruction.

Leaping and scrambling, he dodged puddles and piles of refuse, sidestepped a collision with a skipping child, and crawled through the stamping legs of a coach-and-four. On the other side he was snatched from the path of a snorting, smoke-belching automobile, then broke free to jump on the back luggage rack and ride the car to the first turn, where he let go and half lunged, half ran down a dank, sunless lane to hide in a doorway.

His mind screamed at his heart to stop its whumping for all the world to hear.

Minutes passed. His heart agreed to remain in the confines of its own chamber, and the warning yowl of a cat was the only sound heard in the narrow lane.

Soon the toot of horns on the Bosporus and the faraway shout of draymen wrestling the day's goods into shops provided sufficient noise for David to attempt to peek out of his doorway.

He prayed for courage and leaned out.

The Hunchaks, in hiding, sprang for him, one meaty paw gaining a hold on the collar of his shirt. David twisted, heard the tearing of cloth, and was free.

"Stop, you little mud flea of a Judas! Stop, or we'll crush you flat!"

Shirt in tatters and half gone, David rounded a turn in the

151

lane and almost smashed face first into a wood-and-wire fence as tall as three men. Behind it was a jumble of timber, fishnets, and tangled metal—a scrap pile. He was cut off from escape.

David searched frantically for a way through, terrified that a Hunchak hand was even now reaching for his throat.

"There you are, you little spoiled meat dumpling!" The Hunchaks jostled to a stop and leered at the boy flattened against the fence with his curly hair plastered to his forehead and exposed rib cage rising and falling in ragged spasms of fear.

They came for him. Quick as a ferret, he dropped to the ground and wriggled beneath the fence, losing a shoe but none of his hide. Cursing in frustration just inches from his head, the big Hunchaks tried stuffing their youngest member beneath the fence but were stopped when he let out a howl of pain as a rusted wire imbedded itself in his knee.

The others slammed against the fence and tried to tear it from its moorings. When that produced no immediate results, they took a running leap and began to scale the barrier.

David's chest constricted in terror. He couldn't catch his breath. He was in a dark maze of discarded rope, rotting wood, and sharp iron. It was hard to see, and he was scraped and poked at every move.

Not that he could move. Each way he turned was blocked or too tight a fit for someone his size.

The rattle and crash of the Hunchaks overhead made it impossible to think.

Then they crashed over the top, and the entire pile shifted with a horrible screeching and clanging.

Their weight pressed everything down on top of him.

David's panic came in rapid puffs of breath. A sob tore from his throat, and he prayed for an angel. He had to get out. He had to.

"Do you see him?"

"I think . . . yes . . . no . . . there! No, just an old ice cabinet."

There were six of them; just one of him. It would be only a matter of time before he was cornered, and what was to stop them from killing him here and burying his corpse beneath the rubble?

On raw nerve, David curled his body and found that by doing so, he was able to wriggle farther beneath the pile. The ground beneath was bare earth, slimy with mold, and stank of death and corrosion.

"There! I see something moving ... something black. It's a huge one!"

David couldn't see them, but he could hear them—rats chittering and squeaking, their kingdom of decay invaded by unwelcome outsiders. He asked God to call them to a meal somewhere else while he kept wriggling deeper.

With each twist he made progress, but a sudden clatter and ring from the hunters above would scare him immobile for precious seconds. Every time the load shifted, down came another phantom shriek of metal, as if a train were falling on his head, and with it a very real shower of dirt and insects. Dark, stupefying images played in his mind, pictures of being buried alive, crushed, his flesh slowly consumed by rodents and worms. His father had not taught him the ways of prayer, but his mother had, and with each cry for divine help, he squirmed forward.

How far did the pile extend?

Willing the paralysis and fatigue from his body, David Mugurditchian fought a way out of the prison, pulling himself forward by the elbows. He was oblivious to rocks and glass tearing and grinding the skin from his arms.

Suddenly, unbelievably, he saw through the tangle to an emptiness beyond. He'd reached the end of the pile! Another street!

The young boy's heart soared. Through there, right through that last bit of rusted flues and broken chairs, was sweet escape.

But try as he might, no path yielded an exit from the maze. David probed and corkscrewed into every space, mounting panic again squeezing his heart in its viselike grip. They were coming, and he could not move.

He was trapped!

A loud bang and a grunt sounded just above his left shoulder, and David involuntarily jerked in its direction—right in the path of five grasping fingers. The slender feelers buried themselves painfully into the curly mop of black hair and yanked back. David stared up into the sweating, triumphant face of the youngest Hunchak.

"I've got him, Abraham! Help me here ... help me hold him...."

Thunder sounded from farther above, shuddering through the whole pile, as Abraham the Hunchak crunched down the mountain of debris in aid of his much lighter companion.

Five more fingers descended through a gap in the metal, but two of them entered David's mouth. He did what came naturally.

"Argggghhh!" With a scream, the boy above jerked back, released his hold, and David obligingly released his, the taste of blood metallic on his tongue.

"Don't lose him, mule!" With that helpful encouragement, Abraham lost his footing, launched outward over the lip of the pile, and slammed down hard against the side of the maze. As if he'd triggered an avalanche, the entire load shifted forward and, borne down by the weight of the other four Hunchaks, crashed into the street beyond with a tortured screeching and banging.

David forced his eyes open and saw that his prayers had been answered. The shifting load had torn a knot of iron rods away and left light at the end of his tunnel.

He tumbled from beneath the pile and got to his feet running. The ringing, crunching roar of the avalanche of refuse rang loud in David's ears, but not as loud as the unearthly screaming of a mortally wounded animal—the youngest Hunchak. "My legs! My legs are pinned! Get it off me, please, oh ... oh ... they are breaking!"

David's only comfort was the frustrated shout of another Marxist trying to free himself from the wreckage. "Shut up your braying and look for that boy! If he got away, we may as well go down to the bridge and jump...."

David smiled, praying his thanks.
And ran like the wind.

————

He was lost. Hopelessly and utterly lost. The twelve-year-old boy had escaped six grown men only to lose his way like some infant child who can neither feed nor clean itself.

David Mugurditchian had to stay off the main thoroughfares or risk detection. How could he ask for directions to the orphanage without drawing unwanted attention? He berated himself for not thinking it through before it came to this. The Sarafians were so kind, and Fevzi the Fisher was so much like the father he wished he'd had. And how had he repaid them?

It was a dark and dangerous sector of Stambul into which he had wandered. Sulukule. Gypsy Town. Before the war and the deportations, when Armenian fathers wanted to frighten their children with tales of haunted places, they told of the awful sights in Sulukule. Of strange talismans of dough and curses so coarse that the littlest Armenians were required to cover their ears, even though the storyteller always used an unintelligible "humph" or clicking sound in place of the actual words.

David remembered the stories his parents told. Of evil eyes. Of Gypsy babies born in the open air under wagons. In the same way, Gypsies died. For if they died before they could be taken outdoors, then the tent or caravan where the death took place must be destroyed, a great embarrassment and expense. It was said that Gypsy mothers sometimes suckled orphan pigs, and Gypsy males who wear "the dead man's shirt" are marked for blood vengeance at any time.

He shook the dark thoughts away and tried to concentrate on where he was going. When after an hour he came to the same slim passage between warehouses he had been in twice before, he slumped onto an empty wooden cask and leaned his back against a damp brick wall. He was hungry and cold. There was not enough left of the silk shirt to cover even half his chest and back. David pulled his feet up under himself and sat cross-legged, bent forward, hugging both arms for warmth. Angrily, he knuckled tears from his eyes and closed them to rest.

It seemed they were only closed a few seconds when a deep-throated snarl startled him.

The snarl raised in pitch and intensified.

Forcing himself to remain rock still, David opened one eye a bare slit. At first he saw nothing in the dull light of the passage between buildings. Interminable seconds later, a shadow moved, and an inky black cur stalked forward on thin, stiff legs. On it came, stealthily, a gash of yellowed teeth and patches of flaky pink mange on the head the midnight beast's only coloring.

Nor was it alone. Another shadow detached itself from beneath the stoop of a decrepit rear entrance that looked as if it hadn't been opened this century. As black as the first, the second shadow was smaller but spring coiled, and it slunk forward, its gaunt belly grazing the ground. The growl in its throat, though less intense in volume, held a sinister note unlike anything the boy's ears had ever heard.

David watched through slitted eyes, prayed the rest of the pack was occupied, and forced himself to await his move.

The dogs came as one, steadily closer together, placing their silent paws as carefully as tightrope walkers, feral eyes locked on their prey.

With all the roar he could muster, David jumped to his feet atop the barrel.

The curs sprang for the boy, two streaking arrows with one target in mind.

The smaller canine met with David's remaining shoe and all the force he could deliver in an abbreviated kick. It met on the point of the dog's snout and sent it cartwheeling backward in a yelp of pain.

The bigger dog clamped onto two inches of spare stocking on the boy's other shoeless foot. With one wrench of its jaws, it fell back and took the stocking with it.

Knowing he could lose toes on the next lunge, David kicked the cask from under him and used it as a battering ram to run directly at the scattering hounds.

Quickly they darted in behind the boy, intent on his tender, unprotected hindquarters. They frequently brought down a crippled competitor or a wayward drunk in this way.

David spun like a bullfighter, keeping the barrel between himself and the curs. If one worked its way behind him . . .

The younger dog stumbled and almost fell beneath the tumbling cask. The heavy container rolled over its right flank and leg, and the dog scooted away yelping and limping.

This infuriated the other dog, and it gathered all its strength for one mighty lunge.

David ran at the dog, spinning the barrel ahead of him with both hands, then giving a final shove with all he had in him. He stepped to the side and felt a searing pain shoot from his bare foot into his calf. He'd stepped on a rock or shard of broken glass.

He collapsed like a rag doll. The nimble cur easily cleared the barrel and charged straight for the boy.

In a last defensive gesture, David curled into a ball and threw hands into the air to shield his head from the tearing, deadly teeth.

But the dog hurtled straight into a swinging phalanx of wooden clubs, wielded by three wan and bony boys in rags, a sickly yellow cast caking their skin. They straddled David's fallen form and within seconds routed the dogs and sent them complaining mightily into the gloom at the far end of the passage.

David rolled onto his back and stared up at three of the most unlikely warriors he'd ever seen.

"I am Krikor," said the oldest, a somber twelve or thirteen years in age. "Mother Agop sent us to meet you. Where is Adrine Sarafian?"

"We were detained by some men with a gun and became separated," the shaken boy muttered. "She told me to run, and I did."

"This is Garouj and Levon." Krikor made introductions as if David had said nothing. "And if I am not mistaken, you are David. If I am wrong, then we have just saved a worthless Gypsy for nothing."

The boy on the ground gave them the biggest smile he had on him and sat up. "I am David Mugurditchian. My descendants thank you!"

The oldest of his rescuers glowered. "I know who you are, and it means nothing!" He spit on the ground. "Your first name is noble, for David was king of the Israelites. But your last name comes from a camel's rear and will forever be linked with shame and betrayal. Look at you! Untouched by the massacres, son of a man who fed his own people to the enemy. Your face is so round, so full, and your belly is fat with goose grease. You know nothing of suffering except that which you have caused the true children of Christ, who must go hungry and naked!" The angry boy shook, smacking one hand with the thick gnarled club he held in the other. His companions stepped closer and swung their cudgels so close to David's head, he could hear the ominous whoosh of their passing.

David cringed, then straightened his shoulders and held steady Krikor's look of contempt. He would not let them whip his spirit. "You are wrong! The massacres have left death and destruction in my home as well. My father was a coward and became a traitor to feed his family and to profit from the conspiracy against his own flesh and blood. I make no excuse for that." His lower lip trembled, and he struggled to keep his voice even. "But he died from a shot to the head, executed in front of my eyes, my father whom I once loved. . . ."

The other younger boys, comrades in grief, seemed to soften at the quiet words. They knew all too well the contortions of war and the sicknesses of heart and mind that it spread among decent people.

But Krikor snorted contempt at so frail a defense. "Too swift and merciful a sentence for a Judas with the blood of three hundred on his hands! And now here you come, of his same breed, hiding behind the pitiful costume of a godless Gypsy. What do you want from us? Protection from a death you deserve?" He bristled forward as if to step on David like a dirty bug, the club swinging free and menacing. "Where is Adrine Sarafian?"

David threw his arms up to fend off the blows, misery churning hot in his gut.

This time, the tears would not be stopped.

CHAPTER 13

If only I can reach the caravan . . . the Gypsies will hide me. If only I weren't so stupid.

If only I weren't so intent on my own way.

If only Fatima of the thirteen children were here to throw a hex into the muzzle of the gun I know will spit death any moment and bring me crashing to the street, far from my husband . . . my home . . . my homeland. . . .

If only God Almighty would clear my frantic mind of such stupid superstition and remind me that I am His child and heir of His riches. . . .

Oh, He just has. . . .

Scraps of faith and fright flew down the street with Adrine Sarafian, but run as she might, pray as she might, the rhythmic fall of Chazarian the Hunchak's shoes kept constant pace. He was patient and methodical. Stambul was not about to miss another fallen Armenian. He could well afford to wear her down and take her when the stabbing pain in her side would force her to slow.

David! Had he gotten away, or were those Hunchak horses pulling him apart even now? *O God above, protect your children!* She had to cheat Chazarian, then somehow find what had become of sweet David.

Jesus . . . Jesus . . . Jesus . . . She forced her lungs to draw a full intake of air, timed to a steady declaration of the Name Above All Names. *Jesus . . . Jesus . . . Jesus . . . Friend of publicans and sinners such as I. . . .*

How proud she was of all she had accomplished with her business.

How often the Armenian sisters, meek and poor in spirit, had sought her out to sit at her feet to hear of the great escape from Hekim Khan, the glorious mountains of Ararat, Father Noah's mountains, and to listen to her paint vivid mental pictures of the homeland to come.

How little she had glorified God in those times of self-congratulation and personal adoration. How clever she had been to rally a hundred women and their children for the daring flight across the river. How stoutly she had stood up to the corrupt Captain Ozal of the Turkish army, even to scarring his face in her unprecedented bravery. Wounded, pursued, facing certain death, she had defied hell itself to ride in a coffin to freedom in Russia. And once having tasted freedom, she nevertheless denied herself and returned to Turkey to continue the fight for justice.

Adrine Sarafian ... brave beyond measure ... now wanted for treason!

A door opened in the wall beside which she ran, and before the startled woman exiting with a sack of rice knew what slid by her, Adrine was inside the shop. She ran past the frowning shopkeeper, who shouted at her in Turkish, to a second door set in the back wall, one in a series of doors and gates she hoped connected a small chain of shops forming a single market.

On she ran, opening one door here, closing a small gate there, dashing past laughing children, disapproving mothers, old men playing backgammon in a coffee house, and a baker removing loaves of twisted sesame bread from a clay oven.

She burst into a nut vendor's store, no wider than room enough for three wooden crates of pistachios, sunflower seeds, and a wheat-and-honey confection stacked in wafers. The proprietor, his pinched brown face bent to the task of filling a customer's handkerchief with pistachios, looked up sharply and spoke to the customer in rapid Turkish. The customer stepped to the side for a better view.

Adrine looked into the fiery, suspicious eyes of a uniformed gendarme.

"*Evet?* Yes?" the shopkeeper said.

"*Affedersiniz.* Excuse me," Adrine said in Turkish, quickly exiting through a cloth curtain and colliding with Artin Chazarian.

"Welcome!" he said on the other side of the curtain, gun waving at her breast, lips distorted with the grim greeting. "Can we stop the chase now and go somewhere quiet to discuss your treachery?"

"A gendarme is right behind me!" Adrine whispered through clenched teeth, even as the policeman wrenched the curtain aside and came upon them.

At the same time, Artin grabbed her by the arms and whirled her around so that his face, known to most of the Turkish constabulary, was hidden from the officer.

"You stupid, stupid woman!" Artin berated her gruffly in Armenian, yanking at her arms for emphasis. "You spend my money faster than I can earn it! How am I to meet my debts when you are forever buying trinkets and food that I hate, just to aggravate me?"

The gendarme grinned at the domestic commotion and went back inside the nut shop. Adrine could hear him telling the proprietor it was just two Armenian dogs in love.

The gun motioned for Adrine to start walking. She looked desperately about for an escape. Chazarian shook his head in warning.

He stayed close behind her as they moved deeper into a covered market that was meagerly stocked. She knew this place. Most of the stall owners were half or three-quarters Gypsy and made more money from picking their customers' pockets than from selling them legitimate goods.

Artin herded her past a clothing stall, where a half dozen Gypsy men were in heated debate over the price of wool. Adrine's desperate eyes locked on the penetrating gaze of one muscular young man. He saw her distress.

In an instant, the Gypsies swarmed around the couple, cutting Chazarian off from his "wife," and relieving him of his pocket watch, pipe, and penknife even as they measured him for a new suit. He scuffled with them, protested that he was not interested today, and they slipped him into a beautiful black felt coat, in the process separating him from his gun.

Adrine last saw Artin making short little leaps off the ground in a vain attempt to shake loose from his tailors and see where she had gone.

But even out of sight, she could still hear him shouting. "No, no, you madmen! Stop belching at me in Romani. Take your hands off me. I don't care if this was worn by the kaiser himself, I don't want it. What have you done with my coat? I know a gendarme just over there, and if you don't stop fiddling with my buttons, I'll have you arrested. My vest! What have you done with my vest. . . ."

For all its poverty, Adrine felt comfortable and at home in the Gypsy marketplace. She needed time to rest, to think.

She was drawn to a fragrant leg of mutton turning in its juices on an open spit with a scrawny chicken for company. The chicken hadn't been plucked clean, and seared tufts of blackened feathers gave the carcass the comic appearance of a hapless fowl having flown too close to the flame.

The young chef stopped turning the meat over the coals, sliced a slab from the mutton with a large curved blade, stabbed it, and extended the portion to her, aromatic and dripping with fat.

Adrine needed the meat for strength but smiled apologetically, indicating that her pockets were devoid of payment. He motioned all the more vigorously, certain that she must have something of value. She reached in and withdrew five dark blue buttons, large and shiny in the flicker of the brazier light. He nodded, eyes eager, holding out the mutton on the end of the blade and his empty hand with fingers waggling.

She shrugged, dropped the buttons in the chef's outstretched hand, and pulled the meat from the knife. It was chewy and a little rank, but an improvement over gray goat soup. She finished it and licked her fingers in a show of appreciation. The dark Gypsy eyes dropped, and the head dipped in a slight bow.

She must go. David needed her. She had to make her way to the orphanage. If no David, then she would backtrack. Perhaps some of the boys would help her.

Should she go get Tatul first? There wasn't time. David's life was in danger now. Mother Agop would know what to do.

The late afternoon street was wet and teeming with commerce. Adrine hurriedly drew a shawl close about her head and tried to keep behind the bales and barrels and away from probing eyes. She had no idea where Artin was, or if when he at last broke free of the clothing stall, he would attempt to pick up her trail or go for reinforcements. She smiled ruefully. That might of course depend on how much of his belongings and his dignity he still retained.

A horse-drawn flatbed wagon trundled past, an old man at the reins, two young men seated on piles of finely worked carpets. Another wagon sat alongside a raised platform where two boys threw sacks of cotton batting from the wagon bed onto the backs of two muscled Kurds in soiled undershirts, who then quick-walked them inside a trousers factory. A short, fat man with a rolling gait and a brown felt hat crammed down over his cauliflower ears called, "Hot yogurt! Sweet hot yogurt fresh from the teat!" Adrine couldn't help admiring the old one's advertising sense, even if his promise would be difficult to document. She watched him trudge over the uneven cobblestones a half step from the crushing hooves of the big dray horses, a wooden crossbeam over his shoulders supporting two scummy iron pots in cradles of hemp. The crossbeam bowed under the weight, arcing over the man's rounded shoulders as if a part of his anatomy since long before the war. He walked pigeon-toed, shoe heels worn flat on the outer edges, legs thick and stumpy.

Adrine thought of her stall at the Grand Bazaar, the need to resupply and reopen for business. She had much to do, thanks be to God. Much to do. Perhaps some of the boys could help her with that, too, and earn themselves a little spending money.

She passed a scribe, thin and bald, hands encased in cotton gloves without fingers. He sat by the side of the road on a small stool before an upturned fruit crate, peering at his work through thick glasses. Beside him, watching his every pen stroke, sat an illiterate Balkan laborer dictating a letter home. The shrewd scribe had probably talked the simple man into the deluxe edition with a few added flourishes and curlicues that upped the price from an hour's wage to a half day's. Such was free enterprise.

At the Café Yat Limani, she paused. She shouldn't stop, but after the salty meat, a hot glass of tea would quench her thirst before she plunged into the darkening streets of Sulu-kule. Again she defied the powers of the air, and if the angels feared to accompany her, at least she could manage a drink of green courage. Anna, the proprietor, was part Armenian, and that part always allowed tea to sisters in the faith on a time payment plan.

Adrine ran inside. The interior of the café was plain but clean. Eight small tables for two and four crowded the checkered floor tiles and were mostly full. The lighting was low but adequate, and she couldn't help noticing an impeccably dressed young man by himself at the window, reading a worn copy of Turkish poetry. Florid stuff, full of garden imagery and paradise this, paradise that. Holy wars and pilgrims blessed. Bow, scrape, bow, scrape.

But the fact he was here in a poorer part of the city and not playing backgammon or drinking German beer or smoking French cigarettes was wonder enough. In that he was nicely attired, his beard carefully kept, and the soft gray fedora blocked in the European style was double wonder. He periodically sipped tea from a glass in a most refined manner, not at all the loud slurping found among the local populace lapping at their bowls.

"Hello, Anna," Adrine said anxiously when it was her turn to order. Her eyes darted to the street. Had she been followed? "I am in need of a glass of your strongest, but not too hot. And if I could pay you sometime next week, that would be helpful—"

"I heard of your recent misfortune," plump Anna jumped in. "You drink all you can hold, sister, and when you're back in business, you bring me some of that nice okra, and the tide will go out once again. Why are men such vicious things?" She lowered her voice. "The massacres would never have occurred if the pashas had tended to their beer and gambling and left the running of the nation to their wives."

Anna filled Adrine's glass and passed it to her. "I see you eyeing that one by the window."

Adrine looked flustered.

"No need for guilt," Anna soothed. "But you can be sure he's not so perfect as he looks. God has given every man a sorrow just as He has given every fruit a worm. You go home and put a couple more logs on Tatul's fire and count yourself blessed!"

"Anna!" Adrine remonstrated, downing her tea in a single unfeminine gulp. "Tatul is a wonderful man and I love him dearly. I'm only curious about what that class of man is doing in this district."

Anna sniffed. "Make that three logs on the fire."

Adrine scowled disapprovingly and dashed for the street. She looked cautiously at the traffic flowing past the door on foot, hoof, and wheel, decided it looked safe enough, and stole one last glance at the man in the fedora.

He yawned hugely. There was no surer sleeping potion than the Ottoman poets.

She said a quick prayer for David and lunged out of the tea shop in the direction of Sulukule.

She hurried past a pile of dead sheep, throats slit and chests stained red, waiting to be butchered and next to a pretty wall of carpets hanging for inspection. The brilliant blue of one caught her eye but she forced it from her mind. May Tekir Pasha burn his feet on the ill-gotten royal blue Birjand in his dining room!

"Forgive me, Father," she breathed. "All I have is yours. If you wish that I share it with a madman, then perhaps you can bring him to faith in the Messiah through a Christian carpet!"

Adrine laughed shakily at herself and turned into a side street, away from the bustle of commerce. Her way began to wind downward toward the orphanage in Sulukule on the bottom rung of the city. It would be a safe, temporary refuge for David until they could get the death warrant removed from his head. She thought of dear Cheyrek, the bumpy skin, the long fingers, the memory of him holding her hand and the scented soap to his cheek, breathing her scent, visibly calming.

The eerie stillness of Sulukule felt like another skin, but this one clammy and foreign.

It was some moments before she sensed that someone had fallen in behind her, the echo of hard-soled shoes careening off the two- and three-story buildings rising on either side of the narrow passage.

Her feet quickened and broke into a run, but she was pursued again by an unseen assailant. She crossed two intersecting alleys before chancing to look back.

No one.

She stopped to lean against a wall until her breathing slowed. In what was becoming habit, she berated herself again for seeing demons wholesale. If everyone in Istanbul were after her, who was directing traffic?

She heard organ music in her head, a performance Grandmother had treated her to at twelve, when the first irrefutable signs emerged that the little goose was at last a woman. The beautiful swelling strains carried her to the end of the block and made a concert hall of dank, dark Sulukule. She looked back once more, searching the dim byway for signs she was not alone. Seeing none, she turned the corner.

A warm hand clamped down on her mouth, and her heart threatened to stop. She was staring into the face of the mystery man from the Yat Limani.

"Say not a word, and the pistol stays in my pocket. Cry out, and the matter is concluded in a way most regrettable. Come with me, please."

The words were spoken evenly, without heat, but the hard-edged tone permitted no argument. He pushed her ahead of him until they came to a door recessed into the building wall. He unlocked the door with a key and ordered her inside.

They negotiated a short hallway lit only by a skylight at

the far end. Just before the hall intersected with another, he stopped at a door with a long-ago coat of peeling yellow paint, unlocked it, and nudged her inside. He lit a lamp in the middle of a bare table, motioning Adrine to a chair as he shut the door.

The man remained standing, removing only his soft gray fedora to set it on the table. "Raki?" he asked.

Adrine shook her head. "I don't drink. But you go ahead." Maybe if he numbed himself, she could get away.

"There will be no raki until I have completed my assignment. The first time, I acted alone. That attracted notice, and now I have been assigned to rid the earth of the Turk monster who ordered the annihilation of mothers and babies."

Adrine listened carefully for clues to his identity. She fought to think clearly, to interpret the words. What did she have to do with his assignment?

"You were unexpected. I was about to leave for Berlin, where the target has been sighted. But then I was informed about you and your husband—observed you, actually—and now, regrettably, I must complete one more task before my work here is finished."

"Who are you?" Adrine insisted. "Do you work for Chazarian the Hunchak? Tekir and his secret police? Who?"

The serious young man shook his head. "I am the corrector of the unlawful. I punish the perpetrators of crimes against the innocent. I am called to avenge the blood of my countrymen. When constituted authorities stand by and do nothing, I do that which they are incapable of, or are unwilling to do."

Adrine prayed to understand. "You said that the first time you acted alone. What did you mean?"

The man went to the door, locked it, and leaned against it. He looked more haggard than the man sipping tea over garish Ottoman infatuations. "The Judas lived far longer than he deserved. Justice was far from him. Judas and justice. I brought them together."

Adrine blanched. She was locked inside a room with the man who, with one bullet, had left David fatherless. *Oh, Tatul, sweet husband, forgive me for doubting you and accusing you falsely!*

She had to know it all. "And what assignment did that earn you?"

He peered at the ceiling, but the expression did not change. Somber, intent, no regrets. "I have been chosen to bring Talaat Pasha, the former minister of the interior, to justice. It was he who plotted to eradicate the Armenians, and it is he who has fled to Berlin to escape justice. But justice will follow him there, where it is said he writes memoirs in which he justifies the deportations and blames the Armenians for their own deaths. Hopefully, history will gladly blame Talaat for his own premature finish."

Adrine looked at the man who spoke so tranquilly of murder on assignment. It had been unnecessary for him to explain who Talaat Pasha was. Every Armenian who yet drew breath knew of Terrible Talaat the Butcher. But who among the Armenian resistance felt it was really in the homeland's best interest to slay the former leaders of a misguided government with blood on its hands? "All you will do is perpetuate the slaughter," she said. "You are young. Have you never loved anyone or aspired to something? Can this really be your life's work?"

He swallowed hard, and she thought for a moment that she had touched him. But when at last he spoke, the words held the same determined note, the same lack of remorse.

"I have spoken to you of my aspirations, and I know of none more honorable given the course of events. You ask if I have loved? I love two women, both of whom share in the work and would gladly fire the gun themselves if called. The world community has had ample opportunity to collectively right this wrong, and they have declined. Therefore, I accept!"

Now it was Adrine's turn to swallow hard. It was perhaps the most difficult question, but it had to be asked. "And what is the final task left to you to perform before you leave for Berlin?"

He did not immediately answer, closing his eyes instead as if lost in thought. After several minutes, the eyes opened but did not seek hers. "There is no reason for collusion with the cruel military police force that rules this city with an iron rod. Yet you and your husband saw fit to accept the invitation of Police Chief Tekir Pasha at a time when he has a price on my head for the execution of his Armenian informant. It is not so great a leap of logic to conclude then that he needs a new informant, or what other purpose could your visit at his bidding have possibly served? Who is better placed within the resistance movement than the Fox, that great folk hero of the people, whom most of them would never suspect? Or the Fox's wife, whose thriving market trade places her in the center of the ebb and flow of the Armenian community? Get them both for the price of one, and he will have done a pleasant day's work."

Stunned, Adrine sat at the table wildly seeking wisdom from above. She felt termites of fear gnawing her insides. How could she convince him of any other conclusion? After another long moment of silence, only one question formed in her mind, and in a low, disbelieving voice she asked it. "You are actually planning to kill my husband? To kill me?"

The man left the door, went to the opposite side of the table and placing both hands flat on the tabletop, leaned forward so that she could not mistake his reply. "I am not a killer," he said coolly. "I am an assassin."

CHAPTER 14

Tatul Sarafian, eyes flashing defiance, stood tall and rock firm atop the dais. Now that Martin's auction hall had burned to the ground, they gathered in the dusty bowels of an old Turkish courthouse—condemned, boarded, and ideal for outlawed sessions such as this.

Below Tatul and about the benches around him, a wild tumult of incredulous voices and angry, disbelieving faces reached to the very walls of the hall where young men stood atop the shoulders of fathers, friends, and brothers, all shouting frustration and accusations at the man who sought their trust. All that stood between Sarafian and the storm-tossed sea of barely contained violence was the loyal and faithful band of five, led by the scrappy Andranik. They encircled the dais, shoulder to shoulder, arms folded, stern faces to the crowd. Let no man try them.

Tatul used to be able to count on half the crowd and more to side with him. On this day, given the events of the past twenty-four hours, he could be certain of nothing.

He thrust his arms into the air, fingers wide, waving for silence. The voices fell into an undertow of rebellion, bubbling and boiling to the surface in an effort to suck him off his feet.

He knew they were here for no other reason than to defy Tekir Pasha's order that any more than three Armenians constituted an unlawful assembly. Recklessly defiant. Suicidally determined. He had to channel their destructive impulse. He prayed for Holy Spirit stamina.

"Brothers! Citizens! Heroes of the homeland! As the hosts

of heaven are my witnesses, I mean what I say! After being violated and stripped of our belongings by the constituted authorities of Istanbul, my wife and I did enter the home of Tekir Pasha to argue for compassion on the remnant. God had convinced us that what clubs and guns and fists and fire—and theft—have not accomplished, words could avail—"

"Words?! *Words?!*" someone shouted. "You insult us with words and more words! Did the monster Turks kill our grandfathers with words? Were our mothers and fathers politely asked to hand over their life's savings with honey-glazed words? Was it words with which the Ottoman slayers nailed our babies to boards? The only word a Turk understands is the sound made by a bullet speeding for his manhood!"

The hall crackled with jagged bolts of agreement firing from the floor of packed humanity to the ceiling overhead, where a dozen more Armenian hotbloods hung from the rafters.

"Hear me, brothers, hear me!" yelled another. "Do you know why it is a waste of good ammunition to shoot a Turk through the head or chest?"

The assembly began to shout its rude answers. The man who posed the question grabbed a comrade on either side about the neck and looked madly into the eyes of first one, then the other. "No brain! No heart!" he growled, and the hall erupted in howls of laughter. They were one, resurrected as one from the ashes of their people, ready as one to avenge Armenia without a backward glance.

The sea of deadly intentions swelled again, but the Fox held it back with a wave of a large black leather book.

"Living Word!" Tatul roared, slapping the cover for emphasis. "We, the People of the Book! In the beginning was the Word! ' "Is not my word like fire," declares the Lord, "and like a hammer that breaks a rock in pieces?" ' Words, brothers, are a life-giving force and able to accomplish that which harm and destruction never could! Remember the dry bones of Ezekiel, how the Lord brought them to life with a word? 'I will attach tendons to you and make flesh come upon you and cover you

with skin; I will put breath in you, and you will come to life,'
says the Lord."

"And just what did you gain from your little talk with the
chief of military police?" The question sped from the rafters
like a dagger thrown. "You have just told us that we must
never be seen in public in more than groups of three. The gendarmes could be gathering outside even now, ready to burn
this place down because we dare call an assembly! Our sick are
thrown from the hospitals like human waste. And what have
you done with Chazarian, our Hunchak brother? Where is
he?"

Again, Tatul quieted the tumult, standing above them
strong and immovable as if cut from the granite of their hardened hearts. When he spoke, clear and definite, this time the
Lord's words recorded by the prophet Ezekiel pierced them to
the marrow. " 'Come from the four winds, O breath, and
breathe into these slain, that they may live . . . and breath entered them; they came to life and stood up on their feet—a
vast army.' "

A strange hush settled on the assembly, as if the very words
were meant for Armenia. Tatul ruffled the pages of the Bible
to the book of Ezekiel and read, " 'Then you, my people, will
know that I am the Lord, when I open your graves and bring
you up from them.' "

As if a mighty silent wind swept the hall and removed
them, hats came off, heads bowed, lips moved in silent prayer
for the vast graveyard that was Armenia.

Tatul felt hot tears well and his throat tighten, but he read
on and the words were words of hope. " 'I will put my Spirit
in you and you will live, *and I will settle you in your own land.*' "

Throats cleared. Noses blew. A deep yearning fell upon
them.

" 'Then you will know,' " Tatul concluded, his voice low
and choked, " 'that I the Lord have spoken, and I have done
it. . . .' "

Many wept unashamedly for what had been, for what was
lost, and sought God for a glimmer of what could be again.
Sarafian watched them slip arms of comfort and support

around the shuddering shoulders of broken brothers whose wives and children had been destroyed. He saw an old farmer clasp thick plowman hands to his bony breast and heard the halting petition to the living God to be allowed to work the land again.

Everywhere among the fellowship of survivors, dry bones came to life.

Andranik, hands together in prayer and a smile of encouragement wreathing his round face, looked up at Tatul and nodded.

"Brothers," Sarafian said somberly, and they were still. "It is past the hour when Artin Chazarian demanded that I produce David Mugurditchian. But I cannot and will not. Artin, who came against me, his brother, with weapons and threats, is no different than we. He wants someone to blame, a scapegoat to send out into the desert beneath the weight of the sin of war. But each one of us is as deserving, or more so, to be that scapegoat as young David. We, all of us, sometimes in our lives put ourselves first and think more highly of ourselves than we ought. It is not up to us to visit the sin of the father upon this child. Rather, God wants us to redeem the sons of the wicked and take them as our own. It is into those bones of compassion that He will breathe new life and from which a new and stronger Armenia will rise!"

The chant began immediately, and soon filled the hall with a heat of its own. "Fedayee! Fedayee! Fedayee!"

Tatul Sarafian clasped the Bible to his chest and bent prayerfully until his forehead touched the cool binding. *Lord,* he breathed, *forgive the dryness of my own bones. Protect Adrine and David.*

A commotion sounded far back of the crowd near the entrance to the hall. A familiar voice, demanding, intemperate; another placating, apologetic but firm. The demanding voice would not be deterred, and soon the facts sped about the hall like angry bees: The Hunchaks were back.

Chazarian and his bodyguards made a disheveled entrance, one more comical than dramatic. Tatul watched Artin attempt to stride up the middle of the assembly, every twitch and scowl of his being wanting to part the Red Sea of public opinion his way, but he was prevented as much by his costume as by the now thoughtful demeanor of the crowd.

The trousers were his, but the cheap, ill-fitting, mustard-colored coat and too short sleeves were not. Gone was the expensive vest with red-and-silver threading, as gone as the pearl buttons to his once crisp white shirt. A copious amount of black body hair had been set free from neck to navel, and it was that which now defined the Marxist in a region once graced by an exquisite watch and fob of white silver.

The face above the devastation was livid with rage.

Trailing behind their deplumed leader limped five Hunchak lieutenants in soiled and bloodstained disarray. Though some in the hall frowned at the fate befallen the Marxists, many more fought a powerful tendency to grin at so ridiculous a parade and so thorough a deflation of pomposity.

Tatul himself fought the urge to remark on the scene and graciously waited on Chazarian to speak before he ruptured.

The Hunchak leader did not disappoint.

"*This* man!" Chazarian pointed the finger of accusation at Sarafian high atop the dais. "Seize him, brothers, and make him pay for his treason! He hides the son of Judas, and his wife—his *wife*!—shares in his collusion!"

Tatul, barely hiding a grin, looked in critical assessment at his philosophical opponent and shook his head. "Why, Artin, you are unarmed. Your clothes are someone else's, and your dignity lies about you in tatters. What? No torches, no coming in force against innocent brothers in the middle of the night? And what of your compatriots? They look as if they've tangled with Medusa herself. Can we get you anything? Some water, perhaps? A new identity?"

The emotional tension and mirth in the stifling hall burst like a dam. The laughter and derisive snorting brought a look of stunned disbelief to Chazarian's face. His fists clenched and unclenched at his sides at the guffawing that came from the rafters at his expense. He looked down at the slapping, merry mob and met with nothing but the same.

Upon Chazarian's nod, the five bodyguards jumped from

the speaker's platform into the crowd with fists flying. Young toughs all over the hall were only too happy to join in and managed to pick up a few fights along the way to the base of the platform.

The chief Hunchak stood above the mayhem, wearing a little satisfied smile. Tatul knew what he was thinking. The momentum had again shifted.

After half a minute, Sarafian withdrew the German automatic from his waistband, pointed it at the ceiling, and squeezed off three shots.

The combatants dove for cover.

Again a hush settled over the assembly. All eyes turned to the tall, lean figure atop the dais. Meeting their anxious stares, Sarafian replaced the gun and spoke without looking at the Hunchaks but loud enough for all to hear. "I don't believe Artin has said all he came to say. Please grant him your full attention."

Tatul watched Chazarian seethe at being given "permission" to speak. But he straightened, attempted to close the coat with a button that would not hold, then abandoned the effort. He waited, as if Sarafian would come down from the dais and give him the entire floor, but Tatul remained where he was, raised his eyebrows, and urged the Hunchak on with a diffident nod.

Chazarian lifted his arms, but quickly dropped them when the coat rode up and exposed a belly as hairy as the rest of the man. "Fellow countrymen, I have been plundered by Adrine Sarafian and her Gypsy mongrels!" Several jaws dropped, and he appeared to take heart. "Stripped, threatened, disarmed, and barely escaping with my life, I watched this man's wife command the Gypsies, then disappear with the son of Judas into Sulukule, that cesspool of the strange and the bizarre. But not before she had absorbed the attentions of a muscular Gypsy acrobat, whose every sensuous move she drank in like one who'd gone a week without water!

"I ask you to ask yourselves, What danger are we in from a man and woman who dine with the Turkish police, who give sanctuary to the criminal son of a traitor and consort with godless Gypsies, using them as a shield for their dark affairs?"

Again the hall rumbled with incredulous voices and angry oaths. The people were pulled two ways on the rack of Chazarian's accusations.

"Finished?" Tatul asked, barely able to control his disgust with the Marxist storyteller.

"Oh no!" said Chazarian expansively. He must have caught the faint whiff of a sea change in the atmosphere of the hall, Tatul thought. He watched the old reassurance come flooding back into his opponent, and it looked as if Chazarian had just experienced a divine revelation.

"I have saved the most damning news for last!" He stabbed an accusing finger at the man on the dais. "Mrs. Sarafian's last words before leaving me to the murdering Gypsies were these: 'Take what you want and dump his body in the sultan's well.' They would have if in the course of executing me with my own gun it had not jammed and I was able to make my escape!"

"And where was your fine protective force all this time you were being molested?" a disbelieving Tatul asked. It was as if the entire assembly leaned in for the answer. The Hunchak bodyguards looked anywhere but at him.

Artin took his time replying. "As you can see from their condition, they, too, were taken by Gypsy surprise and barely came away whole." The bodyguards shuffled uncomfortably, as if even they were scandalized by their leader's fabrications.

Tatul placed both hands on his hips and looked at the head Hunchak in disgust. "Are Marxists the world's best liars, or are the Turks? What a difficulty separating the two!"

It was a remark Tatul might normally have to fight his way out of, but this time it earned him a look of abject pity.

"Of course, you do not yet know," Artin said haltingly as if the words were difficult to form. "Perhaps you had better come down to hear this."

Sarafian felt a cold stab of worry. The Hunchak was a prize deceiver, but sorting truth from fiction was a full-time occupation in this city. What did Artin know?

"I'll stay. What have you to say?"

Chazarian looked pained. "When I last saw Mrs. Sarafian

walking into the gloom of Sulukule with the boy, they . . . they were not alone."

"What do you mean?" Tatul felt his skin prickle.

Artin hesitated, then spoke rapidly as if to empty himself of the awful implications. "Dogs. Three, maybe four big curs trotting after her. I begged the Gypsy slime to free us and let us escort her to safety, but they refused. She looked so small, so vulnerable, utterly without defense. What good could the boy do against such a horror? The Turks turn those dogs loose on the street to feed on Armenians. The Gypsy filth just laughed and chattered away in that unintelligible garble of theirs. Sons of imps and witches! They are protected by the Evil Eye, but what defense have we?"

Tatul desperately wanted to deny every twitch of Chazarian's lying tongue, but could he? Adrine must have taken David with her in defiance of Tatul's wishes. No matter how badly she wanted to visit Cheyrek and Mother Agop, she should have listened to her husband. The streets were not safe for a woman and a boy. Especially *that* woman and boy! Tatul would trust a Gypsy over a Turk any day, but over an Armenian Marxist? Did Artin speak the whole truth?

The blighted dogs were a serious public health nuisance. Diseased and mostly wild, their only motivation was survival at all costs. Was any amount of political maneuvering or rallying of the brothers worth risking Adrine's health and safety?

The murmuring and heated debate that peppered the hall fell away from his thoughts. Chazarian, the Hunchaks, even the worried countenance of gentle and caring Andranik were momentarily forgotten.

The Spirit of the Living God, the Word Incarnate, had filled the building with heaven's fire for more than a quarter of an hour today. It was in that power that he would find his wife and son—not his son, another man's son, but one for whom he felt a father's attachment.

An odd warmth filled the Fox. He thought of his two earthly fathers—Serop, the one who taught him to walk, and Black Wolf, chief of the Fedayeen freedom fighters, who taught him to thwart the Turks at every turn. He felt a stream

of holy continuity stretching back to the springs of his fore-
fathers and flowing forward to the sea of his descendants. For
too long he had played the statesman, acted the diplomat. The
Fox had nearly forgotten the cunning with which he had ha-
rassed the Turkish military and bedeviled their efforts to defeat the Russians. But now he felt the power of its return.

He would not be defeated. The blood of Christ was on him,
and for the first time in a long while, he could smell the snows
of Ararat.

He was Fedayeen!

He leapt down to the platform, grabbed Andranik, and
placed his lips against the loyal servant's ear. "Horses," he
whispered. "Get me horses!"

CHAPTER 15

The four boys made their way cautiously along the dank twists and rutted crossings of Sulukule. Their leader seemed a little less hostile toward David once he had explained the trouble he and Mrs. Sarafian had earlier encountered. And when the boy dressed in Gypsy clothes breathlessly replayed Mrs. Sarafian running for her life and the threatening thugs who had hunted David in the tangled maze, the residents of the orphanage visibly paled.

Sticking to the shadows, they skirted angry lovers in heated quarrels and the halfhearted threats of mothers shrilly promising their wayward children all manner of doom and destruction. One child, slipping away from an older sister, made a rude face and skipped off with a chill "Demons ill and devils dread eat your eyes and drain your head!" echoing after him.

David shuddered. He had never ventured into the Gypsy quarter before, always believing—and with good reason, he thought now—that he might not emerge alive from Sulukule. The tales told in polite company were hair-raising enough, and he knew never to get near a Gypsy, let alone befriend one.

But now, desperate and hunted, he was only too ready to dress like a Gypsy and to sneak through their district for cover and protection. He felt guilt but knew no other course of action.

The houses of the Gypsy band were constructed of anything lying at hand. Bits of wooden boards and canvas were hooked, nailed, and tied to hammered tin, sailcloth, or leather to afford something of a shelter but far removed from a watertight home. Sometimes it was the underside of a Gypsy wagon that formed the roof, and the odd pieces of discards that leaned against it made for walls and doors—effectively a two-story domicile, with the parents and babies below and the older children or an adult child's family above. The statutes of Istanbul said that if a house can be roofed between dusk and dawn, it must be legally accepted.

To the derisive Turks, they were the *gecekondu*, the "night-built" houses.

A barefoot toddler, wearing nothing but a soiled grin and his brother's too big coat, pointed at the Armenian boys slipping past his home of scraps and let loose with a string of happy gibberish. The mostly empty sleeves of the coat flapped uselessly. When the boys did not stop, the toddler hopped into a puddle and squealed in delighted shock at the cold water splashing on his naked legs.

"I think I had a little brother about his age," said Garouj in a small, faraway voice. "It seems a long while ago, but my mother said he was so hard to give birth to that my brother was destined to live forever. When the Turks came, he was the first killed because they said he was too little to survive the journey to Syria. It was a mercy, they said, a kindness."

"Shhh," Krikor said, "don't talk."

David felt sick. His father . . . the three hundred Armenian thinkers and dreamers and artists betrayed . . . by Judas . . . shot like diseased rodents . . . killed by Tekir Pasha, the gold pried from their teeth . . .

Then David looked and really saw his companions for the first time. Short, quiet, stone-faced Levon, his face scabbed from dirty nails that nervously picked and scratched; thin little Garouj, whose amber eyes peered quizzically out from a trusting face, so obviously enamored of his protector and champion; Krikor, who was tall for his age, handsome, broad shouldered, and given enough food could one day be a strapping specimen of robust manhood. For now, he was light, malnourished, his skin dry and bug bitten.

A loud, threatening commotion brought the boys to a cu-

182

rious halt. A hulking beef of a Turk was stalking about a small square of ground adjacent to the ruins of the massive land walls that had protected Stambul for a millennium and formed the stone spine of Sulukule. He was berating the noisy knot of Gypsies who had fashioned a clay earthwork against the wall and carefully incorporated a tottering framework of wood, roofed it with corrugated iron, and called it home.

Shouting obscenities in three languages, the Turk paced off the square he owned and, with a mighty windmilling of arms, attempted to point out the violation to the Gypsies following his every stride. Gamely, mother, father, grandmother, five children, and undoubtedly an uncle and cousin or two, crowded close, testifying just as passionately that what was at issue was a "night-built" dwelling clearly within the law.

"Possession! Possession!" crowed the Gypsy father in defense, ignoring the epithets. He and his progeny pressed close to the landholder. "We are here; you are elsewhere. If you do not wish your land occupied, then you, sir, should occupy it. We have no permanent home, so what would you have us do? Build our homes in midair?"

"I do not have to justify what is mine! The police will settle this matter, and we know how often they sympathize with Gypsy scum!" The Turk shoved the milling pack away and strode off in search of legal reinforcements.

The boys, shoulder to shoulder in the dark valley between two buildings, felt a shiver of fear pass between them. A Turk military patrol was the last thing they needed. Krikor signaled for them to move on.

A burst of victorious laughter momentarily stopped them again. The castigated Gypsy family, far from cowed, still held the property and celebrated an additional triumph. One son lifted high a gold watch with a crystal face. Another male hand shot into the air, holding aloft a wad of Turk currency. A sister's delicate hand joined theirs, clutching a knife with a pearl handle. Another sister displayed a jeweled circlet fresh from the thick neck of the excitable Turk. Even the youngest child, scarcely four feet tall, produced an expensive hand-tooled sash that would earn a day's wages in trade at the Grand Bazaar.

The small boy was bathed in kisses and lifted above their heads to the lusty beat of a tambourine.

"Ah, little sheep," cried the father, "such a day! Such fortune! And soon we shall have an entire Turk military contingent to greet and relieve of its valuables! Keep watch, little ones, for soon they come and you shall have new clothes before the cock crows!"

Krikor shepherded the others ahead of him and cast a wary eye from street to rooftop. The light was beginning to wane, and that which was dangerous by day would become doubly so by night. Without their leader having to say a thing, the boys knew instinctively that they must hurry.

With every step he took, David winced, and it was soon obvious that he grew steadily more fatigued. It had been a stressful few hours, and he was probably ready for a safe place to lay his head and sleep.

"How much farther?" David inquired. "Why is it taking so long?"

Krikor stopped and gave David a scathing look. "Do your royal pants need changing?" he mocked. "If you knew anything but your powder and comfort, you would know that we have to take a longer route in case we're being followed. Or would you like to make your bed tonight in the Stambul jail?"

Garouj and Levon, although they said nothing, looked sympathetically at David, and he visibly brightened.

"I don't know why you're so mean," he told Krikor. "I might be able to help the orphanage, or maybe my family can. Adrine told me how little you have." He looked Krikor over. "You're very skinny, and your clothes wouldn't protect you from cricket spit."

Krikor's hands balled into fists and came for David.

Little Garouj stepped between them and put a restraining hand on his friend's chest. "Krikor! David's only trying to help."

"He knows nothing about us, and I'll not eat his food! It has blood on it—Armenian blood!" He glared defiantly at David, then saw that Garouj and Levon had tears in their eyes. He pulled them close to him and hugged them. "Don't," he said softly. "Soldiers of Christ don't cry. Remember?"

They nodded even as tears spilled from them.

Krikor sighed and nodded at David, grave but apologetic. "I forgive your insult. You speak without experience. Perhaps you will find that we have more to offer you than you can give us. Whatever happens, you will find a lot of damaged boys at the orphanage. You might be wise to say little until you know what they really need. Words, wrongly spoken, can harm."

David, lost in thought, at last nodded. "I think I see that and agree with it. I forgive you your harmful words."

Krikor looked sideways at David, the black curly hair, the forthright face, the stouthearted resolve. The orphan leader blinked and smiled awkwardly. His teeth, considering the times, were quite white and straight. "I'm glad I did not let the dogs eat you."

David returned the smile. "Not as glad as I am."

Krikor handed him his wooden club. "Swing this awhile," he said. "We'll keep looking around for one of your own. A lot of the curs see a club and leave you alone on instinct."

"Thanks," said David. He gave the stout stick a trial swing, twisting to face the way they'd come.

Staring at him, not a carriage length away, was a member of the gendarme, the national police. Behind him was an armed security force administered by the army in the aftermath of war. Seventy percent of the country's police force was assigned to Istanbul and the surrounding area. To encounter them, though startling, was to be expected.

"Halt!" the forward officer commanded.

"Run!" Krikor countered.

The boys listened to their leader and bolted.

They rounded the corner, and marching straight at them was another contingent of military police, this one with the irate Turkish landholder—no less inflamed than when they'd first encountered him—at the vanguard. "That's one of them!" he roared, pointing at David, who was still dressed in what was left of his Gypsy garb. "He and those other Gypsy rat droppings stole me blind!"

Krikor quickly assessed the squeeze they were in and

pointed up. The boys lunged for a rickety pile of stairs clinging to a crumbling brick building. They had barely set foot on
the first step when a clamor of shouts and stampeding leather
at their heels buoyed them up the unmaintained latticework
like four corks on a geyser.

The climb was a horror. The frail stairs shuddered and
swayed beneath the pounding of boots, and at each landing,
the boys imagined wide, strong hands first pinning them to
the boards, then lifting them by their throats and throwing
them to their deaths against the cobblestones below.

Up they rose, one, two, three flights to the roof above,
where wheezing and sobbing in panic they raced between lines
of dry wash flapping in the winds off the Bosporus. The rooftop was a web of sagging clotheslines.

Krikor cast about crazily for somewhere, anywhere to hide.
Face etched in frustration, he mentally berated himself for
leading them into a dead end. It was impossible to leap the
wide gaps between the buildings. The best they could do was
play cat-and-mouse among the clotheslines until they were
surrounded and caught.

Several Turkish women in long dresses, heads bundled in
black scarves tied tightly beneath their chins, watched the
boys start and stop in little circles of frenzied uncertainty.
Without pause the women—seven young ones and two husky
matrons—methodically removed shirts from the line,
dropped the wooden pins in linen bags, and, with two practiced moves, folded the clothing into large wicker baskets at
their feet. They worked in an oddly coordinated ballet of
reach, fold, dip, and rise, hurrying against the approaching
night damp, adding other garments to the baskets one by one
and steadily shortening the marching lines of dry cloth
stretching from one side of the building to the other.

They looked into the boys' eyes and saw the desperation.

The thunder of feet crashing up the sides of the old dwelling gained the top of the wall and clattered onto the roof.
Quickly men with rifles took up their positions at the corners
of the building and looked over the side to make sure no one
was dangling from ropes. They saw nothing but other officers

peering up at them from the street below, cutting off that escape route.

On the roof, the burly Turkish landholder shoved the wash aside, roughly searching beneath and behind dresses and underwear for young criminals who picked pockets and laughed about it behind the unfortunate victim's back.

A commanding officer of the gendarmerie motioned for his men to take up positions at the ends of each row of wash. There was not a runaway boy down any of the aisles between lines.

The national police squad stood at attention among the laundry, weapons ready. Their eyes were question marks of confusion. The suspects had vanished.

Near the center of the rooftop, the Turkish commander encountered the women who were calmly and steadily adding their husbands' trousers and children's stockings to the growing piles of clean, folded clothing in the ample wicker baskets. Averting their eyes, unwilling to meet the quizzical looks of the gendarmerie, the women worked on.

"*Bayan*, ma'am, excuse the intrusion. We chased four criminal boys from the street. Three Armenians and a Gypsy, from the look of them. Have you seen them?" demanded the gendarme politely but firmly.

"That is unlikely, Colonel," a matron replied without skipping a beat in her unpinning and folding. "This high above ground, children and laundry do not mix." She gave a child's blanket a snap, reducing it to a small, tight square in three rapid folds. The other women said nothing, methodically removing wooden clothespins, freeing another dress or shirt as they had done a score of times already, then adding the neatly pressed article of clothing to a basket. The aggravated landholder met their stoic silence—and the absence of any boys—by snatching a shirt from a line, wadding it into a ball, and flinging it from the roof.

The commander frowned. "Men, attention! The boys must have entered an open door or window on the way up. Quickly! Each sergeant take his squad inside a landing and conduct a thorough search of every floor. Meet in the street as soon as you have completed your investigation! Go, go!"

They went, pouring over the side of the building like rats abandoning ship. They stormed down the protesting stairs, entered open doorways without knocking, and smashed through unopened doors. Cries, screams, and the thud of police boots running and seeking suspects echoed from inside the ancient tenement that housed the city's poor. Squalling babies and wailing mothers made it clear the residents feared that Istanbul was again under siege.

Within twenty minutes the sweating, hard-breathing troopers descended to the street, and it was clear by their bewildered, uneasy expressions that the boys were nowhere to be found. Last down, the fuming Turkish landholder at his ear, was the colonel, who now had to face the very unhappy municipal security advisor for the entire Gypsy quarter of Stambul.

He reported the sum total of his investigation: seven Turkish women, four wicker baskets of wash, no boys.

"You imbecile!" the advisor roared, spittle flying in the colonel's face. "Why have you come down? You saw them go to the roof. They are on the roof! God did not take them. God would not want them. They did not take wing and fly off the roof, nor did they make a rope out of the washing and rappel off the side of the building to the street below, which we have securely sealed off. Which means they had to have slipped into a vent or a pipe, or that they are hanging on the line along with the rest of the wash. You've got to think like a mongrel! Get your misbegotten tails back up those stairs and do not come back down again without the four miserable vagrants who led you on this merry chase! And if they are dead, no one here shall mourn. This time I will accompany you and see that the job is done right! Move!"

The troopers moved, with their seething colonel leading the way and the security advisor bringing up the rear. At the first step the colonel turned. "Pass this back," he said to the man behind. "I want those street scum shot on sight, no questions asked!"

For the second time that day, the national police pounded

up the rickety stairs of the ancient building, murderous eyes trained on the edge of the roof. Every man hated those worthless boys for making the police into winded fools who could not have apprehended a corpse in a cemetery.

At the second landing on the way up, the police met the washerwomen making their ponderous way down the stairs, each heavily piled basket carried by two women, one at either end.

"Step aside, you stupid women!" the colonel yelled at them. "Official police business! Get out of the way!"

Shouldering them back against the building, the gendarmes rushed past the lowly washerwomen. The men's eyes blazed with fury, intent on the quarry they now believed beyond a doubt to be cowering on the roof, listening to the rapid approach of the feet of death, not so much as a clean apron with which to cover their nakedness.

The security advisor had said it was so.

Once the gendarmes passed, the women resecured their hold on the heavy baskets of laundry and made their way slowly down to the street.

The soldier left in charge of the contingent watching the perimeter of the tenement put up a hand for them to stop. "Your business?" he demanded.

The matron who had spoken with the colonel on the roof turned a motherly eye on the young man in front of her. The pimply moustache on his upper lip was sparse at best. "Kind son," she said, "this clean wash is for the sick women in the adjacent building who are pregnant and too nauseous to do the family laundry. Would you do the mothers of Turkey a great favor and allow us to bring them the news and fresh clothes?"

The soldier smiled warmly and nodded, looking as if he would have enjoyed a hug from her very much.

"Where is your home, my son?" she gently inquired.

"Keskin, kind mother, east of Ankara—"

A rifle shot snapped his attention to the rooftop. A second and a third crackled between the buildings. "Go, mother," the young soldier urged the washerwoman. "Go quickly to the home of your friends and remain with them until the danger passes." He whistled to his men and ran to the stairs, motioning them to follow.

The matron looked at the top of the roof and the young men rushing up the stairs to join the action. She hoped that in their eagerness to capture their criminals they did not mistakenly kill the young man from Keskin, or any other mother's son. There had been enough killing in Turkey to last a hundred generations.

She turned to the other women and nodded. They hefted the piled-high baskets between them and checked the street both ways for wagons or fresh troops. Seeing none, they made for the privacy of the building across the street, where they could examine the laundry away from prying eyes.

They had to shuffle sideways, both hands gripping a handle, to make sufficient progress.

Today's wash was extra heavy.

CHAPTER 16

"Are you God?"

The young man jerked as if jabbed with a hot poker. His high forehead glistened sweat. He seemed to be waiting for something. Weighing consequences.

Adrine Sarafian didn't think him in the habit of executing women.

"Do not question my motives," he said, a perverse calm in the tone.

"Like God?"

"What?"

"We aren't to question God's motives. He is supreme. Sovereign. Unquestionable."

He circled the room, hands tightly clasped in front, carefully tended features leaden with the gravity of the mission. Eyes hard with the vexing question he'd been asked, he stopped, his rigid back to her, his head sharply tilted as if examining the crease where peeling wall and cracked ceiling met.

What was he waiting for?

Adrine stole a glance at the door. Could she rise from the chair, skirt the table, open the door, flee down the hall, reach the street without capture?

Not unless he let her.

The thought of him toying with her was a thought no less chilling than the image of her dead body, bloodless and alone, discarded in a cold room of an abandoned building. Would it be found before the rats . . .

"Yes, I am God. In a land where the divine folds its arms

while the innocent are plundered, I become God. He allows Armenians to die; I defend them. He looks away; I even the ledger."

"And if each of us were to do that?"

The narrow back stiffened. "Each of us is responsible to do what we can. When a way opens to us, we take it, or we lie awake nights cursing ourselves for missed opportunities. Cowards hesitate and foul their own nests; the brave act."

"And if they act in a lawless manner?"

He twisted his upper body and gave her a scathing look of annoyance. "You can ask that in a land of lawlessness? I remember when Armenian women baked bread and told their men how virile they were. What did your mother and grandmother teach you?"

Adrine avoided the accusing question. "I see a man who doesn't know what else to do but act as the Turks acted in the feeble hope that just a few more select murders will even the score, avenge the dead, perhaps cause the Turks the remorse they deserve."

The assassin shrugged. "God lays down His scepter for a season; I take it up. A hundred years from now, who will bear the sting of criticism—the Turkish executioner with blood on his hands or the Armenian death angel who brings those bloody hands to justice? You became confused in your politics, and now I deliver a corrective. Once you are corrected, I will find your husband and bring him back for correction."

Distract the man, Adrine thought. *Keep him thinking about the perplexities of the Armenian plight. Show him something of value— pique his curiosity—then seize the advantage before he has time to make good on his threats.*

"But the Armenian church—"

"What of it?" he snapped, staring at her, hands on hips in exasperation. The way he stood, the flaps of his coat held back by a scholar's hands and wrists, she could easily see the butt of the pistol that had moved from pocket to waistband of expensively tailored gray trousers. Someone was funding the assassin, possibly from America. She had no doubt the gun was the same one that ended the life of the Judas.

It looked identical to Tatul's.

"The church teaches nothing of assassination. It is the ultimate judgment, and we are not to judge," she said evenly.

The look regarded her with cold speculation and her statement with contempt. "The Armenian Apostolic Church has remained independent through nearly two millennia of persecution and triumph, the two as interwoven reeds made stronger by their shared unity. But if I take you to next Sunday's ritual of praise and adoration, we will be treated to shambling worship and mumbled devotion. What happened? I'll tell you. Four years of soul-stealing horror!"

The room felt dry and chalky as a box of brittle bones. The space between walls, between floor and ceiling, seemed less than when they'd entered. Adrine needed to get out before the bitter assassin sucked the room of all its oxygen.

It was her duty to live.

Slowly she removed the hand-painted enamel watch from her pocket and made a show of opening the handsome lid, checking the time, running a finger over the concave interior in which Tatul's piece of paper, his emergency message, remained tightly folded.

The assassin's eyes followed her every movement. "That is an impressive timepiece," he said. "May I look at it?"

It was such a regular request, and so politely given, each felt a breath of normalcy stir the dust of their confinement.

"Here, I will show you," she offered, keeping the watch close to her, beckoning him nearer. To Adrine, it was surreal, the killer and his target, both still alive, marveling together at the watchman's artistry. What *was* he waiting for?

He drew near, lulled by their conversation, and bent to see what she kept so carefully cupped in her hands. As if outside herself, Adrine saw a woman lunge forward and shove a neatly dressed man backward, off-balance, saw him fall to the floor, fumble for his weapon, saw and heard a wicked muzzle blaze white-orange, and felt the spray of plaster and wood that came from a bullet digging a home near her head.

She tipped over the table, heard the lamp crash and explode in flames, wrenched open the door, and half ran, half fell down the longest corridor on earth. Far longer than the short one she'd entered by, yet the same. A second bullet reached the outside door before she did, but the brain-surging shock of being shot at nearly tore that door from its hinges.

He WILL kill a woman! He offered me a drink, debated me, asked to see my watch, then shot to stop me forever!

She ran for her life, but it was with all the grace and speed of a wounded ox. The bullets had missed her body but buried themselves deep within the command center that ordered her limbs to move.

The last dim light of day turned the streets and warrens of Sulukule a ghastly gray. All the Gypsy tents and earthen hovels looked shut and shuttered against the creeping evil of nightfall. Usually the Roms danced and laughed in the face of iniquity—even invented a little of their own—long into the night watch, but with this sundown they wanted nothing to do. There were some times best surrendered to unseen forces, and this was one of those.

The assassin was closing the distance. She could hear his rapid breathing, his echoing footfalls, and imagined she could hear his thoughts. *It is not my pleasure but my duty to cleanse the land of the guilty and all who give the appearance of guilt. I must be on that train to Berlin in the morning or answer to my patrons.* It was then she saw it.

A light. Music. A small audience of whistling Stambullus danced wildly, stomping their feet and swaying drunkenly to the fiddle and the squeeze-box. Beyond them a young girl of no more than fifteen, lithe body wet with exertion, hair wild, feet and legs naked, one shoulder bare, snaked provocatively in a swirling blur of twisting limbs, red lips, and redder nails.

Adrine flew to the light like a moth to flame. She recognized where she was. Two streets beyond the merriment was the orphanage, Mother Agop, safety. *God, my Father!*

The assassin caught her by the hair and yanked her over backward. Adrine hit the cobblestones with a jarring impact but managed to keep her head protected. Momentary numbness washed over her, rapidly replaced by the sensation of a thousand needle pricks traveling down her left arm and side.

Gone was the warm welcoming light. She stared into the dark shroud of a Sulukule night, which was rapidly descending like the lid of a burial box.

The merry music of her salvation became a hollow din. She heard someone's labored breathing and felt hands lifting her by the arms. Unconsciousness wanted her, and she wanted it.

But something inside refused to surrender her senses. She struggled against the hands and took a stinging blow to the ear.

The gun, blue-gray in the faint light, swung level with her right eye. At that close range, the barrel was a gaping hole, and she stumbled forward as if sucked toward its evil maw.

"Stop this!" she tried to shout. "I am not the enemy. . . ."

A wall of red fur rose in a blur, a staggering railcar of an animal suddenly filling the world with a thunderous roar and the thick stench of rotten fish and ursine musk.

The German Mauser clattered to the street unused.

The only sound louder than the roaring of the bear was the screaming of the assassin.

On her back in the street, Adrine watched in numbed horror. The bear lumbered forward on hind feet, as tall as the buildings of Sulukule. It caught the gunman from behind in an embrace elemental in its power, crossing massive paws in front like a mother protecting a child. The great dripping jaws spread wide and the mighty neck bent in a terrifying bow to take the head of the shrieking, sobbing avenger.

"Gah! Gah!" The stern command was soon followed from the dark shadows by a short, stout Gypsy spilling rags from every pocket of a stained wool coat. The familiar long pole rested on one shoulder; the ever present bulging sack drooped from the other, both as necessary to the man's anatomy as hand or foot.

Barg the Gypsy bear master.

The bear closed its jaws and settled back on its haunches, hauling the assassin with it as if reluctant to part with so new and interesting an acquisition. The shaggy head tossed from side to side, spittle flying, emitting little guttural bursts of protest. The coal black eyes longed for something that Barg so rudely forbade.

The assassin, wild-eyed and drooling, arms stiff as sticks, emitted his own little whimpers of protest from the arms of the Russian bear.

"Gah! Whish!" Barg ordered, sweeping the pole off one shoulder in a dominating arc. The bear rolled its eyes and bent its head coyly, an overgrown child insisting on its way. Barg would have none of it. He jabbed his pole into the bear's throat. The beast peered forlornly at its master, saw the firm set of grizzled face and piercing eyes, and with a grunt of dissatisfaction, released its hold.

The young man, neat clothes now in smelly, damp disarray, jerked forward on the frozen limbs of an animated scarecrow. With a shudder, he found his senses, and without the gun or a backward glance, the divine assassin from the Yat Limani tea shop ran back the way he'd come on feet that suddenly sprouted wings. His work in Istanbul was over.

With customary gallantry, Barg extended a soiled end of the pole that served as a third arm. Adrine grabbed hold and stood to her feet.

"I warn! Fair caution!" Barg gabbled in a broken mix of Turk and Armenian seasoned lightly with Romani, poking his pole at a jagged scrap of board affixed above their heads to a weathered grain sign dangling from the building by a loop of rusted wire. The board was spattered with bear dung, a common Gypsy practice. Bits of rag, animal waste, carefully arranged branches, or an ancient shank of mutton, appropriately displayed, conveyed considerable information and warning to the practiced eye. "I warn!" Barg said again indignantly, and Adrine nodded that his testimony was true.

Adrine felt a rush of affection for her unlikely champion. She wished she knew Romani, the ancient language of the Gypsy clans that was better committed to memory than to books. She would tell the old "one-who-knows," as the nomads called their learned elders, that he was sent from God. Barg would laugh at that. They knew no god but the open road and the day's take. But at least the eccentric little man would hear the gratitude in her voice.

She would attempt something. "I . . . I thank you for saving me from that man," she spoke slowly, watching Barg watch every move of her lips. "He wanted to kill me."

Barg's eyes grew big and incredulous when the meaning sank home. A leering, gap-toothed grin spread across his face. He tucked the pole under an arm, picked a scab beneath his nose, and pointed at Adrine's bosom.

"He after those!" he declared, throwing his head back and laughing uproariously. "What good to kill female? The female only thing make difference between man"—he pointed to himself—"and monster"—he pointed at the huge bear that had backed against the building to rub its spine over the rough brick with huffing moans of pleasure. *Close your eyes*, thought Adrine grimly, *and it would be difficult to tell the animal from its master.*

Adrine felt the Gypsy's gaze read her discomfort, and she knew it was time to move on. Trying not to let her indignance show, she slipped a coin from her pocket and thrust it forth, palm up, as she might an apple for a horse.

Barg's eyes narrowed, smile fading. Had she offended him? People said it was impossible to offend a Gypsy with money, but that was rude talk.

Swifter than a snake, Barg's rough, callused paw encircled her slender wrist in an icy clamp. The bear's shaggy head snapped to attention, and it sat forward in anticipation. "My Shik Shik need female," he said, low and ominous, glancing back at the rollicking band of minstrels and their sweaty entertainment. Desperate, Adrine followed his look, wished the party would move closer, prayed for knife-sharp wits.

"Female make circus finished!"

It was a few seconds before she comprehended. *Complete*, she thought. *He needs me to complete his act.* She would be an invaluable asset to cook and dance and tend his bears and—she didn't want to think of what else she might have to tend. She did not owe her deliverer that.

Barg stole her thoughts and frowned. "Barg not need woman; Barg have bears! *Bears* need woman! Clean cage, feed, dance pretty with the bears, make lots stinking money!"

He leaned close, and she smelled a body that had not known water since the days of the sultans.

"Or I sell you to ugly man without wife. Make lots babies, make Gypsy blood!" She could not look at him but tasted bitterly the irony of an old Gypsy bachelor uttering a bizarre blessing on the womb.

He released her. "You think Barg not marry?" he asked, the indignity of the very idea clouding his countenance. "I marry plenty. Two, three, four, I think. Wife now ugly as crow. All bad. Barg only marry bad females out of families not know how to raise wives." He looked sad and wounded, a forgotten and unlucky man in the company of bears.

Shik Shik stopped scratching and ambled over to sit companionably near its master, as if sensing his need. Other bears in the shadows growled hungrily, but clearly Shik Shik was the favorite. One thing more was obvious. Little, elderly Barg assumed grander proportions in the presence of his menagerie.

Adrine doubted there was a wife for Barg, but if she did exist, their love had surely died, and she had long ago lost him to the only creature he could control.

———

The clatter of hooves shattered the Stambul night. Tatul and his loyal men sat on the lunging beasts as if carved from them. Eyes set, faces hard and determined, they raced through the streets, urging their mounts to make haste for the orphanage at Sulukule. To be sure, they searched the outside of every shack and manor en route. Tokapi Palace. The Sirkeci Railway Station. Suleyman's Mosque. Homes. Tenements. Businesses. Squares.

Like the Fedayeen the brave ones rode, stirrups high, coats flying straight out behind, whipping and reining their mounts in a furious and concentrated effort to find the first woman of Armenian independence, the only one wise and beautiful enough to complete the legendary Fox, and the boy she sought to protect at all cost.

No one hailed the riders. No one questioned their mission. No one dared block their way.

Fully loaded weapons rode with them, but the gendarmes, the secret police, the military gunmen—Tekir Pasha's executioners—all kept their distance as if they knew who chanced the back roads and thoroughfares of dark Stambul. To confront the Fox that night would exact a terrible toll.

Even the feral curs of alley and sewer remained hidden or scattered before the riders and the heaving chests and flying legs of the mounts they rode.

But no heart beat stronger or truer, nor ached more painfully than the lion's heart that thudded deep within the chest of Tatul Sarafian. God had gifted him with the dearest, most selfless woman ever formed, and he had taken her for granted. He had grown ever more preoccupied with the antics of Marxists, the convolutions of political oratory, the hypothetical raising of a nation from the ashes of an unimaginable slaughter, until he could scarcely remember, or took time to remember, what they had come through to earn a position and a voice of sufficient volume to even be heard in the swelling confusion of postwar Istanbul. The harder he rode, the more he begged God to save what He had begun. Tatul had been blind to that which was in front of his face all along: Armenia would rise, one family at a time. Hadn't sweet Adrine said those very words?

A remnant had been spared. Dazed, traumatized, weak in power but sufficient to birth a republic, they had survived near annihilation. Now they must come together before God, bathed in the blood of Christ, to make their homes, quietly take up the pen, the play, the plow, raise children and teach them to build a future upon their faith, not the bitter past. "By His stripes are we healed" the prophet Isaiah said. Without the stripes and the leadership of the One who bore them, the healing would never begin, no matter how much speaking or legislating anyone did.

Tatul had learned his lesson, and if the Lord would spare his wife and give them another beginning, Sarafian the Hot Wind would lead next by example. He would find employment, anything, no matter how far down the Turks tried to keep him. Quietly, with a minimum of words, he would conduct his business and be a faithful husband to his wife instead of inciting others and inviting a killer's bullet. He would help Adrine build her business so that A Taste of the Homeland would bear witness to the world that Armenia was far from destroyed. Husband and wife would spend more time in the marriage bed, and by God's blessing, they would have a child. In him—or her—would be the seed of the new republic!

He whistled sharply and pulled his mount to a snorting, stamping halt. The others circled round him, eyes questioning. He looked into their faces—Andranik, Vahram, Hovsep, Bayard, Ephraim—and felt such love for their sacrifice. Tatul shot out an arm, palm down, into the circle. The others quickly followed suit, hand upon hand. "Our Father in heaven," Tatul began. The others' voices, deep and caring, joined in. "Hallowed be thy name . . ."

When they had finished praying, Tatul stood in his stirrups, looked at his loyal friends, and nodded. "Sulukule!" he shouted.

"Sulukule!" they shouted as one.

And as one, they did ride.

———————

Rising fear—and the situation she was in—made it difficult to breathe. Adrine didn't want to fear anything, for the Scriptures said to cast her cares upon God the Protector and Jesus, His Redeemer. But the heavy night air hung with the black crepe of Barg's rapidly deteriorating mood.

Shik Shik had herded Adrine out of sight of the celebrating Gypsies into a twisted cove between two buildings. The narrow space contained Barg's full circus—a collection of handmade wooden cages that were occupied by four more growling, snorting bears with dispositions decidedly against being confined inside a box in a dank alley. He must have cast a special spell over a few Gypsy children to get them to gather enough meat and meal to feed that many bears. The heavy stink of bear hides and the piles of fly-flecked feces made the space close to intolerable.

Tonight the bears were fed a small portion each of goat entrails. Adrine's stomach remained close to the center of her body despite the bucket of aromatic viscera she carried and from which Barg lovingly ladled the scant meal.

She was anxious to leave but was afraid to say so or to walk away. A threatening tension fell over everything. She shuddered with the memory of the young man half disappearing into the furry arms of Shik Shik. Glistening teeth and twenty claws, each longer than a man's finger, kept her from doing anything sudden.

Inexplicably, Barg brightened. "Tomorrow no rain, good day. Much crowd at Bazaar. Shik Shik wrestle with Big Gaja. You dance, shake plenty, stinking money fall like rain. Now, I tell my *hira*," Barg said in an alcoholic slur. He'd begun drinking from a squat brown jug after licking the cork that kept the contents in.

"*Hira* is Rom for my stories." He thumped his chest. "Stories of Barg's fortune." He belched long and noisily, setting the menagerie to grunting in reply. He stretched alongside the small warming fire with much groaning and creaking of limbs. He motioned Adrine to an upturned vegetable crate, which put her in painful reminder of the produce stand in desperate need of her attention.

At any moment she expected Tatul. He had rescued her before when it took a miracle from the mountains to give her back her hope and her humanity—and that belonging to another hundred women enslaved to a mad Turk military captain. Perhaps he had found David, and together they would come for her.

She wished Shik Shik were in a cage like the others. The massive he-bear lay untied against one cage as if friends with the occupant.

"In Ger-many—you know this Ger-many?" Barg inquired, taking another long pull on the jug.

Adrine nodded and looked about for the best escape. She noted the bears seemed to grow still now that their master was lying down. She noted, too, that Barg watched her studying the camp.

"Dragon caves. Ger-man dragon caves. Barg only man brave to go inside. Floor of caves deep in bat dung. Past knees." He swiped at his legs to show the depth of the guano. "Under dung Barg find"—another suck of the jug—"find skulls. Heads like this." He smacked his forehead with the flat of his hand and made an angling motion to indicate the steep frontal slope of the hidden skulls. "Cave bears. Old, old bears. Dead before these." He waved at the animals around them. "Much bones; much skulls. I tell people in valleys, stupid people all over, these heads of dragons. Because of shape, believe Barg. Give Barg money. Put ghosts of dead in caves. Barg do and keep dragons in. Fill tambourine heavy; money falls out. Train monkey to pick up stinking money."

He stopped, tired from the weight of his own legend. He licked the top of the jug and sucked at a damp spot on his coat sleeve. His heavy eyes closed. "Woman get Barg more." He waved in the general direction of some decrepit, blanket-covered shelves against the wall of the building opposite. Adrine rose, stepped around the reclining bear master, and with one eye on the slumbering animals, pulled back the blanket.

Jugs in assorted sizes lined the cracked and rotting shelves. She chose the smallest, shook it to make certain it contained liquid, and with pounding heart let the blanket drop back in place.

"Monkey steal from Barg." The old man's voice grew steadily fainter. "Keep coins to buy sweet things in village. Monkey not taste good. Not manly like fresh bear meat. Barg like bear more than stinking monkey."

The small brown jug in her hands rose high in the air above the mumbling man in the brown wool coat.

"Shoosh! Skah!"

So startled was she by the sudden, unexpected command coming from a very awake Barg that Adrine stumbled backward, lost her balance, and fell to the ground. Her jug sailed into the wall behind and smashed in a burst of clay shards and strong drink.

Shik Shik the bear was up in an instant, rising to a height half again as tall as the tallest Turk. With a savage roar of genuine primal hatred, it came for her on hind legs.

She squeezed her eyes shut and prayed Barg would issue the command to leave her alone. But it did not come. Instinctively, Adrine rolled into as tight a ball as she could make of herself.

The bear clamped its jaws on the back of her dress and hoisted her high into the air. Barg danced in the firelight yelling angry encouragement to the enraged animal.

The bear shook its mouthful like a rag doll. A loud tearing and Adrine was suspended in air a split second before crashing to earth, much of her dress dangling from the jaws of Shik Shik.

Adrine scrambled behind the shelf of drinking jugs but the bear still came for her. With a single swipe of the mammoth beast's paw, the flimsy shelving splintered into a thousand pieces.

Adrine, exposed, cowered against the wall and waited for the death blow to fall. "Jesus . . ." was all she had time to pray.

"Gah! Whish!" The disgusted command was as musical to her ears as "Go, in the name of the Father, and of the Son, and of the Holy Ghost!" The towering creature protested vehemently and Barg's magic pole moved in a series of jabs and whacks that sent the giant grumbling back into the shadows.

Barg hopped in anger. "Stupid woman!" he railed. "Beautiful was the plan. Barg decide to let you live, to be part of circus. But you stupid like wife. Only difference, you not ugly!"

Adrine, shaking from her close encounter with a mountain of fur-wrapped muscle, tried to keep up with the rapid spewing of frustration. One thing was clear. Barg had come to a major decision.

Crestfallen that he had failed to successfully woo her with the charms of an international entertainer and ghost tamer, Barg surrendered to the inevitable.

Rapid footsteps approached. A half dozen men in the uniform of the National Police rushed into the circle of firelight and seized Adrine.

Shik Shik growled low in his throat. The other bears stirred. "Gah!" soothed their master dejectedly.

She watched them deposit a handful of gold coins into the calloused hands of the bear trainer. He met her reproachful gaze with just six words: "Monkey steal. Monkey never attack Barg."

Firmly, the gendarmes led Adrine to the open door of a waiting vehicle. She prayed for her husband and Mother Agop to step forward and vouch for her. For Grandmother to lead her to safety. For God to strike her captors immobile.

Instead, two forbidding soldiers of the Turkish army followed her inside the automobile and sat one on each side, close and hard muscled. She was acutely conscious of their thighs touching hers, of her bare legs so sparsely covered by the ragged ends of the torn dress. But the men seemed not to notice and sat silent as stone, hard, unyielding eyes fixed on the windshield ahead.

Before the door closed, Barg approached and bent to look at her, the grizzled face of a legend now a twitching mask of regret. His last words to her were completely unexpected and made her cry. "*Ja develesa*," he called gruffly through the door. "Go with God."

A cry of frustrated anguish tore from her throat, and she reached a hand toward the awful little Gypsy who now seemed quite the lesser of two evils. Rough hands grabbed her, threw a blindfold around her eyes and cinched it tightly at the back of the head. Shoved forward, Adrine felt a sturdy rope looped around her wrists and cried out when it was pulled secure and the restraint bit into her flesh.

The car started with a jerk and sped away.

Away from Sulukule and the clattering approach of many hooves.

CHAPTER 17

Tekir Pasha slowly circled the sea of woven pillows in rich blues and bright saffron. He stood straighter and looked younger, more focused, than he had since the so-called Judas had been murdered. The finely manicured hands behind his back twirled a short gold chain usually found around his wife's ankle.

Neva lay back against the pillows, feet bare, jumbo olive eyes following her husband about the room. She extended comely arms to him and cooed little murmurs of invitation from behind the veil that kept her identity his and his alone.

He stopped circling and watched Neva's attempts to seduce him from deep within the pillows. The chief of military police weighed the two excitements: the thought of Neva's fragrant embrace, and the carefully laid snare even now tightening about the Fox, his lady, and the rest of the misbegotten Armenian infidels who soiled his city.

Neva's moist black eyes begged him to leave his medals and fringe and golden military strategies to join her in an interlude of passion.

Tekir Pasha's face remained immobile, studying her, curious that a creature so strong in many other ways as a woman would let her guard come down so far when it came to intimacy.

Neva wasn't even the most desirable of women. He had been with others far more satisfying. Neva's best features were that she said little and possessed a craven willingness to live among the pillows if he was so inclined. He rarely was.

"You should not be so swift to entice," he told her, circling the table again, watching for the warm eyes to go cold. A moment later they did, and he felt a surge of mastery. It was his job to retain control. The second he failed to exercise control, valuable people like Mugurditchian, the informant, lost their lives.

He saw defeat in her eyes. He saw subservience. Good. Now he could devote his undivided attention to the tightening snare.

Adrine Sarafian was on her way to safe hiding, well away from the death and destruction soon to befall the young vermin at the orphanage in Sulukule. Tatul Sarafian was on his way to the orphanage in the mistaken belief that she was there. Capture the Fox, reunite him with his lady, show them the destruction of their precious breeding ground for future Armenian anarchists, then force the Fox, just before his own death, to watch Tekir Pasha take the lovely Mrs. Sarafian for his latest trophy.

The smashing of the Fox and his lady, coupled with the destruction of an entire orphanage of beggar boy infidels by the score, would utterly break the back of any further Armenian resistance in Stambul. The good Turk citizenry would rise up as one voice and hail the chief of police for restoring order and making the greatest city on earth safe again.

It was his duty.

A lecherous smile spread across the security commander's narrow features at the thought of claiming so fine a feminine trophy as Adrine Sarafian.

At her husband's knowing look of pleasure, renewed hope lit Neva's eyes among the pillows.

It died quickly when he turned without a word and left the room.

CHAPTER 18

The auto halted abruptly, and the blinded Adrine Sarafian sat in magnified darkness. She fought against a rising panic by guessing how far they'd come. En route, despite the pain at her wrists and the back of her head where hair was caught in the binding about her eyes, she forced herself to listen to passing sounds, to record every turn the vehicle took on the map of her memory. If she was accurate and her prayers were heard, they must be somewhere near—

The door opened and in rushed a thousand aromas. Baking bread. Cut flowers. Summer figs. Outdoor restaurants. Strawberries. Ginger, cloves, nutmeg, cinnamon, and curry. Hanging meat. Sharp cheeses. Onions. The sea, the salt, and the night damp.

With the smells came a thousand sounds. Tinkling cymbals. The fiery beat of the *zurna* (clarinet), *darbuka* (kettle drums), and *kanun* (zither). The cry of vendors haggling prices with their dismayed customers. The call of the water, tea, and juice sellers. Laughter. Singing. Boat horns on the distant Bosporus.

They could be in only one place. She had guessed right— God be praised! They were at the Grand Bazaar.

Adrine fought her fear to think of where in the bazaar. Judging from the lack of fish on the air or the sounds of the fishmongers shouting the allure of fresh turbot, they were likely at either the opposite end near the Street of Jewels or closer to the middle and the clothing emporiums. There were entrance gates at both.

A thick cloth was pulled over her head, and by its weight she guessed it was a Muslim chador. It would conceal her bound hands and much of the blindfold. Arrests were commonplace in Istanbul every day. "Devout" women in religious garb were sometimes caught for overzealous shopping, in which items inside their righteous costumes had been "forgotten" and not paid for. Adrine, escorted by two stern military gendarmes, would draw little attention.

But why here? Why not the police headquarters or—she paled at the thought—the local prison? She needed to swallow and pray, but neither came easy in her sightless ignorance. A Turkish prison, she had heard, was the entrance to hell.

Silent as gravediggers, the men beside her pulled Adrine from the auto and propelled her by the arms. By the switch in bartered shouts from the whistles and banter of the open air to the more conversational tones of indoor haggling, Adrine knew they had entered the bazaar itself.

Then she understood with a happy familiarity where she was. She heard the swish of cloth brushing against her head as they negotiated the crowded aisles. They were in the clothing sector, where foot traffic burrowed through a jungle of dangling dresses and pants.

Adrine almost laughed from the relief of gaining her bearings and the thought of what the passersby must be thinking. *Look at the thief. What's she wearing under that chador? Selim Hamam's fine trousers? Four pair and who would know?*

On they went down the endless lanes. Everywhere could be heard the chanting of Greek, Arabic, and Turkish, with bargains to be had at every turn.

Adrine carefully counted their paces, tensing as they drew closer. *God help me if I am mistaken.*

"Genghis the Mongol!" she cried as loudly as she could. "Good health, good friend! Good profit!"

The men beside her stiffened and tried to rush her away, but the crush was too great. A thousand different faces crowded in on them.

"Where is a good man when a good one is needed?" Her tone sounded desperate. She struggled rashly against her captors, caring little but to get away. "Good Genghis! Speak, man, or lose a sale!"

From behind, about two stalls away, came the answering cry rising above the din. "Ho, good woman, has your husband sent you past sundown that needy of a Genghis caftan? Is that you, good woman, or do the zephyrs taunt me by the imitation of your voice?"

The good-natured banter she normally enjoyed with the Mongol dress merchant suddenly assumed a deadly importance.

"The gold-and-red embroidered one," she called. "Does it still sag forlornly from the rafters awaiting my form, awaiting a change in heart of the one who prices it beyond what the gods can pay?"

He had followed the sound and was drawing closer, a big broad man with beefy hands and brow, his eyes permanently shut.

Genghis the Mongol was as blind as she.

He parted the crowd like a jolly fat Moses and stood beside them. "You are here, charming Adrine?"

"Here!" she said, a rush of relief deluding her into a false security. She felt the very real press of a gun in her side and took a sharp breath. The four of them were jostled by the press of humanity. A shot here would unleash a crushing stampede and few survivors.

"What? Why do you stand here shouting so rudely from a distance? Is that someone with you? I heard about the sons of harlots who attacked your stand. Their mothers are dogs. But Genghis will help you. Here, take my hand, and I will lead you safely to the sparkling shore where your caftan awaits!"

"I . . . I cannot, good thief. I must get our fish for breakfast and steer for home. Ask Jesus for my swift return and may you dream of low prices and caftans that do not require a month's wages." The gun jabbed her insistently, and she was half dragged, half carried from the spot by her captors. They grew increasingly rough. Hopefully, Genghis, a nominal Muslim, would think her encouragement to petition Jesus, and her odd attitude in general, sufficiently strange for comment to his fellow merchants. The news would spread, and Tatul would hear.

"Who is with you?" she heard from behind, the concern evident in the big man's voice. "You will not have a man who is blind, but you give no thought to keeping company with a man who is dumb? Speak up, good man, or this lady's caftan doubles in price!"

They left him there perplexed, a giant wide island in a flowing stream of humanity, berating their rudeness until the caftan in question had risen in price fivefold.

Adrine felt the anger in the men beside her. What might they do once they had her out of sight? Though the gun had been removed, she could yet feel its lethal impression in her side. *O God, please remind Genghis that I would not be here in the clothing district to buy fish at night for a morning meal, and ask him what I am doing here after dark anyway and why those men did not speak.*

It was her last thought before the sounds of the market vanished as she was knocked unconscious by a swinging blow to the head.

———

She awoke, a swelling knot just over her right temple, her head thudding with the supreme ruler of all headaches.

Wherever she was felt empty of any other life. At first.

Then something furry brushed against her arm, and she choked back a scream. She was locked in with a bear!

But bears did not purr. She laughed aloud, so great was her relief. The cat must have liked the sound, for it placed two paws on her shoulder and began to knead.

Adrine was on her back, bound hands beneath her almost numb from lack of circulation. She wasn't certain, but she thought her entire head had swollen the way the blindfold seemed to cut all the deeper.

Sitting upright, she waited what seemed like many minutes for the incessant pounding inside her brain to lessen, which it eventually did.

She gathered her legs under her and rocked up on her knees. Again she outwaited the pounding that came with every effort. The comforting purr of the cat she could not see took the edge off the unsettling darkness and reminded her of her own brave Giaor, the mother cat that had survived the military slave camp along with her mistress and was given a good home with a caring Turkish friend and her little boy.

While on her knees, Adrine prayed for courage and a way free. For Tatul. For David. For Armenia.

She could hear something.

The muted sounds of the market traffic just beyond a partition.

A wall . . . a door?

She wobbled up on one foot, then the other, rising slowly against the thudding pain.

Can't think . . . hurts too much . . .

The purring increased, and Adrine could feel the happy feline rubbing against her ankles. But she almost could not convince her legs to move, so numb were they and so fearful was she of what she would encounter even if a way out of the room could be found.

But move she did, slowly, a shuffle step at a time, her feet out ahead to keep from crashing into any barrier that might block her path.

The cat went ahead, and she decided to follow its purrs.

She jumped back, but it was only a cloth curtain hanging over a doorway. Cautiously, she slipped through and sensed light ahead.

The sounds of the market increased and with it the sound of something else. A heated argument.

Adrine froze.

"You fool! If we kill her, we steal the pleasure that is rightfully his, and Allah or no Allah, he will hunt us down and remove our pleasure. Think on that!"

"Maybe she's already dead. You hit her too hard. I think maybe her skull is broken!"

"Shut up! Why don't you go and see if she breathes, or are you afraid of the dark?"

In a panic, Adrine crouched low, debating whether to go back through the curtain or find something close at hand to hide behind. Bent down as she was, her nose was assailed by the pungent aroma of pepper. Cayenne. She backed up slowly and felt rough wooden containers. Spice Street!

"You are lazier than a dead Armenian, which is what I think she is. You had better pray to Allah I am wrong! They will be here anytime, and if all we have to offer is a corpse, we may as well join her."

She flexed life into numb fingers and grabbed as big a pinch of pepper as she could hold. Someone nearby was getting up. Adrine hated to do it, but there was no other alternative. She bent her face to the ground and let the cat rub against her. Quickly she turned, and when the cat stuck its curious nose near her bound hands, she flicked the pepper between her fingers into the cat's face and ducked behind the containers.

The cat yowled as if set afire and raced in circles sneezing and pawing at its muzzle. The men, startled at first, soon began to laugh. "Cat just like you!" chortled one. "Sticks his nose where it shouldn't go!"

Adrine heard both the pained yowls and hoots of laughter move a little farther away. She prayed the men were distracted by the crazed cat and not paying any attention to the darkened corner where the spices were stored.

Carefully but quickly she moved ahead, feeling her way, bumping along until she rounded a corner and was met full strength by the cacophony of buying and selling.

Which side of Spice Street was she on? She dared not ask anyone until she was far enough away to be certain the gendarmes were no longer in the area and she didn't mistakenly direct the question to one of them.

Thinking of the children who wandered the luscious mysteries of the Grand Bazaar blindfolded in a game of "find the way out," she used nose and ears to direct her. At first she bumped into people, but she kept her head down and spoke to no one. Soon it seemed that people stepped out of her way, for she had a clear path.

She came to a divide between stalls and got a waft of fragrant pine. The woodturners' shops! Beyond them, the stench of smelted metal, beyond that the musty aroma of leather. She knew where she was!

It meant she was sixteen streets—no, seventeen—from the outer perimeter of the bazaar. More importantly, if she went straight up Leather Street, she would exit near Produce Street and Tansu Bir's. If only the cheese merchant had not closed early, he would help her.

It was then her sharpened ears heard the approaching commotion. "A woman in dark chador, about this tall. Slender, perhaps bumping into things as if drunk. Have you seen her?"

"Are you deaf? I said she's wanted for murder. Spread out! Help us find her!"

Adrine heard the soft snuffle of a horse and backed up to feel the rise and fall of smooth ribs. The horse nickered, and she followed it to its tail and the tongue of the wagon behind, then to a leather bridle and a waiting customer. She had barely enough time to slip under a stack of hay.

"I don't know! She's disappeared. Search the leathersmith's. Set the place on fire if you have to. I WANT THAT WOMAN!"

———————

Tendrils of fog slithered between the ruined walls and huts of Sulukule. The dogs of night nosed the refuse of the Gypsy camp, feral eyes blinking yellow with moonglow. An emaciated dam lifted a feeble pup in her jaws and carried it into the street to die. She laid it gently on the wet cobbles, licked its face and pink belly, then returned to a protesting litter of three to give suck.

A growing thunder caromed down the winding track bordering the Byzantine bulwark of decaying rubble that housed the Gypsy families of Istanbul. Dark eyes of the hunted peered apprehensively out, searching the night in fear of assault. Lights were quickly snuffed, and babies nearly smothered to silence.

The breath of Sulukule was caught in one collective gasp. Tatul Sarafian whipped the reins and drove the steed forward in desperate urgency. If anything happened to Adrine, he swore he would do what the Romans failed to do and bring the fortress walls crashing down on the sultans' misbegotten city.

Adrine. Sweet Adrine.

From out of the fog, like specters of war, a wall of uniformed men blocked the street and leveled rifles at the fast approaching horsemen.

For one brief moment, the Fox thought to defy them, to charge straight at the police and their bullets and to trust God that at least one of the dauntless Armenians would clear the barricade. But he could not guarantee which of them would go down, and it was not in him to sacrifice so loyal a following to one man's love.

He reined in his horse, as did the others, sparks flying from the hooves of their heaving mounts. Sarafian stabbed the air with a hand to restrain his men from drawing their weapons. He would give the Turks no excuse to cut them down like rats in a well.

From the shadows of the side street at which they gathered came the restless snufflings of Barg's family of bears.

The seconds ticked by in the early frost of night, trails of steam rising from the nostrils of men and horses.

The captain of the gendarmerie stepped forward and spoke in a loud commanding voice. "You have enjoyed the good offices of the Young Turks and the nationalist government that seeks to show compassion to the infidel in its midst. In defiance of the security laws of Tekir Pasha and the military police charged with keeping order and civil tranquility, you continue to incite anarchy. You are guests of this country, and yet you respond with arrogance and disobedience. You are found in contempt, and still you gather with impunity to plot your seditions!"

Tatul had heard enough. His tongue slapped reason aside. "You speak of order and tranquility as if the heathen Turk were intimate with either virtue. Yet was it not our guardian Turk government that did nail innocent Armenians to crosses with taunts of 'Let your Christ come help you now!'? Was it

214

not the compassionate Turk who beat the soles of Armenian feet until they burst from the swelling? How many yet starve to death in the deserts because you will not feed the prisoner in your midst?

"In the name of God, why? We are citizens of Turkey as are you. What do we seek that so threatens you? Cultural freedom? Equality before the law? Freedom of speech? Freedom from unjust taxes selectively imposed on Christians only? What, man, what is it that makes you hate us so?"

The captain coldly stared Sarafian in the eye. "You are an unlawful assembly. Choose from among you who will live and who will die. Three Armenians only may continue to draw breath."

He spoke the awful words calmly, as if announcing a new ordinance for the regulation of fireworks.

Barg the bear man rose shakily from his bed by the fire, instantly sober.

When no Armenian moved, the captain barked, "Choose NOW, or all shall die!"

Tatul Sarafian stared at the rifle barrels drawn against them and the grim faces taking aim, intent on Turk supremacy at all cost. He thought of how far they'd come, how far they had yet to go. And yet, what did it matter without Adrine? What would anything matter without the courageous, tender woman with whom he wanted to have babies, with whom he wanted to sit by the sea eating baklava and watching the sun settle into the Mediterranean?

Perhaps the only real answer was to draw their weapons now, to die in a hail of lead, and to hope that the echo of battle would be loud enough to reach the ears of Woodrow Wilson.

Tatul looked around at the dank, anonymous little street of Gypsy squatters and smiled grimly. However fierce the fight, it would not be heard above the howl of wild dogs or beyond the excited chatter of Gypsy scavengers picking over their dead bodies.

He saw Andranik's hand slide slowly down his leg where a pistol lay hidden in a boot.

"We have chosen!" The Fox turned his mount to circle his

men and come to a stop even with the other Armenian horsemen. Andranik left the pistol and watched his leader. The Fox
looked down at the captain, and a flash of understanding
passed between them. "One dies, all die!" Sarafian said loudly,
proudly. The Armenian brothers straightened at the words,
their jaws solidly set in a common resolve.

The captain shifted, unnerved. His men tensed to halt so
brazen a show of anarchy. "Three only!" the captain shouted,
his voice high with strain. "It is the law!"

Tatul Sarafian reached an arm to Vahram on his left and
they clasped wrists. Vahram's left arm went out to Hovsep,
who linked wrists with Bayard, Bayard with Ephraim,
Ephraim with Andranik, until the six brothers on horseback
were joined as one. Tatul felt the tremor in Vahram's arm and
hand, and used it to steady his own. "We are ready, Captain,"
Tatul said, "ready to die."

The captain swore. "Cursed infidels! Death you have chosen, and death you shall receive!" His arm rose and with it the
saber of command. "To whatever God you pray," he practically
screamed, "pray NOW!"

The six brothers of Armenia shut their eyes, tightened
their grip on one another, and waited for the saber to fall.

A hellish roar exploded from the murky recesses of Sulukule, and behind it lumbered four Russian bears led by the
snarling rage of Shik Shik. As they had been trained, the un-
chained beasts raced for the immediate threat—men with
weapons drawn.

Surprised, the Turkish gendarmes panicked. Fingers
jerked. Rifles blasted. Terrified shrieks and primitive roars tore
the night. Horses, spooked, reared on their hind legs, neighing
and foaming in primal fright.

The captain of the guard watched a rifleman go down, the
face disappearing beneath a monstrous head of fur. The bear
tore at its victim, flipping the man into the air as easily as
straw. Horrified, the captain wildly slashed the air about him,
not caring what his saber struck.

Bringing his rearing mount to earth, Tatul Sarafian held
tight to the reins and fought for control. He twisted about,

yelling for his men. Andranik knelt on the cobblestones, gripping a bloodied arm. Hovsep and Bayard were nowhere to be seen, their riderless mounts dashing about the street, eyes wild with alarm. Vahram and Ephraim remained astride, fighting mightily to control their bucking, skittish animals.

Tatul leaned forward over the horse's withers and tried to reassure the creature under him, but the chaos of gunfire, shrieking men, and snarling bears was too much for the frightened mount. The horse whirled in circles, stumbled, and nearly went down.

Sarafian stared suddenly into the perspiring, fear-crazed mask of a gendarme youth and, as if time stopped, saw the muzzle of the boy's rifle swing up and take aim.

CHAPTER 19

Krikor Andonian listened to the sounds of death not far beyond the walls of the orphanage. Tears leaked into his ears. He swiped at them angrily.

On the mat next to him, little Garouj shifted uneasily in sleep, turned, and threw a thin, bug-bitten arm across Krikor's chest. The sight of that skeletal limb, yellow and arrested in growth by lack of nutrition, made Krikor sob. He tried to do it silently and nearly choked on his grief.

Garouj's arm rose and fell with Krikor's watery gulps. It barely felt warm against his skin. The pale light from a sputtering lamp added to the arm's jaundice.

The older boy turned to face the younger, protecting him, drawing him close until their hearts beat as one. Krikor buried his face in the musty nape of Garouj's neck, wanting his mother with a longing so powerful he thought he might be sick.

Garouj stirred and pulled away from his protector's tight hold, returning to his back, then onto his right side, his back to Krikor.

The older boy sat up and looked across to David Mugur-ditchian, who slept alone on the bare earthen floor, curled in one of Mother Agop's thin shawls. Krikor dug in his pants, extracting a fat bug looking for warmth. He mashed it beneath the heel of a bare foot, then flicked the flattened carcass away with thumb and middle finger.

He decided he liked David and believed the curlyheaded boy must have been adopted. It helped Krikor like him if he believed that not a drop of Judas blood circulated in David's veins. Besides, adoption meant the boy they saved from the dogs had once been an orphan himself.

From beyond the wall came a rifleshot and an awful roaring of bears. Without Barg the bear man and his shaggy dependents, Krikor had little else to live for. It took him beyond the gloomy orphanage. He dreamed of the circus and becoming part of it, of eating fire and letting someone throw knives at him for the thrill of the crowd. Perhaps he could command the bears like Barg and be known as Krikor the Magnificent. He had almost convinced the smelly old Gypsy to let him feed Shik Shik.

The thought of losing that dream gripped the boy's heart in its icy cold talons. He should pray.

Krikor Andonian got on his knees and swayed there a moment, hands clasped to chest, listening to the sounds of breathing and nightmares. The air stank of sour flesh and urine and the liquid mess that protected their eighty wasting bodies from who-knew-what sicknesses. Whimpering disturbed the rest of the old warehouse, and somewhere a bat chittered in the darkness.

"Father of the heavens," Krikor prayed, with lips scarcely moving, "give us this day our daily bread and help us believe in your mercies even when there are so few to be seen. Forgive me my bad sins, especially for wanting to kill David. Be with my . . . my family and let someone beside me still be alive and help us to find each other soon."

A horse thundered past on the street. A man screamed as if dying.

Krikor squeezed his eyes hard shut and wet his lips. "Please, please, good Lord, end the terrible fighting out there. Don't let it in here. Protect me and my brothers and the dear women who keep us. And Mother Agop, bless her name! Please don't let Barg come to harm or the bears. And that kind Mrs. Sarafian. Please, can she bring us more vegetables and sweet fruit to make us well?"

He needed to relieve himself. He thanked the Lord for an

end to the war and closed in the name of "Jesus, my Christ" and two amens.

For a fleeting moment Krikor thought of making water in the little closet by the back entrance where he had done so many times after first arriving, until his nerves calmed enough and he had regained control of his bladder. But no, street fight or no street fight, he would go outside by the wall and not foul his home anymore. Hadn't he just prayed for protection?

Out of habit, he went by way of the little anteroom where Cheyrek and the nameless boy they called Euphrates slept. Cheyrek liked to wander.

He was not there. Euphrates snored softly, his pale face pinched in a troubled expression. But Cheyrek's place next to him was unoccupied except for a pile of ragged but carefully folded clothing.

Krikor frowned and looked over at the stairs. They'd been warned not to go up there unsupervised, but Cheyrek either didn't understand or chose to ignore the warnings. More than once he'd been stopped halfway up the stairs and returned to his mat and watched until he fell back to sleep.

At the foot of the stairs, Krikor hesitated. He saw no one in the moonglow that shone through the upper windows and partially illuminated the passage. Why go up there if Cheyrek had simply crawled into bed with someone else? The boys, especially the little ones and the more severely traumatized, often did that for comfort and reassurance.

"You're scared." He breathed the words without thinking. Though no bully, even taller ones, even dared challenge him beneath the sun, Krikor had his night fears.

A rush of cold, moist air rolled over him, and he knew. The building was big and drafty, but this was outside air coming in through the second-floor door to the roof. Someone was out there, and that someone had to be Cheyrek.

Krikor wished with all his might that Adrine Sarafian would come. No one had the calming effect on Cheyrek that she did. No one.

He thought to call Mother Agop but didn't want to risk waking the rest of the boys and causing them unnecessary concern for the remainder of the night.

Slowly, carefully, so as not to make the stairs creak, Krikor ascended to the second floor. When his head came even with the floor, he saw Cheyrek through the open doorway.

Naked except for a pair of holey stockings, the boy stood on the raised ledge that rimmed the roof. Face tilted to the dim glow of the moon demanding to be let through the thickening fog, arms outstretched at his sides, legs spread wide, Cheyrek swayed in the darkness like a fragile flower in search of daylight.

Krikor rushed onto the roof, then slowed so as not to startle his friend.

Up the street beyond the boys the clash of police and rebels was dying; those combatants still moving were more concerned about surviving their wounds than in pressing their grievances.

"Gypsies," Krikor said softly.

Cheyrek turned and smiled agreeably as if expecting him.

"Always turning the night merry, those Gypsies," Krikor said more loudly, hoisting himself up to stand on the ledge with Cheyrek.

"Dance!" The naked boy stomped and dipped as if taking up the beat of an unheard tambourine. It was the first word Krikor had ever heard Cheyrek Effendi speak.

Krikor took up the movements, fearful they would be spotted from the street but using the dance to move gradually closer to the emotionally disturbed boy.

They moved in unison, an ancient Armenian dance of gratitude to celebrate a bountiful harvest, a full barn. The whole time they gave God thanks with their waving bodies, Krikor's heart was in his mouth, the ground two stories below a dizzying blur. He watched Cheyrek's stockinged feet, ready to lunge should he misstep.

Krikor closed the gap between them and was alongside Cheyrek at last. He braced to sweep his friend from the ledge when the other boy threw his arms wide and grabbed Krikor in a clammy embrace. Krikor hugged him tight and fell backward off the ledge.

They crashed to the roof with Cheyrek giggling delightedly, and Krikor trying to extract himself.

Voices sounded from below. A sudden flood of lamplight up the stairwell. The pounding of feet coming their way.

Krikor removed his shirt and quickly tied it around Cheyrek's waist in front, leaving only the back exposed. "Modesty, Cheyrek. We must return to modesty." And to think how long it had taken them to get the rocking boy to part with his clothes. The younger boy looked down at the impromptu apron Krikor had fashioned and smiled.

A burst of excited voices reached the top of the stairs. Krikor sighed. It looked as if sleep for the rest of the night was definitely out of the question.

One thing was certain. He needed to relieve himself more than ever.

CHAPTER 20

Tekir Pasha, commander of the Istanbul gendarmerie, rubbed soft hands together in delicious triumph. The news, despite unforeseen complications, was better than women or wine or a day at the camel fights.

He buried his face in a riot of flowers and breathed deeply of the bouquet's ambrosial aroma. The man in uniform waiting patiently by, hat beneath his arm, showed no emotion.

"I'm a genius!" Tekir gloated. "The woman baits the man. While she is whisked into hiding, he falls headlong into the trap. Fool!" He took another deep drag on the floral array. "*King* of the fools!"

The man at attention nodded. Austere yet agreeable, just the way the pasha preferred his employees. "You are most generous, Commander, not to fault the men who have temporarily misplaced the woman."

"Fault them?" Tekir Pasha's face rose from the yellow-and-orange profusion. The carefully tended eyebrows dipped down like two slashes of charcoal. "No, I do not fault them. Women are the most treacherous by far of Allah's creatures. But I will behead the two misfortunates at midnight if she is not found and place their heads alongside *The Canon of Medicine* here in my parlor. All who then enter may be reminded that it is by both superior intellect and ancient ruthlessness that the Turks are lords of this land!"

Another agreeable nod.

"I want you to employ muezzin criers to pass through every street in the bazaar proclaiming the death of Tatul

225

Sarafian. His wife cannot remain long hidden once that news is out. Lay the blame for the tragedy on the Gypsy bear man. Perhaps the Armenians will do for us what we have thus far been unable to accomplish by law, that is to run the Gypsies out of Istanbul!"

A nod. "Anything more, Commander?"

The chief of military police shifted in his seat and absent-mindedly chewed one of the blossoms he held in his arms. "One thing more. I do not wish the sun to rise on the orphanage at Sulukule. Take all the forces you need to storm the place and do not take thought for sparing lives. They are vermin, and all they will do if allowed to escape is breed more anarchists and assassins.

"On second thought, I will lead this charge, for this will be a lesson to the infidels. Gather your forces. We will launch the assault from here. When it is decreed that no more than three Armenians shall gather in one place, this will help them understand that they are subject to the law. There are those who make the laws and those who must obey them." He smiled at the man in the uniform, hugely enjoying the recent turn of events. He shrugged playfully. "Allah be praised. He has decreed that we are the lawmakers!"

The man in waiting snapped his heels together, bowed slightly, and made to leave.

The police commander held up a hand. "One thing more has occurred to me just now." His eyes narrowed shrewdly. "Spread the word through Sulukule and the Armenian quarter that the woman is also dead. Dead in theory, dead in fact, I like to say. At your earliest convenience, make it true. Once the Armenians are sufficiently demoralized, then perhaps we can enjoy some well-deserved peace in Stambul, yes?"

The man, upon hearing this, bowed again and smiled agreeably. "As you say, Commander. As you say." He backed from the room and swiftly left the carved and marbled home of his superior. He was scowling like a man who'd been given but a few hours to live.

Adrine Sarafian dozed, forgotten beneath the hay in the stable of the Grand Bazaar.

She awoke with a start. The police had not found her, nor set the leathersmith's on fire to drive her from hiding. She had escaped their notice after shuddering for her life in the stifling, dusty confines of the hay stall. The blindfold bit into the flesh of her head, tight as a tourniquet.

A horse chewed complacently on the fodder and with another chomp and a swing of its head, she was exposed.

But what was the message ringing up and down the streets and stalls of the merchant paradise accompanied by the tolling of a bell?

It sounded like . . . Tatul?

The call drew closer, nearing her hiding place.

"Arise and mourn! Take refuge in Allah! There is a death among us! One so young, a son of his people! Arise and mourn, for Tatul Sarafian has gone to the bosom of Abraham, mauled by the circus bears of Sulukule . . ." Clang! Clang! The bell tolled. "Tatul Sarafian is lost! Pray for the disposition of the dead!"

Lost? Dead? Tatul . . . gone?

Her body went slack, and Adrine thought she might faint. All feeling left her except for a hard, stony lump where her heart had been. Good, brave Tatul. The bears? He must have come looking for her and . . . *dead*?

Inconceivable.

And as quickly, she knew that he'd been killed, taken from her and his people by Tekir Pasha with no more thought than he would have given the removal of a cyst.

Hot tears spilled from her, and the horse backed in surprise from the woman in the hay.

"Are you the murderer they seek?" a gruff voice sounded at her ear.

Startled, Adrine uttered a muffled cry. She smelled a hard-working man and the leather and boot grease of his trade.

"Tied up like that, I doubt you're able to plot anyone's demise," he said sardonically. "There's so much death anymore. What if I free you? Will you repay me with a knife in my back?

Poison in my cup? A rope at my neck?"

She struggled against her bonds and uttered a string of unintelligible words. Rough hands fumbled with the blindfold and a sudden stab of light signaled her sight had been returned. She felt lightheaded.

Eyes adjusting, she found her field of vision filled by the large head of a heavily muscled blacksmith. Dark skin, broad flat brow, large lips, and wide, expressive eyes told her he was not from Istanbul. That and the huge gold ring that pierced the septum of his nose.

"Death," he reminded her. "If I free your hands, will you leave my horse without a stabler, my patrons without the blacksmith and leather maker they so admire, me without the heartbeat to which I have grown so attached?"

A thick wave of despair brought more tears. "God would not permit me to end the life of one so kind."

With one upward slice of a wickedly curved leather-cutting tool, Adrine was freed of her restraints, and there was a renewed flow of blood to her throbbing arms and hands. The big stablekeeper gently applied salve to the abrasions at her wrists and temples but could do nothing for the wounds she bore inside.

"Good. I had to promise them hand-tooled leather vests to dissuade them of the notion that one so bloody as you would be within twenty shops of this humble stable. Hope you like this potion as much as my four-legged patients do." The blacksmith smiled, glancing over his shoulder and about the marketplace, eyes alert to danger. "Those are better than ordinary welts you've been given."

"I . . . I thank you for your kindness," Adrine responded shakily. "I have recently learned that my husband is dead."

The blacksmith's already dark countenance darkened further. "Tatul Sarafian? The champion of Armenia? *He* is your husband?"

Adrine nodded, afraid to attempt more words.

To her shock, the big man bent one knee and bowed humbly before her. "Lady, I am your willing servant. How may I assist?"

They were soon on their way to Tansu Bir, the cheese merchant. Adrine was so heavy with sorrow, she wondered that the wagon, pulled smartly by the kind horse that had shared its hay, could even move beneath the burden of her heart.

Out the back of the bazaar, to the end of the mammoth market, up the long side, and around the front. Adrine stayed hidden beneath a heavy blanket smelling of horse sweat and oily leather. They actually sniffed the cheese stall before sighting the hanging strings and bladders of goat, sheep, and cow cheese.

Adrine squeezed the blacksmith's thick hands appreciatively, tears in her eyes.

The big man looked at the ground. "I am so sorry, lady. The good die too soon. The evil are kept alive by sheer deviltry."

She wore the blanket inside Tansu's tiny shop. Through a blur of tears, she watched the cheese merchant and the stable keeper confer, heads close. An awful idea sprang unbidden among her jumbled thoughts: *What if Tansu and the blacksmith really work for the chief of police and are right now agreeing on the most efficient way to transfer me back into custody?* Adrine shook her head. The chaotic times poisoned every thought and friendship. She needed to beat back such dark absurdities.

Slender, scarred fingers clutched the ornate pocket watch. Trembling lips kissed the smooth enameled hunt scene touched by his fingers and once cradled in the palm of his strong hands. *Open the inner lid of this watch only when you, sweet Adrine, know inside you that I am dead.*

The hand holding the watch began to shake. Lid closed, it was their word; lid open, it was a lover's admission that the dream had ended.

Adrine squeezed the watch tightly in a bloodless fist and bit her hand to keep from crying out. Two truths were inescapable: he had never been *this* late, and the only thing that would save any shred of whom she'd hoped to become was to cling to God and read Tatul's last words.

"'For we are to God the aroma of Christ among . . . the perishing,'" she whispered, her nail working open the watch's inner compartment. A thin sheet of onionskin, many times folded, lay tight against the gold underside of the lid. A round impression left by the inner casing scored the fragile note as if pressing against her heart.

God the Father, his work was too dangerous. Why didn't we leave for America when it would have been so simple?

Why?

She would die with that single word on her gravestone.

By the thin shaft of light that came through the door of the shop, a sorrowing Adrine asked God to help her read her husband's last message.

Adrine, my enchanted one, how sorry I am that you are forced to this and that you have so little to show for having been wed to me. I desired for you the emerald Tokapi dagger for your protection, the tiles of the Blue Mosque for your private dressing chamber, and the grand marbled fountain of Suleyman the Magnificent for your formal parlor.

Instead, I leave you this simple watch and remind you of the hidden backside of Stambul. There, dug in the old land walls at Sulukule, are caves large enough for a bear. It is a good place to heal. They make good hiding places, and if you hadn't insisted on a normal home near the sea, that is where I would have liked to live—the wilderness in my Fedayeen blood!

The American poet Emily Dickinson—the rough Fedayeen are all balladeers at heart!—called God's love the "imperial thunderbolt that scalps your naked soul." It wasn't until we met that I fully understood the meaning of that. God came to me through you, and now I have gone to Him because of you. Not my death—that is man's doing. But my soul flies to Him, and I am at rest. Thank you, my little grape, for so inexpressible a gift. Left to myself, I would have done as so many and trusted to my own understanding.

Be not sad. When I found you, your heart beat with the strength of ten men. Draw on that strength again and Armenia shall be free! Hold this paper to your lips, and you shall be kissed by the Fox.

The last two words of the note were smudged and barely discernible. Just as Tansu turned toward her refuge, she saw that they were "Eternally yours." She pressed the words against her lips and let the hot tears flow.

For several moments, the cheesemonger allowed her her privacy.

"Come, I take you to the orphanage in my wagon," the kindly Tansu said at last, his face a troubled map of uncertainty. "That is, if you do not mind a smelly cargo of aged cheeses for traveling companions."

Adrine gently pressed her stomach and forced herself to calm. "I am quite accustomed to the mold that makes you famous, cheesemonger. It has helped keep my family alive. . . ." She choked on the last words and wept. Her "family," the source of strength that made her believe in a New Armenia, was now dead, and she was suffocatingly alone in a land that knew her not.

She pressed a trembling hand against her stomach as much to steady the shaking as a mother's reflex.

Carefully she refolded Tatul's note and replaced it in the lid of the watch. She had wanted to tell him the thing he did not know. But she had wanted the setting to be perfect, not in a house stripped of its furniture or in a place inhabited by a loaded German Mauser. On a windswept bluff, maybe, high above the sea, or by a slender brook with her head in his lap, far from political debate and physical threats.

Now she could not.

Tansu pulled the weeping woman to her feet and strong arms bore her to a wagon, where she lay down under a canvas next to a thick wheel of pungent cheese. In how many wagons across the nation did the hunted lie, praying to escape detection? Mercifully, her desperate cries of anguish could not be heard over the lumbering of the wheels.

CHAPTER 21

Two hundred of Tekir Pasha's handpicked troops boarded open trucks to eradicate the orphanage at Sulukule.

"It is a matter of highest urgency," the pasha addressed the men. "An issue of public safety. The health risks to Stambul are great. You have been issued protective gauze and are expected to use it. You do your fellow soldiers and family members great harm if you yourselves fall victim to whatever defects attack the infidel males. Remember, these are not children. They are diseased parasites, and the risk they pose to every man, woman, and child in this city will be reduced by your actions today."

The men nodded uncertainly, unsure that Armenians were disposable debris. They held to the swaying side slats jutting up from the wooden beds of the troop trucks and avoided one another's gaze. The few who might have questioned if the Gypsies or the Greeks or the Cypriots would be next prudently kept the question to themselves.

———

Gunpowder hung heavy in the stagnant air. Barg, the master of the Gypsy bears, pulled back from the still form, blinded by tears. Sticky with animal blood, he stumbled between the dead bodies of national policemen and the unmoving mounds of fur that had been Shik Shik and Hagia. Shik Shik had made Hagia pregnant, with twin cubs from the size of her. Two Turkish marksmen's bullets at point-blank range had wasted four red Russian bears. One of the marksmen lay where he'd fallen, his face half torn away by the raking claws of the mortally wounded Shik Shik.

Barg's children were dead. To the old Gypsy performer, it was no less devastating than if a son and expectant daughter-in-law had been executed before his eyes. He groped the ground for his hat but couldn't find it through the tears. All he'd had to look forward to that was fresh and new was the birth of those cubs. He believed in the ancient presumption that bear cubs were born shapeless and were licked into form by the mother. He wanted to be there when that happened. Hairless, blind, and toothless, the tiny blobs would be raised to amaze audiences from Krakow to Baghdad.

Cold and lifeless, they would amaze no one.

Not knowing what else to do, the stricken Barg secured the latches on the cages of the two surviving bears—worrying loudly in noisy agitation—and lay down alongside Shik Shik and rubbed a grizzled cheek against the dead bear's wet nose. He waited for the great pink wash of a tongue to slurp its master's sagging jowls, but the tongue remained locked in rigor.

He had tried to help the Armenians. He knew what it was to be despised and driven from one's home. He was sure he had seen the one they called the Fox, whose pretty woman the police had earlier taken away. But his stupid reflexes were too slow, and he had waited too long. Now he did not know what had become of any of them.

In the distance, the shifting whine of laboring trucks grew steadily louder.

Nearby, he heard a human moan, then a gurgling rattle from punctured lungs. Barg got up from the ground and walked over to a badly gunned man, who in the confusion had been mistakenly shot by his own and left, his head now barely moving, his flattened lungs struggling for air.

And dressed in the hated Turkish uniform.

Barg felt a most awful surge of suppressed rage, the rage of all Gypsies for centuries despised, the rage of a father whose children had been slain, the final rage of a man too long ridiculed and rejected.

Trucks laden with national military police streamed down

three side streets and converged beneath the weathered grain sign spattered with a warning writ in bear dung. On his knees before them, a worn little Gypsy elder straddled a bloody figure in uniform, and with an old man's hands choked the last of the life from the tyrants of Turkey.

"Horse and cow, you Hun, you murdering Ottoman Hun!" gasped Barg, eyes enormous, blood roaring in his ears. "All I ever want is horse and cow and to be left alone with my wild children. Why you not leave us plenty stinking alone?" The thick, arthritic fingers dug in the young neck but found there no life left to take.

Tekir Pasha, commander of the Istanbul police force, leapt from the cab of a truck and raised his pistol.

A single shot silenced the bear master forever.

Adrine watched the wagon pull away with gratitude and dread. Tansu the cheesemonger had made it quite clear he hated the idea of Adrine Sarafian wandering among the caves of the land walls like some outcast leper. If she was in that much danger, he would do all within his power to see that she was smuggled out of Istanbul, since she and her husband had been responsible for the safe passage of so many others. She could come live with him and his family for as long as it took for her to find a place of protection.

Adrine would hear none of it. "Without my husband," she said, "I do not know what God intends for me. But one thing I know: I cannot abandon the boys at the orphanage. I feel they are in terrible danger, and I must at least see with my own eyes that all are safe."

Her dark, red-rimmed eyes begged him to understand. "I need to think. I will do that thinking where the military police are least likely to search. I've heard from the old Gypsy women that the caves in the land walls are inhabited by the ghosts of Gypsy kings and one-eyed dwarves. You know as well as I those stories are for the benefit of the superstitious Turks, to keep their prying noses out of Gypsy business. Tatul liked the irony of despised Gypsies finding refuge inside the walls meant to protect the bigoted Turks. That is where I go to think."

Tansu, having failed to dissuade her, slumped defeatedly in the wagon seat.

"Be bright, cheese thief!" Adrine hissed at him. "Go back to robbing your loyal customers, and when I emerge from the wilderness, it is back to you I shall go! You will one day cheat me again, never fear."

He jumped down from the wagon and hugged her awkwardly. Returning to his seat, without a backward glance, he snapped the reins, and the wagon with its cheese man looking nervously left and right, left her by herself in the night.

Adrine turned in the smudgy small glow from the oil lamp in her hand and headed along the rough path at the base of the walls. She heard shouts, silence, then a shot in the distance. *God, protect Gypsies and orphan sons!* She stopped a moment, forced herself to breathe, then hurried on. Despite the dark unknown, she felt strangely warmed by the high thick walls. They made her feel watched over and afforded her plenty of hiding places if danger approached.

A few twists and turns and she would be at the warehouse full of boys, her final destiny. If the pasha was determined to hunt her down, he would find her tending the sick and holding the disturbed ones. She prayed to find David there. She thought of Cheyrek, the silent one. Would her presence pose a danger to him or the others? God could protect them from any threat. Would He?

It shocked her to think that way, but the losses were too great. God had given her Tatul and now, in the blink of an eye, he'd been killed. A Gypsy bear mauling, they said. She laughed bitterly. No bear had ended her dreams. Tatul Sarafian had been mauled to silence by a corrupt system that could not tolerate an "infidel" race. Or by those with Armenian blood who used Turkish tactics and succeeded only in bringing down Ottoman wrath on all Armenians. She hated not knowing who her enemies were.

But whoever they were, they had dealt her a blow from which she might not recover. Just as a man and woman were beginning to build a fragile existence together—the first signs of life in a land ravaged by hatred's fires—they ripped him from her and tore her relationship with God. How could it be otherwise?

Would she become like the embittered old ones who refused to worship because God had allowed the Armenian slaughter? They all had suffered terribly. So many loved ones vanished. But if they did not have God, what did they have?

She stopped and leaned in toward the wall, raising her lamp at the mouth of a small depression in stone. Small bones littered the space; bits of coarse hair stuck to the rock and brush.

Dogs.

Adrine's breath caught. Of course the wild curs of Istanbul would find the secret places of Sulukule as shielding as she. And they were not likely to move over at her coming. Was there no safe place on earth for an Armenian?

But no dogs were present. She found a sturdy stick and spent a minute or two berating her impulsive ways, then remembered Tatul's tender words. *"Be not sad. Hold this paper to your lips. . . ."*

She unfolded the sheet again and with trembling fingers pressed it to her lips. *Sweet Tatul. I have something to tell you at last and no ear to whisper it in. What cruel irony is this?*

Suddenly weak at the knees, Adrine held to the side of the depression and slid down among the bones. Blood raced in her neck. A throbbing beat against her temples. "God's love . . . the imperial thunderbolt that scalps my naked soul." She said it angrily, mockingly. "God's love. God's love. God *is* love! O priests of my childhood, of what nature is this love that gives and takes, that gently forms and viciously crushes the life from the love between man and woman? Between father and child? Or grandmother and granddaughter? Could one person find another without your divine meddling? Can one feel this kind of pain unless you give both the cause and the torment? Why have you given life only to scalp it bare?"

It was as if the questions would not stop. About her existence. About God's. About life and death and suffering. Heaven and hell. Starvation. Torture. Insanity. The ravine of the dead near the garden of her grandmother in the village of Hekim Khan.

And always ending with why. Why didn't God send a hungry wolf dog to finish her off?

Eventually spent from asking, Adrine leaned back on her elbows and stared at the stars. They winked at her as they had done ten years before when she lay on her back among Grandmother's poppies. *"Each one of those is an angel,"* Grandmother had said once in that raspy voice of hers, pointing at the brightness of heaven. Another time she had said that each prick of light was a small hole in the sky, and what you could see was the Christ Light of the New Jerusalem shining through.

And here she was after all that, wondering if any of it were true. She was full of too much grief to feel shame for thinking it. Little girls didn't know enough not to believe. Big girls knew too much.

It was almost as if Tatul spoke from the darkness. *"God came to me through you ... thank you, little grape...."* Without meaning to, she held her stomach and wept.

If she lost her faith in God, she might as well throw herself into the sea. Yet, without a star of Bethlehem to guide, she felt that this night she would lose her way whatever happened.

A voice, loud and commanding, bitterly familiar like the nausea of rancid food, reverberated from somewhere ahead. She could not make out the words, but there was no mistaking the authority.

THE PASHA.

Not knowing what else to do, she pulled herself up and moved off toward Sulukule. "Is this the belly of the fish?" she mumbled, hoping God heard. "Have I two more days in here?" After nearly twenty-three winters of hearing the story, she finally, on this bleak and lonely night without hope, understood why Jonah had run scared from God. He had more questions than answers, and God's only real answer to any of them was "Trust me."

A feral snarl tore the dark void on her right. She jerked the stick up to protect her face and neck and crouched in a defensive posture. The wall at this point jutted toward the sea, down and around a wide spine of prehistoric rock, then returned to the main path farther on. A second, equally well-worn path, traversed the declension, and it was somewhere from deep within its darkness that a man's terrified yell echoed in the night.

A horror of barks and howls ricocheted up the ancient defile between wall and rock formation.

A pack of them.

The man cried out in pain, then shouts of desperation.

"*Yok! Yok!*" The Turkish "no." Pleading.

She hesitated. *Turk.*

A man in trouble.

Adrine hurried along the gradual slope, lamp held high, stick tapping against trail and rock, out front a fragile probe.

Man and beasts grew louder.

A stone flew from the dark and struck the wall above her head. Chips of antiquity rained against her back.

She stopped, her heart banging against its chamber like a bat in a box.

Ahead, the blacker black of a cave scoured from the rock spine.

The snarls intensified, hellishly loud.

A scream and a curse produced a sharp yelp of pain. A second stone must have found its mark.

" 'Do not fear, for I am with you; do not be dismayed, for I am your God.' " She spoke the word of the Lord from the prophet Isaiah, but her voice sounded strangely distant. " 'I will strengthen you and help you; I will uphold you with my righteous right hand.' " Adrine quickly shifted the stick from her left hand to her right.

The cave mouth loomed ahead black as coal. She felt sick with anticipation, her feet unwilling to turn back. If it took her the rest of her life to explain it . . .

Adrine fought the fear. Another minute's hesitation, and she would run for her life.

A feeble glow within the cave. Another's lamp.

She rushed forward, illuminating the mouth of the cave,

then the interior with her stronger beam. Rapidly the cave walls narrowed, and there at the end of the hewn hollow were its inhabitants.

Five emaciated curs, ears flattened, tails curled between spindly legs, faced a Turkish gendarme lying on his back, uniform shirt sleeves tattered, strong young arms running blood. Near the gendarme was a sooty lamp, offering a bare flicker of light, and just beyond it a rifle. The man, eyes bulging in fear, spied the female specter looming behind the menacing hounds and stretched an arm toward the weapon.

Two dogs darted in and snapped at the arm. The gendarme yelled, fell back. The dogs lunged.

Without thinking, Adrine swung her stick against the cave wall and shouted, "Where were *you* when God laid the foundations of the earth?!" Why had she said that?

Five hounds' heads whipped back at the sound. As if by silent command, the dogs turned to face her, the instinct for self-preservation glowing red in wolfish eyes.

"Hyah! Hess, hess!" she warned, jabbing the stick at the precious little air between her and the wild hounds. She backed. They advanced. Instinctively, she hurled the lamp.

It shattered beneath one of the dogs, setting it afire and sending the entire pack yelping for the exit behind a streak of yellow flame. A gun exploded in the little grotto. Adrine threw her hands over her ears and pressed against the stone, eyes tightly shut.

For a long while, all that could be heard was a terrible ringing in her ears and the fast-fading howls of distant pain.

And breathing. The labored breathing of two people who had survived a stiff scare.

She opened her eyes.

He lay there looking at her in an inscrutable mix of wonder and curiosity.

And suspicion.

She met his gaze and smiled weakly.

He returned a spark of a smile, and she felt an awful strain melt away.

"Alone?" he asked in Armenian, his voice gravelly.

Adrine tensed. Whether intended, the question summed up her existence in one hated word.

"No." She answered the way Armenian children had been taught. God was her constant companion, wasn't He? And Tansu hadn't been gone long. Maybe the wagon had lost a wheel and even now the cheese man was searching for her among the ruins of the fortress walls.

The gendarme peered into the dark behind her to see who else might be there. "You appear alone to me," he rasped.

The gendarme's back was against the rear of the cave, the rifle across his lap. Her eyes strayed to the deep, bloody gashes on his arms, the shredded uniform. He was certain to be badly infected by the filthy bites, if he didn't die first from loss of blood.

His eyes followed hers. He lifted the blood-soaked cloth and winced in pain.

"May I bind those for you?" she asked hesitantly. "My dress is not very clean, but cleaner than what remains of your shirt."

She started forward, knelt, and met the barrel of the rifle pointed at her bosom. She held his agitated gaze. Moments later, the rifle dropped to his side, untouched.

"You are the Sarafian woman who escaped from the bazaar." His relief was obvious, but his knowledge made her wary. "You are very beautiful—for an Armenian."

He apparently still felt he had to maintain superiority over her, though his circumstances were far from it. His soft, anxious voice was laced with the pain of his wounds. So young he was, and his eyes those of a frightened animal.

"I ran here when the Gypsy bears attacked and the great Fox was met with a barrage of bullets."

Adrine started. "My husband? You have seen him? What bears do you speak of? Barg's circus bears?" She thought she could smell his blood in the small cave. He looked as if what he'd seen caused him additional pain.

"Your husband fell from his horse into the guns and the bears. There was blood everywhere—"

"Stop! I do not wish to hear it."

The policeman's hand lifted her chin, which had begun to tremble. He held her tearful gaze and met her sorrow with his own. "He faced us bravely. I ... I fled my post. He ... he did not run away." The young gendarme bit his lip and turned his face toward the wall.

He wept.

Her fingers on his hot skin were gentle and light. She tore the sleeves from her dress and made strips to cover his injuries.

"Go to the caves of Sulukule, a good place to heal, little grape," her husband had said.

Adrine bit her own lip.

CHAPTER 22

"Exit the building with your hands on top of your heads!"

Tekir Pasha lowered the megaphone and waited. Down the street behind him a few of his men collected the dead.

Shots fired. The caged Gypsy bears that remained ceased to move.

The fog had lifted. The crumbling warehouse stood silent, square and unimaginative. At its back were the ancient corroding land walls that reared another two stories above the second-floor roof of the orphanage. Atop these were scores of square, polygonal, and crescent-shaped towers that in the night gloom looked threatening still, ready to repel the boldest barbarian in a long line of Persian, Slav, and Bulgarian attackers. Twenty-two sieges laid. Twenty-two sieges repulsed.

But now came a threat from within, against which the walls of old were useless.

The pasha was highly agitated. He had neither the woman nor the body of her husband. He made the Turks who survived the debacle at the bear man's swear until their guts bled from the strain that they had heard a gun fire and watched the Fox pitch from his horse headlong into the street. The body had remained still as death.

So where was the body now? It was then that the mewling fools told conflicting stories of the smoke and fog, the confusion of trampling horses, the terrible fear shed among them by two powerful red mountains of slashing teeth and claws.

They were liars, and he knew it. One of them had defected entirely, was last seen running for his life to the sea. The pasha could do nothing now but make absolutely certain not a shred of anything went wrong at the orphanage.

Tekir Pasha left every one of the two hundred men at his back guessing what their commander might do.

He raised the megaphone to his mouth, hesitated, and spoke Armenian out of necessity. It felt bitter on his tongue, like sauce gone bad. "It is futile to resist. I am Tekir Pasha, and I command the military police of Istanbul. If you defy me, you defy the lawfully constituted authority of sovereign Turkey. I wish to get you the proper medical care you need to survive. Exit the building now, and you will come to no harm!"

Silence.

He could burn them out. Use battering rams and break right through the flimsy walls.

"First line riflemen—positions!"

A row of twenty men stepped forward, dropped to one knee.

"Aim!"

Twenty rifles snapped level at the boarded windows and thin shell of the orphanage.

"Fire!"

Twenty rifles exploded as one, the reverberation deafening in the close confines of Sulukule. Glass shattered; wood splintered; an entire corner of the building sagged where the rotted construction blew away.

The megaphone rose. "Perhaps now you can appreciate that this is police business. You have to the count of five to exit the building. One . . . two . . ."

At the count of three, a tall woman in faded pantaloons, a long-sleeved blouse, and a head covering of yellow emerged from the arched entrance. Large feet bare, erect as a fir tree, Mother Agop stood stern faced, her back close against the bullet-scarred warehouse, as if by taking a deep breath she could hide it from their view. The woman raised long bony hands from her sides, palms out, as though preparing for crucifixion. "You have come with arms against babies? They are boys, unarmed little boys!" The words were Turkish and the voice hard, deep, disbelieving.

Tekir, with relief reverting to Turkish, kept the megaphone between them. "We have come to give medicine, to take the children into custody for their own sakes. Armenians may no longer gather in groups larger than three individuals. You are clearly in violation of the law."

Mother Agop rocked up on her toes and raised a raw, long-jawed face to the starry heavens. The moonlight streamed about her, illuminating a lean, lissome form and making a shroud of the thin cloth that contained it.

"We have no Armenians here," she said dreamily, as if addressing the cosmos. "We have only little boys made in the Supreme One's image. Like you, they have two arms and two legs each; hands that fold in prayer; an eye on either side of a nose; two ears from which they hear; feet that stink; and teeth for chewing. A heart beats in each chest, and a brain nests in each head. With just a little encouragement, they will laugh and cry and sing and blow the down off a thistle with lips not unlike yours. Tell me why they now lie facedown, slobbering desperate prayers into the floor, hands over their ears, frightened tears making mud?"

Tekir sighed. He would not long tolerate this foreigner telling him his business. "Perhaps it is because their adult keepers break the law. Do you practice their lessons in the Armenian language?"

"Yes," the tall woman replied, her face set with pride that her pitiful charges received an education at all.

"Illegal!" barked the police commander. "No public instruction in any language other than Turkish is allowed."

Mother Agop dropped her gaze to glare straight at the man with the megaphone. "I assumed ours was private instruction, sir."

One man snorted in amusement at the woman's pluck. The pasha turned on him with a malevolent stare and pointed. The gendarme lost humor quickly. "I want that man confined to quarters when this sorry affair has ended," the police chief told his second in command.

Tekir turned back to the woman, megaphone ready. "Do you practice the infidel religion inside those walls?"

"The boys are taught their catechism along with their history," Mother Agop replied evenly.

"Illegal!" he shouted in a strained voice. "No Christian instruction is permitted outside government-approved churches."

Mother Agop bristled. "Will you next tell us how we are to eat and sleep, what bodily functions our bodies are permitted to perform?"

So livid was Tekir Pasha at the sarcasm in the question that he nearly grabbed a rifle and brought the conversation to an end. Instead, he waited until the red streaks ceased to knife across his vision and he could again think rationally.

"Mother, bring the children into the street. I want every one of them out here in plain view right now, or I will be forced to send my men inside the orphanage. I cannot guarantee the outcome of that."

Mother Agop responded, eyes aglitter, by singing at the top of her lungs in the Gypsy language, Romani.

The megaphone quivered as Tekir attempted to quell his anger. "Do not shout in the obscure and mythical language of detestable vagabonds! It is a criminal language used to plot legal infractions and seditious acts. What are you saying, madwoman?!"

"She say," came a thickly accented voice from behind using Turkish, " 'Thanks be to God of sun, moon, stars. Thank God for air; thank God for sight; thank God for day; thank God for night.' "

Tekir Pasha whirled about and saw that a sizable crowd of Gypsies, young and old, had gathered on the periphery to watch. Fat mothers in long dresses with fat infants hanging from every crook made him seethe. Where did they get the food to look like that? Whose pockets had they picked? "Here, you people, this is police business. You must not loiter. Go back to your homes!"

"This home. You bring guns to our home. Why you do?" Angry shouts and Romani insults followed. It didn't take a police training manual to see that things were rapidly deteriorating.

The police commander spoke low to his second in command. "I want half the men to keep their rifles trained on that pile of scurvy Gypsies. They are not to advance another step. Do you understand?"

Face clouded with doubt, the subordinate nodded.

"The rest of us will accompany this insane woman inside the orphanage," Tekir continued, "where we will make an example of their Armenian defiance. Do you comprehend? But under no circumstances are any of the lessons we teach to be taken outside the warehouse. If upon hearing the lessons we teach, the Gypsies become unruly, they should also receive instruction in civil obedience. Spare no one the lash, or our authority will be undermined, and you shall be held directly responsible. Any questions?"

"No, Commander, no questions." The man's troubled countenance said otherwise.

The second in command turned and shouted orders, which were relayed down the ranks by three men under him. Half the men turned, dropped to one knee, and, faces grim, aimed their rifles at the Gypsy families. Children screamed and mothers shrieked in alarm. But though they backed away, and some hurriedly left, most did not go far. Their people had been hunted across the face of Europe, and they were weary of the chase.

Witnesses. Tekir fumed but there was nothing to be done. The Turks needed to act, act fast, and keep the rioting to a minimum. Even though the Gypsies appeared unarmed, it would only take a weapon or two in their hands to turn the street into a bloodbath much worse than that which had taken place earlier in the evening. The French, English, and Americans all had minimal troops in the area, and Turkey didn't need any more negative war crimes publicity.

Up came the megaphone. "Mother, remain where you are. We will move forward, at which time you will take us inside to the children. No further delays will be tolerated."

Tekir set down the megaphone, raised his arm, looked

about at his troops, and let his arm fall. He and a hundred men moved forward.

Mother Agop gave a curt nod, turned, then climbed the twelve steps leading to the main hall. The pasha, close at her heels, wrinkled his nose at the strong odor of urine and un-washed bodies.

At the top of the steps, they entered the expanse of the warehouse that was home to eighty Armenian males. Mother Agop stepped aside and lowered her head. She folded thin, work-worn hands and brought them to her lips.

Tekir stared in disbelief. Even in the feeble moonglow from two grimy ceiling windows and a couple of sputtering lamps, it was plain to see.

The hall was empty.

Littered about the floor were eighty tin cups radiating out from three central pots. Some of the cups still steamed with thin gruel. Several lay overturned in haste, their liquid spills spread darkly like a wet plague.

A quick door of escape, boards kicked and yanked away, gaped in the back wall.

"Go, go!" Tekir yelled at his men. "Track them down! Leave me with a rifle!" Had the vermin enough time to make good an escape? But where could they go in the dark? They would follow the land walls to the inlet of the Golden Horn. Beyond that was the open sea. "Send the vehicles to the water and cut off their escape back into the city. We can drown what we can't shoot."

The military gendarmes streamed through the hole in the back wall until only the pasha and Mother Agop remained in the building. She saw in his eyes that she had transgressed beyond clemency.

Calmly, quietly, Arpi Agop, Armenian by choice, knelt on the bare floor of her orphanage with her back to the police commander of Istanbul. She made the sign of the cross before folding long arms across her chest to still the shaking of her hands.

Tekir Pasha looked at the thin neck and quaking shoulders and felt his fatigue. Disciplining the infidels was such a tiresome business.

CHAPTER 23

"You have my blood on you." The wounded young gendarme's words came softly. He was standing now. He pressed far back into the unyielding hardness at the narrow end of the cave as if willing the earth to open. The bleeding had slowed, but the makeshift bandages from Adrine's dress were already stained dark.

Adrine waved her hand dismissively, letting him know she wasn't bothered. She thought of God's ferocious love for her over the years and how it had shown itself in her grandmother. She recalled the healing tree in the old woman's yard and the hundreds of strips of red, white, green, and blue cloth that accumulated there over the years. Each one tied to a branch, the faded strips of cotton and muslin, wool and linen formed waving prayers of healing for sick relatives or petitions for increased business at the shops of friends. Adrine's own birth earned a special swatch of red-and-white-striped cloth on the healing tree because she'd been born so colicky. It was a pagan superstition swallowed whole by God's people.

Tie a pretty blue strip today, Grandmother. I know you'll have to stretch to reach a branch without a rag on it, but little goose needs it more than she's ever needed anything.

"You should have let the dogs have me!" the gendarme rambled. "I won't be welcomed back to my regiment. I abandoned my post."

She nodded. "Perhaps I did too." Her willfulness had drawn Tatul into a death trap, and in the short blast of a marksman's rifle, she was left alone.

Adrine smiled weakly at the young man and folded her arms against the chill of the cave. "My husband always admired the style of the sultans. He told me that Suleyman the Magnificent was forever going in and out of the city, off to this battle, returning from that one, every time a massive show of pomp and might. There would be six thousand light horsemen dressed in scarlet followed by ten thousand foot soldiers in yellow velvet, then four captains with twelve thousand men each in battle dress just ahead of sixteen thousand slave warriors wearing violet silk."

There was a small light in the faraway look of the boyish gendarme's eyes. He was transported away to the sixteenth century. He was a foot soldier in the service of the mighty sultan.

"One thousand pages of honor followed in gold cloth," Adrine continued. "And then the grand majesty himself, resplendent in a gold robe, would ride regally astride a white charger with six ladies in silver on six white horses. The whole grand show concluded with two hundred thousand camels carrying the army's munitions and food supply."

Slowly the Turk stepped from the end of the cave and brushed past her as if sleepwalking—or marching in the sultan's gaudy procession. He stopped abruptly, and she watched his back, the rifle at his side cradled in limp fingers. He turned and looked at her sadly. She read the unvoiced questions in night black eyes filled with regret. Could it have been different between his people and hers? Who could have prevented it? When?

Boy-man whiskers. The stink of blood and sweat and something else.

Fear.

The muzzle of the rifle rose, but it was symbolic, no hatred in it. "You're a fugitive Armenian," he said, one corner of his mouth twitching nervously. "I should shoot you and take your shoes." Was that the beginning of a smile on his unseasoned face?

She raised her stick loosely in both hands, a kind of symbolic shield of defense. "You're a warrior Turk," she said, her insides a sour mix of kindness and sadness. "I should charge at you and beat you with my stick."

Even as she said it, they heard footfalls pounding against stone. The young man, alarmed, looked up as Adrine brought the stick solidly down across the weapon and knocked it from his grip.

A streak entered the space between them, and a fist ricocheted off the point of the gendarme's chin. He dropped like a puppet with cut strings, striking the ground blissfully unconscious.

An apparition engulfed her. The lips of a phantom sought hers. The strong arms of an angel wrapped her in a vigorous embrace.

Wildly weeping, she struggled against the spectral vision until convinced by its ardent ministrations that it was Tatul.

And then her joy would not be denied.

With a cry of recognition, Adrine flung her arms around her beloved and kissed him as if he were risen from the dead.

He laughed and whirled her off her feet in a dizzy dance of pleasure.

Soon she saw that Ephraim, Bayard, and fuzzy Andranik all stood awkwardly by while the Sarafians danced in a cave in the rock. She cried out again and gave them each a kiss without releasing a bit of her hold on Tatul.

"They wanted me to believe you were dead!" she sobbed into her husband's neck. "I ... I ..." She stopped. How to say the awful thing? Unable to speak, she held out the handsome pocket watch instead.

Tatul understood and put tender arms about her. "Shoosh, my downy pigeon. I was much overdue, and truth be told, we may have passed through Sheol to get here. I counted on your reading my note so that we could find each other among the caves." He looked as if the weight of a hundred wars had been lifted from him. "Can you forgive me, Adrine? I shouldn't have left you unguarded while I kept at my precious discourse. A reborn Armenia will never be spoken into existence, but raised only by steady hands and devoted example."

She nodded with eyes full of grace and bathed him the more in kisses. In time she stopped, pulled back, and her face crumpled. "Oh, Tatul, David was not found." She told him of the pursuit by Chazarian, the kidnapping by the stranger at the café, Barg's strange and pitiful behavior, and how she was finally snatched by men in uniform, wandered blind through the bowels of the Grand Bazaar, and finally made her escape thanks to the blacksmith and the cheesemonger.

By the end of the incredible telling, Tatul's dark eyes and jaw muscles busily processed anger, frustration, and shock. "The Father loves you more than I," he said huskily, sad for the fear and danger she had endured, fiercely proud of the way she had endured it. "Please forgive me for not sparing you such madness."

Adrine laid her head against his chest. "Oh, Tatul, do not feel guilty. Who can save us from the evil one but God Almighty? We should rejoice that we have been spared to continue the work!" She was silent a moment, then said in a very small voice, "My husband, I was so afraid that I questioned everything I have ever known about God and knew an aloneness deeper than any in the days before you came to our rescue in Hekim Khan. Only then, after doubting my Lord, were you returned to me. It is a miracle!"

For a minute, he could not speak. How long before the sword was removed from them? He held his wife until the beat of her heart slowed and she again smiled up at him.

"We must go to the orphanage before Tekir does them harm. I pray David made it safely to Mother Agop."

"Yes," Tatul said somberly, nodding to the three who had escaped with him from the massacre in the street. "I pray that same prayer. The boys would be an easy target for someone as unstable as the pasha. As for us, Hovsep and Vahram were lost." At the stricken look on her face, he drew her close. "Barg, too, and some or all of his bears. Tekir is determined to make an example of Armenians, and all who help them, no matter the cost."

He told her the rest of his story, how in the midst of the gendarmes and the bears and the general confusion, he and his three companions were "swallowed alive" by a Gypsy family and kept in their hovel until the streets cleared of police. One thing was painfully apparent. There was much more troop activity on this night than Sulukule warranted. Tekir was up to something, and they both feared it had to do with the orphanage.

"Come, let us stay to the wall, lamps extinguished, weapons ready," ordered Tatul. "When we reach the orphanage, we shall place the boys on the roof, guard them, and get word to the American, French, and British consulates that innocent children are in imminent danger of attack."

Adrine cast a regretful eye upon the unconscious gendarme and prayed that he might meet God's mercy before the pasha's retribution.

They hurried from the cave, rejoined the main path, and half ran up a rise in the trail where the main fortress wall humped over a small flattened hill.

Another rifle shot cracked a hole in the night.

Sounds carried farther on the night air, including the tramp of human feet coming at them from over the hill.

"Troops?" Tatul whispered, bringing them to a halt with an upraised hand. But there was something different about the sound. They drew their weapons and waited.

And prayed.

At the crest of the hill, one shadow moved. Three. A dozen.

Pouring at them down the hill, double file, they came.

The children.

The boys. The orphans of Sulukule.

And with them the three young Armenian *myrigs*, as thin and faded as their charges, softly clucking encouragement in an urgent attempt to keep order.

"Mrs. Sarafian! Mrs. Sarafian!" It was David Mugurditchian running toward her in the moonlight, with a smaller boy clinging to his back for dear life.

Then a voice she did not recognize also came toward her at a run, calling her name. "Mrs. Sarafian, here!"

And before she knew it, her neck was wet with a young boy's tears. Her *yavrum* could speak. Her Cheyrek was silent no more.

But for many moments, his Adrine was.

CHAPTER 24

The headlights glowed like an ancient dragon's eyes, the whine and snort of the troop vehicles growing swiftly closer along the road parallel to the footpath at the base of the fortress walls.

"The killers are coming!" a boy shrieked, his terror slicing through them all. The orphan fugitives began to cry and stumble.

"Quiet, little brothers!" Adrine called. "Hold hands, brave ones. You are God's heroes of the homeland!"

Guns fired somewhere behind.

Several boys hit the ground as if shot from the sky and threw their arms over the backs of their heads.

"No, no!" Tatul shouted. He ran from one boy to the next, yanking them to their feet. "They're firing into the air. They want to frighten us into stopping. But they don't know where we are, so keep moving. Krikor! David! You keep them moving. Ephraim! Bayard! Bring up the rear. Andranik, you stay with Adrine and me. Run, men, run! Swift as horses, now, all of you!"

The scared boys bit their lips and moved as best they could over the rough, strange terrain, pushing, pulling, propelling one another to escape, to live.

The trucks were almost even now, but separated from the fleeing boys by darkness and the craggy ruins of a crumbling inner wall.

They heard the vehicles brake to a stop. Boots hit the ground. A shout of "In there! Cut them off if you can. . . ."

Ambush.

"Here! Through here!" Tatul hissed, shoving the boys nearest him through a ragged hole in the outer wall. "Adrine, go with them—David, with her. Stay next to the wall!" Adrine and David each grabbed two hands and spurted through the opening. The men and older boys urged the younger through after them.

Krikor was the last of the boys to disappear into the hole. Before he did, Tatul rested a hand on his shoulder and, despite the thinness of bone and flesh, touched cords of strength. "Fly with the angels," he said tightly. "Remember, Satan has a limp."

Krikor smiled back at him and nodded. "God's aim is true," the boy completed the old adage.

Tatul hugged him and sent him through. "Men," he said to the faithful three still with him, "it is time to confuse the hounds."

The Fox and his little band raced along the inner path, bent low to the ground, and darted down into a small draw where the path dipped slightly before straightening out. At the street they heard the trucks shift gears and move off slowly, drivers scanning the night for signs of the fugitives. Behind, they could hear the tramp of running feet. The military gendarmes would soon appear.

Tatul looked up and saw silhouetted against moon brightness the jagged outline of a deteriorating needle of ruined wall towering above the draw. Stambul's postwar municipal priorities did not yet encompass public safety issues like aging walls. Tatul pushed against the base of the needle and saw the top sway precariously. He motioned to the others to brace against the base and await his signal.

They could hear the troops slow, then stop at the hole in the outer wall. Before they could make the choice, Sarafian made it for them.

"I hear soldiers!" he yelled, the words of one echoing like the cries of many among the jumbled and failing stoneworks. "Faster, or we'll all be shot!"

With a shout of triumph, the gendarmes charged down the draw.

The needle of stone leaned out at an impossible angle a split second before raining down on the charging gendarmes.

A rifle discharged, thundering loudly in the narrow confines of the draw.

The trucks screeched to a halt. Shouts. "What?! Have you found them? Where?"

The last thing Tatul and his men heard before ducking through the hole in the outer wall were the moans and curses of the injured caught in their own ambush.

Gunfire. Always more gunfire. Can't stop. Mustn't stop. Run!
Ahead, the inlet waters of the Golden Horn glittered with the fire of stars and moon. Adrine's throat swelled with emotion. What was real? The beauty of the sea or the blood in the streets?

Here and there the light of a boat, a bonfire on the far shore, a strange unexplained twinkling just off the near shore.

She felt a stab of pain low in her abdomen. She fell to her knees, bent over, willing the pain to pass. Where was Tatul? She had something to tell him.

Young hands held her. Voices asked concerned but unintelligible questions. The sparkle of heaven and sea swirled together in one kaleidoscope of light and dark.

"I . . . I have not eaten in some time. A little dizzy, that's all."

She wondered whose voice it was.

The questions turned frantic, the hands pulling and pushing. She took a deep gulp of air and rose to her knees, angry to be down. Adrine looked again at the sea, and by its jeweled loveliness was able to stand and press on.

A gust of salt air slapped her to reason, and with an awful clarity she heard a mocking in her head. *And what will you do when you reach the water? Where will you go? How far can you and your bony urchins swim?* The voice was Tekir's. The asker had the face of an evil imp.

"Mrs. Sarafian, where are we going? Are they going to shoot us?"

She felt a strong young arm around her waist and looked into the dark concern of David Mugurditchian's handsome eyes. "We are going to meet Jesus. He waits for us at the water's edge." She heard the words and thought they might be hers.

Someone called from above and behind. "Adrine!" Again, "Adrine!" That had to be God's voice.

Tatul caught her as she went down a second time and lifted her into his arms. His powerful grip felt as if it would never again yield her up to anyone or anything. She pressed her face hard against his chest and listened to the great rushing of blood and breath that reminded her just how alive they were.

"Where is Arpi?" Adrine asked, waking to the fact she had not seen her friend with the others.

"She remained at the orphanage," Tatul said, not looking at her. Adrine's heart sank. He did not need to elaborate.

"We're almost to the sea," came Andranik's voice from the dark, frustration in every word. "What then?"

"We should stop here, Tatul. Let's shelter the boys behind the ramparts and pray that the Lord of the loaves and fishes will multiply our ammunition in a similar fashion." The suggestion was Bayard's, not a hint of sarcasm in it.

Ephraim agreed. "We could possibly scale the wall along here. The boys could lie flat at the top. It's impossible to hit from the ground, and we can shoot anyone who attempts to storm our position."

Tatul's momentary silence told Adrine that he was thinking through the options, meager as they were.

"They would simply wait us out—starve us if necessary. I do not believe that God will allow these, the littlest Armenians, to perish within sight of the Golden Horn Bridge. If, when we reach the shore, God does not part the waters, we will turn toward the city and take refuge in the Fethiye Mosque. The Muslims will not kill us in their own mosque."

"*This* is your plan?" a laboring Andranik rasped incredulously. "They burned our churches to the ground with our loved ones inside. Tekir will not permit religious restraints to prevent the enforcement of his precious laws!"

"Stop here!" Tatul's order passed to the front of the procession. "Gather the boys and have them lie down in the tall grass." He set Adrine on her feet and watched the boys go to their bellies in groups of four and five, away from the trail, the older shielding the younger from danger. He marveled at how quietly and resolutely they did what needed to be done.

Tatul took Adrine's hand and started forward, eyes peering curiously out at the play of light and dark along the near bank of the waterway. The other men started to follow. "No, good brothers, I would ask that you stay with the boys, help keep them still, their heads down. I wish to talk with my wife alone."

The three looked at each other questioningly but did not protest. In the end, if the Fox said fly, they would run, arms flapping, into the wind.

"Are you well, my little pigeon?" Tatul asked, still studying the Golden Horn.

She nodded, fighting tears. She had so much to tell him, but these were the least promising conditions in which to say the words. They should hurry on. But would there be another opportunity? "I have my husband again. All is indeed well." She squeezed his arm. "Tatul—"

"There!" he said sharply, pointing at the Horn. "Follow my arm. Can you see it?" There was guarded excitement in the question.

Adrine sighed. It was enough to know he was alive. She sighted down his arm, trying to focus where his finger indicated and seeing nothing but shapeless blobs of shadow and shading, uncertain what was land and what was sea.

"There! See, there!" He jerked his arm to the left, and she could feel the tension in it but saw nothing more distinct than the last amorphous cluster of blackness and what she thought was a brief prick of insect light.

"Nothing but shifting shadows and the spark of a glow worm—"

"Yes, that's what I mean! See, there ... and over there!

They're too evenly placed along an identical line to be natural. Either that's Holy Spirit fire, or those are signals. And see those dark shapes there, there, and there? How similar they are?"

"Signals? Who—"

"Lamps!" Tatul said with increasing agitation. "Adrine, those are boats just offshore, and onshore smaller ones, rowboats probably! I think we . . . I think our . . ." He turned. "On your feet, boys, quickly. Up! *Up!* To the water as fast as your legs can go.

"God Almighty has landed!"

CHAPTER 25

The high grass whipped the fugitives in the arms and face, but they were oblivious to the sting and ran all the faster to the safety of the sea.

Dark figures hurried toward them from the Golden Horn. The boys caught sight of them and faltered.

"Police!" someone yelled, reversing direction. "Hide!"

"NO!" shouted Tatul, herding the wild orphan lambs of Sulukule.

Adrine ran after the errant one and caught little Levon by a frayed sleeve.

"We may trust these shadows," Tatul reassured. "We may even know them."

The nearer the shadows from the water came, the stronger the confirmation. The breeze that bore them carried with it the aroma of fin and scale, brine and engine oil.

The two groups met when Fevzi the Fishmonger grabbed Adrine and Tatul in an awkward embrace. He was the pungent essence of fish entrails and fermented rice, and he gripped a stout cudgel in one beefy hand.

"Ah, Sarafian and Sarafian's Lady! I and my fisher brothers were just on our way to defend your honor and to determine if we could be of service should the sons of heifers decide to trouble the orphanage." He looked around at the dazed youth staring wonderingly up at dozens of rough seamen. Here and there a thick calloused hand tousled a boy's head, and a few old sailors, overcome with the plight of the children, knelt in the grass and enfolded several youngsters in their arms.

With a cry of recognition, David Mugurditchian ran and wrapped himself around Fevzi's neck and sobbed in relief. The kind old Turk was emotionally shaken and kept patting the boy's back.

"How many are you?" Tatul asked, keeping one eye cocked at the end of the land walls and along the street coming down from them. "How did you hear?"

Fevzi did not let go of David. "Twelve boats; six, seven men each. Tansu Bir felt so uneasy at leaving Sarafian's lady alone, the old goat horn came to me and sounded the alarm. He had it that the Fox was dead and that his lady came to the wall to throw herself off for grief. We determined to look for her and to approach the orphanage from here, the least public route. It is good fortune that Tansu came to me, or I would have thrown him from the wall and made the market a safer place to buy!"

Adrine laughed. "Fish peddler, no one is a greater menace to fair trade than you!"

Fevzi snorted. "This from the mouth of a woman who yet owes me six ears of corn! Now, say, who pursues you?" His voice was laced with anger and a determination as stout as a fisherman's rope.

"I'm afraid you have come against the pasha himself," Tatul replied.

"Then we invite you for a boat ride," Fevzi responded without hesitation. "We have Greeks and Cypriots, Italians, and a Mongol as ruthless at cards as Ghengis Khan at war. But all these men of the sea, I have found, have soft hearts for babies and the oppressed. Come, we will take you far from here, up the Bosporus into the Black Sea. From there, many a village will welcome your family, large as it is. We will fatten the boys on crabs and bread, and when they have recovered, we will find homes for them. Yes?"

Tatul and Adrine were moved by the kind Fevzi's offer. "Yes, good friend," Tatul said, "but surely some of these men have families of their own. What of the separation and trouble this could bring them?"

Fevzi blew rudely through his nose. "Apologies, Sarafian's

lady, I have the manners of a dogfish, but that is what Fevzi thinks of trouble. And so do my friends. I am old and the sea is my mistress, but not so old that I do not see that the past ways are changing. Turks are tired of war, tired of the heavy hand. We will take care of monsters like the pasha. He will change or he will go." The fisher's tone left no doubt there was a great deal of ocean for Tekir to be lost in. "Come, to the boats!"

With that cry, Fevzi and his men helped shepherd the boys to the water, where half of them rapidly filled four rowboats precariously full and were quickly transported to the fishing vessels waiting in deeper waters.

In two trips, all the orphans and their sea captains were safely aboard. Seventy displaced seamen gathered on the shore, hefted clubs and guns, and turned to face what evil the night had for them. Fevzi, still without his own vessel, made ready to join them.

David clung to his arm. "Must you go?" he asked tearfully.

Fevzi nodded and looked to the walls where the light of torches and lamps could be seen snaking down the hill. The head lamps of the dreaded police transport trucks pierced the dark to the left. Tekir and his gendarmes.

Fevzi shouldered his club in one hand and touched David's wet cheek, giving it an affectionate tweak. "Yes, we need to get an unruly fisherman's carouse going, for them to bring to an end. Police do not like us to have too much fun." He smiled and patted David's sadness. The boy held tightly to the weathered wrist with both hands. Garouj, Levon, and Krikor stood anxiously by. "I will get word to your mother that you are well and will return once your friends are safely settled," Fevzi said. "I will follow in a day or two."

"Thank you," David said, brightening noticeably. "Tell her . . . tell Mother I love her. Tell the jailers to treat her with kindness—" His voice broke, and he looked away.

Fevzi kissed him roughly and turned to the Sarafians. "Go with God," he said, voice low. "Do not come back here. Make yourselves a home where madness is not mistaken for reason. Give your love a chance to bloom." The old fisherman, unaccustomed to so much "woman talk," made a great show of clearing both nostrils. "Pardon, Sarafian's lady, I know better how to behave around the bluefish and the mackerel. I wish you both great happiness." Without a backward glance, the fishmonger stepped into the rowboat and was gone.

"*Ad mortem fidelis!*" Tatul shouted after him.

"Faithful until death!" Adrine echoed. Tatul looked at her with a mix of longing and admiration. It was the first time he had heard the cry of the Armenian brotherhood from her lips.

The engines of the rescue flotilla coughed to life, and one by one the little fishnetters turned east for the Galata Bridge and the mighty Bosporus. A stiff breeze made them all shiver, but because it smelled of freedom, they felt strangely warmed.

"We need to help Fevzi obtain another 'little camel of the sea,'" Adrine said, nestling against Tatul inside his coat, David's jumbled black curls resting against her stomach. The thrum of the boat engine penetrated flesh and bone. She gave a burdened sigh. They were still hounded, forced from their homes, driven out of business, a people without a country. Could they ever stop running?

At least this time the enemy was not their own. Neither was the friend.

Tatul was too quiet. He had said nothing since Fevzi left for shore. "What is it, my Fox?" Adrine asked.

"Serop, my father," he replied, heavyhearted. "I wish he were standing there, face into the wind. . . ." It was ugly, scraping talk that infected the wounds of war. Living Armenians did not speak of the missing and dead for fear the wounds would never close.

A little boy slipped a slim hand into Tatul's. "My sister . . ."

Adrine caught her breath. It was Cheyrek's bedmate who had told the awful story of the incident at the River Euphrates but could not remember.

"My sister's name was Sione. She drowned."

Tatul nodded. They continued like that, the little hand in the big one, faces to the moon, saying nothing, their silence a roar of words.

In a little while when the boy began to sway from weariness, Tatul motioned to David to take the child and lay him down out of the wind. Looking as if he'd been up for days, David hugged the younger boy and lay against him until both fell deeply asleep.

"Sometimes I think it better for fathers to die when their sons are young, for they are yet heroes then."

Adrine felt a chill pass through her. "What are these thoughts, my Fox? Your father, dead or alive, is a hero of the homeland."

"My father went meekly to slaughter. He made no resistance. Was he forced to dig his own grave as so many were? He was my god, Adrine, the author of my life. And now he lies so completely trampled into the earth between here and Syria, it is as if he had never existed at all!"

"No, Tatul, that is a lie!" Adrine felt a chasm of sorrow and anger of her own. But down that way lay death and bitterness. Her father, her mother, her—NO! She would not think it, for to do so was to give the Turks the final triumph. She would live and dwell on the New Armenia and give thanks to the Lord of their rescue. In those things dwelt the enemy's defeat.

She turned and softly caressed his grizzled cheek. "You are the continued existence of Serop Sarafian. He lives on in you, my husband. In you! I look at you, and I think he must have been a great man, a man of passion and principle."

A strong and steady hand closed over hers. "The boys," he said, willing to change the subject. "We must find them nuts and bread and fruit."

"And milk!" Adrine exclaimed, eager to speak of the future, shaky as it was. "They have forgotten the taste of milk."

"And occupations," said Tatul. "They must have a means to pay back such kindness and make their way. They can learn to polish shoes in the city, to wash dishes. In the country they can make dolls from rags and graze other people's herds."

"Yes," Adrine said happily, "and while we are keeping them fattened and busy, we will write to Frank Davidson and ask him to help us find sponsors in America. Then we will send them to a new life far from the ache of Armenia!"

The rush of words, strange in her ears, produced an ache

of their own. She would not meet her husband's gaze. Was she changing? Had recent events taken too much from her? Was she thinking of abandoning the homeland and emigrating like so many others?

If she looked at Tatul, she knew what she would see in those fiery eyes. Resistance. Defiance. Shock that she sounded ready to board the next steamship out, yet sympathy for his wife and her not unreasonable need to build a life in a safe place.

"I am sorry for your business. It was a good one," he said, with regret in his voice.

"It will be again," she said, hoping he could hear that she had not given up, would not run away.

She could not stand to see the Fox cornered, forced to choose between the homeland and her. "It is only that I believe some of these boys need to go where industry is rewarded, where wages are enough to live on, with enough beside to send for the restoration of the homeland. We who remain will need their help." She felt his embrace tighten and swallowed her own misgivings.

"President Wilson is the friend of those who remain," he said. "Frank will nip at his heels until the yavrums are shining shoes at the White House! I love these boys!"

Adrine shared her husband's emotion. She tipped her head to the sky and drank in the bright constellations. "As much as you will ours?" she softly asked.

"Ours?" He barely breathed, and she felt his muscles go rigid.

"Here." She guided his hand to her belly. "Fatima, the old Gypsy woman, says there are two, and that by the way I walk and the fact that a male goat crossed my path the week of conception, they will be boy giants whose fists will blacken the eyes of despots everywhere!" She laughed. "I have already felt them butting heads!"

It was the first time she knew Tatul too befuddled for sense. "Two goats . . . two persons . . . t-two conceptions?"

Adrine laughed again, merry with motherhood. Men and boys stirred and quizzically looked their way. She whispered,

"Names, my Fox. They have to be named. I refuse to call them Little Fox and Foxtail. And what if Fatima suffered from indigestion and they are girls? What then, my fine Fedayee? Can you feel them?"

Tatul's hand pressed gently against her belly. He nuzzled her ear, and she felt the hot breath of his answer.

"They sleep now, Mother Fox, safe inside the den. . . ."

She squeezed his hands. "Oh, Tatul, my husband, think of them working the soil of the New Armenia. Learning the history of Old Armenia. Marrying and having babies of their own. Think of me, a sweet old grandmother clucking at my own little geese within the shadow of Mount Ararat!"

He laughed and held her tight. "Well, old one, where will you keep your teeth at night?"

She slapped his hand. "Noah would never let you aboard with a mouth like that. So, my tart-tongued husband, you must make a cradle for two and get us a cow. Twin sons won't allow me a moment's peace!"

Tatul leapt to his feet, shouting at crew and passengers, at Europe and Asia and the heavens above. "I am Tatul the Father! Tatul the Rich!" While the others, curious and smiling, muttered and tried to make sense of his rantings, he bent and gathered Adrine to him, weeping and laughing and shouting God's praises.

"Arouse, Stambul! Fire the cannon! Awaken the world! Pass the news! Bring the boats alongside, for we must praise the God of our rescue and give thanks to the Savior of people and nations!"

And there, between land and sea, hatred and love, heaven and heartache, Tatul Sarafian saw in the faces of the rescued a New Armenia full of promise. The People of the Book would one day thrive again.

AFTERWORD

U.S. President Woodrow Wilson left office in 1921 at the end of his second term. Suffering the debilitating effects of a stroke, he died three years later. Ill health in the latter years of his administration may partially explain why he was unable to press more successfully for justice in the case of postwar Armenia. Though Wilson was awarded the Nobel Peace Prize for his role in the Treaty of Versailles, the treaty was subsequently rejected by the U.S. Senate.

But a lack of will to save Armenia existed as much in Europe as it did in Washington. The Allied Powers had proclaimed at the Paris Peace Conference that the Armenians should have a homeland. But sadly, they lacked the resolve to ensure that one was actually established.

Several European nations and hundreds of Americans, however, did individually come to the aid of Armenians as mission and relief personnel. Orphanages were built, medical care given, and food dispensed. Two hundred orphanages alone were staffed and operated by Americans, helping rebuild shattered young lives.

Referring to the efforts of the Near East Relief agency, U.S. President Calvin Coolidge took note of the Christian solace that made so profound a difference in the recovery of the Armenian people:

"Not only has life been saved, but economic, social, intellectual, and moral forces have been released. New methods in child welfare, in public health and practical education have been introduced. A new sense of the value of the child, a new conception of religion in action, and a new hope for a better social order have been aroused. All this has brought enduring results, a promise of a brighter future to replace the despair of years of fear and hopelessness. The work ... has demonstrated practical Christianity without sectarianism and without ecclesiastical form, recognizing the rights of each and all of their ancestral faith, while expressing religion in terms of sacrifice and service that others might live and be benefited. Its creed was the Golden Rule and its ritual the devotion of life and treasure to the healing wounds caused by war."

It is an example today's Christians would do well to emulate.

The fledgling Republic of Armenia, a mere shadow of its former territory, was declared an independent state following the collapse of czarist Russia in 1918, but it continued to be tormented by Turkish invasion. Finally, hundreds of thousands of homeless refugees and a shattered economy were no match for the Turkish army under Mustafa Kemal Pasha, know later as Ataturk, meaning "Father of Turkey," who forced surrender of the ancient Armenian homeland and its resident "foreigners" from Mount Ararat to the south. Subsequently, thousands more Armenians died from starvation and cold until the republic acquiesced to Bolshevik protection.

It would be many decades before Armenians again took control of their own destiny. But finally, on September 23, 1991, Armenia declared its independence from the Soviet Union, and the modern Republic of Armenia was reborn.

Today, the spirit of nationalism burns brightly in Armenia. The desire for a full accounting of Turkish atrocities in World War I is a deep and sometimes wild torrent among Armenians everywhere. Until the government leaders of Turkey admit to systematic genocide and take national responsibility for it, old wounds, hatred, and bitterness will remain.

Confession. Contrition. Forgiveness. Healing. On such as these, the hope of a new and thriving homeland rests.

Almighty God, bring it to pass.